"You came

"Like take out," she said, licking sugar from the rim of her glass. His eyes rose from the phone. Her smile was half hidden by the glass, but her gaze was telling a story all of its own. "Does that mean you plan to eat me?"

A semi-smile joined his slow blink. "We're flirting today?"

"Not me," she said, tipping her head back, arching her body his way. "That's where your mind went, Casanova."

Dipping a fingertip into her drink, Roxie took her time about sucking it clean. He put the phone down and rested his hands on the bar, trapping her between his arms.

"Your mind isn't as clean as you let on," he murmured.

Also by Scarlett Finn

NOTHING
To hide

SCARLETT FINN

Contents

1

"Because I own nightclubs, people assume I must be a depraved, perverted playboy living a debauched life."

Zairn Lomond: playboy extraordinaire. What else did she know about him? Hmm... Nothing. Roxie Kyst's only reason for joining the Talk at Sunset audience was to support her roommates. They'd saved every spare dime to travel a couple of thousand miles to be in the same room as Lomond for a few minutes.

"And that's not the case? No debauchery?" Drew Harvey asked his guest. "Zairn, I'm disappointed."

Zairn Lomond lifted his arm to drape it along the back of the couch behind the stunning actress at his side. Judging by the elated smile on the woman's face, she didn't mind. Why should she?

"Drew," Lomond said, an arrogant slant to his lips. "You've partied with me... Have you ever seen anything debauched?"

Drew Harvey paused. A tight smile teased his lips, damming a laugh. "I plead the Fifth."

Everyone laughed, Lomond included. "It's all relative, right? My life isn't like most others."

"Like any other," Drew said.

Led by a vast number of women, the audience had gone crazy when Lomond first appeared. Her friends' idol had a magnetic kind of ease, she'd give him that. His appeal came in more than just his appearance, he oozed charisma. From that angle, she got why Toria and Jane went cuckoo for him. Not that she'd follow suit. Going cuckoo for a guy wasn't her style.

"Have I seen some wild things?" Lomond asked, without disguising his smug nonchalance. "Sure. Have I been a part of some extreme setups? Yeah. That's life. It's the life I live."

"Knox Collier is one of your best friends," Drew Harvey stated. "The Collier family own a vast percentage of the world's media."

"Yeah, you'd think they'd go easier on me," Lomond said, earning himself another laugh.

"Some might speculate that your Collier connection is exactly why you're targeted so frequently in the press." Lomond responded with a slight twitch of his shoulder. "Do you have an opinion on that? Have you considered severing the connection?"

"You think breaking with the Colliers is likely to improve my image in the press?" Lomond asked, shifting to sit straighter. "Look, I'm in the public eye and have connections to some newsworthy people. I chose this life, and everyone is entitled to their opinions. Free speech is our right and sometimes that speech isn't in my favor. I don't lose a lot of sleep over it, Drew."

"You're credited with a lot of high-profile matches. Unofficial word is, you've been responsible for some famous marriages, got top actors and actresses involved with movies that made their careers and/or earned them Oscars. Same for producers, directors, the whole range. You can make or break a career. It's said everyone influential owes you a favor... and that you have dirt on hundreds, thousands of people, including those in the business and political worlds."

"I know people who have dedicated their lives to information gathering. Personally, I don't bank data."

"But would it be fair to say?" Drew asked, receiving the same shoulder response as before. "You have power in prominent circles. Know something about everyone from movie extras to presidents." Little response, just a slow, controlled blink. "You are facilitator to the world's rich and powerful, right?"

"Crimson venues pride themselves on showing our guests a good time. If someone needs something specific, we'll find a way to provide it."

"And with a network like yours, I imagine there's little you can't provide. Maybe it's jealousy. Could that be why the internet is rife with questions about your business and lifestyle?"

"People like to speculate."

"Yes… especially when there's a premature death involved."

A tense, more somber air crackled through the studio.

Jane leaned in to whisper, "He's talking about Dayah Lynn."

"Dayah's passing was a tragedy," Lomond said. "We mourned her and cooperated with the investigation."

"Your reputation took a hit after that incident. Is that why you came up with the idea of opening yourself to extreme scrutiny?"

"As much as I'd love to take credit, the contest wasn't my idea," Lomond said. "But we at Crimson have nothing to hide."

The host adjusted his angle to address the audience. "We teased a challenge earlier in the show. One lucky member of our audience will be invited to tour the Crimson network with Zairn as he opens his doors to winners of the Crimson Experience." Drew looked at Lomond again. "What exactly is the Crimson Experience?"

Offering a snicker, Lomond eased into his arrogance. "It will vary depending on where we are."

"Contests are running across the world as we speak, aren't they?"

Lomond nodded. "Yes. Winners will be contacted after the deadline this weekend."

"But our winner from the audience, he or she will accompany you on the whole tour. It's what? Three months?"

"Almost three months on the ground. Longer if you factor the travel time. We'll spend around a week in each city and end right here in LA," Lomond said, smoothing a hand down his thigh. "A documentary crew will follow the winners as they receive their experience in each city."

"The documentary will air next year?"

"Yes. The person who wins tonight will be able to direct a supplement to the documentary. Streaming a video diary as often as they want. The world will be able to follow progress and keep up with the news as we travel."

"Proving you have nothing to hide?"

"And having some good times along the way," Lomond said, focusing on the host even while the actress wriggled closer.

"It's an excellent prize," Drew Harvey said. "Comes with five-star hotels, all expenses paid and an allowance for clothes, hair, make-up, whatever they need."

"That's right."

"And unrestricted access to you and your team."

On another easy smile, Lomond's eyes glittered with innuendo. "Unfortunately, there will be some restrictions."

The host laughed. "Right."

"But the winner will be involved in our daily briefs and given the VIP treatment at every venue. They'll also have unrestricted backstage access. They'll meet the guests—"

"Famous guests?"

"Yeah, whoever we have appearing or who's in for a good time."

"No doors closed in their face."

"No," Lomond said. "They'll have complete access and will be invited to contribute to the documentary. They'll be interviewed for it throughout and after their experience comes to an end. The winner will have full editing rights over their own comments too."

"Approval before air?"

"Exactly."

"So nothing can be doctored or manipulated?"

"We have nothing to hide," Lomond said again.

"*Nothing to Hide*" would be a good title. Except Roxie's suspicion ticked up the more often it was said. Anyone that adamant and arrogant would believe himself above typical rules. Lomond probably thought the winner would be too star-struck to dig in and ask the hard questions.

Drew Harvey switched to talk to his audience again. "How does that sound?"

The room went wild, further stoking the ego of the man on the couch. He chose that moment to notice the actress. Her breasts were squashed against him, it was a miracle he hadn't noticed her before. Of course Lomond wasn't repelled by her proximity, he smiled and winked before leaning in to whisper something. The beauty laughed and stroked his arm.

Roxie didn't get it. Well, she did get it. Both of them were Hollywood hot and knew it too. In their positions of society, there would be few scenarios, if any, where they didn't get exactly what they wanted.

"As if that wasn't enough..." Drew Harvey shouted over the audience, calming their cheers. "At the end of the experience, before they return home, the tour prizewinner will receive all secondary prizes given tonight and, as a reward for their hard work, fifty thousand dollars!"

More cheering and clapping. With good reason, the audience dialed it up to eleven. Fifty thousand dollars was a lot of money. Was it bribery? Who wouldn't give someone a positive review in exchange for that amount of cash?

The host tapped Lomond's leg to get his attention away from the woman on the couch. The two men exchanged some unheard words and then got up to approach the audience.

"Okay, take a seat! Take a seat!" Drew Harvey called. Roxie hadn't realized so many people were standing. "It's unusual for us to do this, bear with us... Every member of our audience will win something tonight. And, believe it or not, the final decision was to do this by the Oprah method. You'll find an envelope under your seats. Don't open it!" The audience did as he said. "If you have a red envelope, stand up!"

Jane stood up, excitement shimmering around her. Blazing anticipation was buzzing around the room, upping the temperature of the air.

"Open those red envelopes!" Drew paused for a few seconds. "All of you are the proud owners of a pair of tickets to the Crimson Resort in the Bahamas! Flights and hotel stay included!"

Lots more cheering. Jane dropped into her seat, showing them the glitzy invite.

"Next, gold envelopes, stand up!"

Leaping to her feet, Toria held her envelope high. The gold prize was a pair of tickets for the grand New Year re-opening of the New York club. According to the host, it had been closed for months undergoing a multimillion-dollar refurb.

Her gregarious roommate was perfect for the prize. Jane, the most demure of their trio, wouldn't be comfortable getting VIP treatment, not if she was singled-out. In contrast, Toria would lap up any and all attention, in the most fabulous way.

The green envelope holders won a thousand dollars; blue envelopes got masses of merchandise. Next, Drew Harvey told those with purple envelopes to stand... or, at least, she figured he did. Without Toria and Jane nudging and pushing at her, the cue would've passed her by.

The lights on the host and Lomond became more vivid when the audience were plunged into darkness. A spotlight formed over her. Damn, did it have to be so bright? Roxie held up a hand to block the brilliant white light's glare.

"The five of you come on down!" Drew Harvey yelled.

Five? Roxie wouldn't have seen the others even if she had looked around. Jane jumped up to get out of the way and pulled Roxie onto the stairs, giving her a push to get her moving.

Drew Harvey spoke again, "Stay with us, folks! You'll find out which of these lucky people are about to have the time of their lives!"

2

Roxie stood on the stairs while Drew Harvey waited on pause, presumably for the commercial break to start.

The lights came up and a woman wearing a headset rushed over to gather the five purple envelope holders.

"Come with me," Headset Gal said, gesturing at them.

The five followed her onto the set. They wound around cameras, hopped over wires, and dodged people until they came to a side curtain leading into a wide corridor. They hurried along in double-quick time and were funneled into a bright room with white walls and a bunch of computers set up in the middle.

"Sit down and fill out what you can," Headset Gal said. "You have twelve minutes."

The woman shuffled out and the door was closed.

Sealed in silence, their quintet looked at each other for a few seconds.

"Jill Alcott," the brunette opposite Roxie said.

"I don't think they want us to make friends," one of the guys said, rushing to seat himself at a computer.

"He's right," the other woman said, dashing to another terminal. "We only have twelve minutes!"

The reminder got everyone moving; her with less impetus. Curiosity won out, so Roxie took her place at a computer to see what awaited on screen. Fifty grand was nothing to sniff at. She wouldn't mind travelling for a few months either.

The club appealed to a certain extent. At home, she and her girls went to nightclubs all the time. Every week, often more than once. Exclusive extras weren't required to have a good time. As long as there was music and a good atmosphere, she'd have fun.

No one could see each other's screens; the monitors had been positioned to ensure that. She guessed they shared the same questionnaire.

Name, age, marital status, occupation, number of children. Easy. Straightforward. Beyond the basic biography stuff, all of the questions were multiple choice. A quick scan revealed that in addition to three or four specific choices, every question had "*all of the above*" and "*none of the above*" as optional answers too.

Favorite color? The options were the colors of the envelopes. Roxie went with "*all of the above.*" Favorite ice-cream flavor and genre of music got the same response.

"Oh my God, it asks for favorite sexual position!" Jill exclaimed.

The men straightened up, encouraged by the inclusion apparently. They exchanged a look before returning to their screens, no doubt to search for the question. Roxie kept going down the list, answering questions as they were numbered.

"What do you think they're looking for?" Jill asked. "What do the questions mean?"

"It'll be some scientific thing, like the answers reveal a lot about us," one of the guys said. "I'm Dale, by the way."

Roxie didn't think to respond to him until she noticed he was looking right at her. "I didn't ask the question," she said. "Jill did."

Smiling, he didn't look away. "Just wanted to introduce myself."

Creepy, but okay. Weirded out, she drew her attention back to the screen.

"I think we're supposed to be honest," the other, more fresh-faced, woman said. "Not try to figure it out."

"How old are you?" Dale asked. "Are you even legal?"

She did look young.

"Bet Lomond picks her to get in her pants," Mr. In-A-Hurry said then stood up to offer his hand to Dale. "Ron."

"Dale," he said again. They shook hands. "And, yeah, you're probably right."

"I'm nineteen," the gorgeous blonde said. "I'm an adult."

Just barely. She snorted. Oops, had that come out? Yeah, everyone was looking at her.

Clearing her throat, Roxie returned her focus to the screen.

"If he's picking based on who he's sexually attracted to…" Jill said. "Why are we filling out questionnaires?"

"He can't do that," Roxie said. "If she was already the winner, they'd have spotlighted her and been done with it."

The others pondered for a minute, so Roxie went back to the questions.

"What's your name?" Ron asked the young woman.

"Bree."

"She could be a plant," Dale said. "Sent in to throw us off."

"You would do him though, right?" Ron asked Bree. "For fifty grand, I don't think anyone would say no."

Roxie was incredulous. "Do you think any studio or show could get away with prostituting the audience?"

Mystifying. Some people were… Surely everyone got to that conclusion on their own.

"We have to get through these questions," Jill said. "I don't think we're supposed to talk to each other."

"Everything is a test," Ron said, nodding. "That's the truth. We live in a reality TV show. Life is reality TV."

Life was reality, not TV. Dwelling on reality was no fun for anyone. The pursuit of liberty and happiness went hand in hand, but she never worried about being watched or coerced into contrived setups. Pushing out her lips, her eyes slunk left to right. She'd never worried about it until right then anyway.

"It could be the one who answers the most questions wins," Dale said.

"Or the fewest," Roxie said to be contrary.

Dale was smiling at her again. Still creepy. The guy could be perfectly nice, completely harmless. But with the creepy smiling, he didn't stand a chance.

"I bet the resort is amazing. The Bahamas, I've always wanted to stay at a luxury resort," Bree said, pausing to swoon. "Zairn must live an incredible life. Imagine."

"Endless money," Ron said. "Endless pussy."

What else could a man want? Women on the other hand… In her experience, men only wanted their women to have a good time if it suited them. Suited the guy that is, not the woman. Double standard. Her ex, Porter, came to mind.

Continuing with the questions, she ignored the speculation bouncing between the guys and Bree. Risqué conversation didn't bother her, few things did, but guessing was pointless. Jill was keeping her head down too.

The conversation came to an end when the door opened and Headset Gal leaned in. "You're done. Hit submit at the bottom and come with me."

Roxie scrolled down and clicked submit as instructed, then fell in line with the others as they filtered out. Instead of returning the way they'd come, Headset Gal directed them the other way to continue along the corridor.

Nearby voices were muffled. Everyone they passed was silent. Her group went around a curve just as the unmistakable sound of applause rose. Each of the quintet was pushed through curtains into the glare of more bright lights.

The applause died down as her eyes adjusted to the illumination. The purple envelope posse stood at the back of the talk show set flanked by the host to one side and the couch guests to the other.

"Welcome, all!" Drew Harvey said. "We're going to reveal our winner in one short minute. Our computer geniuses are cracking the numbers as we speak. Zairn, what do you think of the line-up?"

Inscrutable Lomond perused the line. "Some I could work with."

With no interest in his inspection, Roxie drew her eyes away.

Drew Harvey went to gorgeous Bree first. Shocker. "What's your name?" he asked, shoving a microphone in the young woman's face.

"Bree."

"What would it mean to you if you won, Bree?"

"It would be incredible! Amazing," Bree said, vibrating with excitement.

Winning would be exciting, so long as it didn't mean surrendering freewill. Jill seemed like a nice person and Bree would get a lot from the experience. As long as a female took the prize, it would be a good day.

Ron made some joke about being Lomond's wingman. The audience laughed. Dale nudged her to share his eye roll. And he thought she'd appreciate it? He'd been happy to talk about ogling women with Ron earlier.

"And here it is…" the host said, returning to the side to put the microphone down. He pressed his finger to his ear, probably for effect. "We have a winner. Z, man, you ready for this?"

Drew Harvey tossed a smile his apparent friend's way, though the playboy didn't react. Playing it cool seemed to be Lomond's specialty… when he wasn't busy flaunting his ego.

"Roxie Kyst!"

Her name. Did he say her name? It flashed on a screen above the band. That was her name. Roxie had won.

Someone hugged her, then someone else.

"Congratulations, Roxie. You're in for a wild adventure! Our other four finalists do not go home empty-handed. You get all of the other prizes, resort holiday, tickets to the opening night in New York, all the merchandise and one thousand dollars!"

Still in a daze when the embracing ended, Roxie was dumbfounded. Cheering and applause rose. Her ears rang with it as the host thanked his guests and said goodnight.

3

When Roxie shook herself back to the moment, Drew Harvey was chatting it up with the rest of the final five. The guests from the couch were nowhere in sight and the audience were talking amongst themselves, gathering their things.

Her friends were standing up there, waving at her.

It was over. The show was over.

Jumping to action, Roxie hurried across the set to vault up the stairs in the direction of her friends. Jane and Toria were bouncing in the middle aisle by their seats, waiting, eager to grab her into a hug.

"You won!" Toria screeched. "You won! You won!"

"Where did they take you?" Jane asked.

The three of them parted, though their hands stayed linked.

"We did a survey thing on computers."

Whatever her answers, they'd been honest, which was apparently enough to grant her the win.

Something touched Roxie's shoulder. She turned to find a group from the audience peering at her.

"Congratulations," one of them said. "You must be so excited."

"I… yeah," Roxie said, still trying to convince herself it was real.

"She's the best," Toria said, leaping forward to put an arm around her. "The best!"

"You're so lucky," another audience member said.

For the next while, Roxie fielded questions and listened to people gush about the prizes. She didn't even know how long they'd been talking when the group parted to bring Headset Gal into view.

"Miss Kyst, would you come with me?"

The group lit up. Her hand was grabbed, and someone squeezed her arm; another someone touched her back. Apparently, her body had become public property.

"Oh, wow, this is it! You're going to meet him!"

Headset Gal wasn't as excited as the others around them. The employee's day job involved meeting all sorts of rich and famous people. For Headset Gal, this would be just another day at the office.

"All of you need to register for your prizes," Headset Gal said.

The woman went backwards down a stair with an air of expectation that anticipated Roxie would follow.

Instead, she lingered. "Can my friends come?"

The woman blinked and glanced at her friends. "No, this is only for you... They have to register for whatever they won too."

Roxie hugged each of her roommates. "Go back to the hotel. I'll grab a cab when I'm done here."

"Will you?" Jane asked. "Maybe your prize starts right now."

Despite their hope of an answer from Headset Gal, all they got was impatience. "I don't know," she said. "It's my job to put you in the room. I don't know what'll happen in there. I am not the top of the totem pole."

Toria hugged Roxie from behind to murmur in her ear, "Wow, she's warm and fuzzy."

"Okay," Roxie said, twisting in her friend's arms to kiss her cheek. "You have fun. I'll give you a full report when I'm through."

Following Headset Gal down the stairs, Roxie glanced back to wave one last time. Wherever they were going, she was on her own. That was fine. Roxie was confident with her independence. It just would've been easier to talk about whatever happened if someone experienced it with her.

Headset Gal led her the same way as before with the quintet. Roxie was expecting a similar setup wherever they were going until the moment Headset Gal stepped aside. Brought up short, she hadn't expected such vibrant décor. Bold colors on the wall contrasted with the velvet couch and armchairs.

"Just wait in here," Headset Gal said, reversing out of the room.

The abstract prints on the wall had more color than form. But, oh, the candles on a far shelf tempted her over. Scented candles were kind of Roxie's thing, so she'd love to… They were fake. Huh. Being surprised was sort of stupid; it would be against health and safety regulations to leave naked flames lying around in empty rooms.

Returning to the long table by the door, she squeezed the fruit in the bowl to check it was definitely real before helping herself to a grape. There was wine too, red, probably expensive. To drink or not to drink? Until she knew what was going on, it wouldn't be smart to liquor up.

The door opened.

Assuming the entrant would be the famous sponsor of the prize, Roxie was wrong again. It was a woman, maybe about her age, blonde, perky, beautiful. Short, something they had in common. Carrying a leather binder… hmm, intriguing and, perhaps, ominous.

"Miss Kyst?"

"Mm hmm," Roxie said around the second grape she'd just popped into her mouth.

"I'm Astrid, one of Mr. Lomond's assistants," she said, gesturing at the couch.

Roxie went in that direction. "One of them?"

"He has several."

"Why does he need several?" Roxie asked, tucking her skirt under her thighs as she sat down.

The assistant sat beside her. "He's a busy man… A man in demand."

"Sure," Roxie said, her nodding slow and deliberate… and maybe a little sarcastic, if a gesture could be called that. "In demand… Hmm… Wonder why a guy who's so in demand needs a shadow."

"Mr. Lomond puts his business before everything else," Astrid said, unzipping the leather binder to produce a stack of papers. "We need a few signatures."

"Signatures," Roxie said, taking the documents. "This should be interesting."

Sliding her feet from her shoes, she wriggled deeper into the corner of the couch, tucking her feet under her ass.

"You're reading?" Astrid asked after a few seconds.

"I'm reading," Roxie said without taking her eyes from the words.

"There are ten pages."

"Some small print too it looks like," Roxie said, her smirk drifting up to Astrid for a few seconds. "I have to know what I'm signing."

"It's late."

"I can take it away and bring it back another day," Roxie said. "If you'd prefer. I wouldn't want to inconvenience your boss by causing a delay."

"Mr. Lomond's no longer in the building."

Deciphering the legalese would take some time. "So I'm just delaying you."

"I don't know how long we can stay here," Astrid said and shot to her feet. "Wait here a moment."

The woman rushed out without waiting for a response. It was fine. Reading was one of Roxie's favorite things to do... it was her job to do it well.

In the initial pages, rules were listed. Stay with the group while in foreign countries. Respect customs. Don't talk to the media, other than the documentary team. Blah, blah...

During Talk at Sunset, Lomond's words were "nothing to hide." According to what she read, they weren't opening all doors as had been implied. Anything of a personal nature was not part of her remit. She got that. Everyone was entitled to their privacy.

When the door opened, Astrid appeared again. "We can do this back at the hotel."

"The hotel?" Roxie asked. "What hotel?"

"The Grand Hotel where Mr. Lomond is staying."

Roxie got up, observing Astrid's uncertainty. "Are you sure I'm allowed in the same building as him before my signature is on these pages?"

"I got permission from Og... if you're really asking."

The poor girl didn't have a good sarcasm-o-meter... which didn't bode well for the level of humor in the Lomond camp. Maybe spending a few months on his tail wouldn't be so much fun after all.

"My purse is at my seat..." Roxie said. "Unless my girls took it with them."

Astrid hugged the binder to her chest. "Everything you need will be provided. In the documents, there's a section dedicated to your necessities. Whatever you require, likes, dislikes, allergies, medical provisions, list everything and it will be taken care of. Over the next couple of days, we'll deal with employment needs, talk to your employer, take care of your bills, anything that needs to be done. We'll iron out all issues. The official tour doesn't start until we reach Boston. If you require your own staff—"

"Geez, lady, you come from a whole different world." Shuffling past the low coffee table, Roxie joined Astrid. "Let me check if my purse is still out there."

"We'll take care of it," Astrid said. "Follow me, there's a car waiting for us."

So efficient. As she hurried along behind Astrid, Roxie was impressed by the blonde's quick issue of instructions on the phone. The assistant requested whoever was on the other end of the line to track down Roxie's purse. She paused just long enough to request the details of the hotel the trio of roommates shared.

A shiny black car was waiting outside; a driver stood by the open back door. A life of luxury was apparently what she'd signed up for. A different world, definitely a different world.

The Grand Hotel suite was a little too nice. With separate living and bedroom areas, the sleek, sophisticated décor screamed hands-off. In her Chicago apartment, the armchairs didn't match the couch. Almost everything was purchased used or at a discount. Her home was clean, but only because Jane was obsessive about dust.

Rather than focus on her transformation into Eliza Doolittle, Roxie read the legal documents until a knock on the door interrupted her. On the room's threshold, a smiling guy handed over her purse with all its contents. Young and sort of twitchy, he was polite and strode off with purpose like delivery of the purse was just one of many tasks he had on his to-do list. Or maybe he had better places to be.

The hour was late, so she elected to read the rest of the documents in the tub with a glass of wine. She called her friends too, to let them know that she was okay.

Returning to Toria and Jane's hotel didn't appeal. The soapy bubbles piled on the surface of her sumptuous pool were too indulgent. It wasn't actually a pool, though it may as well be. The tub was big enough for half a dozen people, maybe more, not that its capacity mattered. Roxie had it to herself and didn't plan on sharing any time soon.

Leaving the bathroom, her scrutiny progressed to the bed, which could probably accommodate the same number of people as the tub. Wearing only her robe, she climbed under the covers and closed her eyes.

Her next flicker of awareness came the following day. Sleeping late was her norm. Her friends hadn't called, of course not, they knew better than to assume she'd be awake in any single-digit hour. Yes, she was nocturnal and owned it.

Room service was next on the agenda. After enjoying her first meal of the day, Roxie used every complimentary product in the bathroom and did her hair with the provided tools. The high life wasn't so bad.

Putting on the previous night's clothes felt sort of shady in the way it would if she was creeping out on a guy. Technically, Lomond had paid for the suite. Good thing she hadn't needed to give it up to get a night's sleep.

No one stood guard outside her room. Not that she expected they would, but it meant there was no one to ask if she was supposed to be available at any specific time. She couldn't hang around the hotel indefinitely. No one told her to stay locked up in the suite. She needed clothes and to talk to her friends. They were only in California for another three days, that day included. Sitting idle was eating into her vacation time.

Using the cash in her purse to grab a cab to her girls' hotel, she rushed up to their room. Her keycard granted her access to stride on inside. Except… there was no one home.

Hmm, disappointing.

While waiting for them, she changed her clothes and fixed her makeup. Then she stood in the closet, staring at her open suitcase, strewn with the tentacles of clothes she'd tossed aside or back to the pile. As always, Jane had offered to unpack for her over and over again. Roxie didn't see the point when it would all just be packed again in a week.

If the plan was to stay in the fancy Grand suite, she'd need her things. Given how boring the day had been so far, Roxie would rather stick with her girls… if she could find them. Her cellphone was dead. Irritating, but not unexpected. Remaining optimistic, she connected its charger and waited.

Her trusty laptop kept her busy. She did a little work, purchased a dress, and read the news. A couple of bills needed to be paid, but she'd get to them… soon.

An hour went by. Should she be worried? She was starting to worry.

Snatching up her cellphone, she hit call on Toria's number. A beep came from the door. Leaping from the bed, Roxie tossed her phone down at the same time the door opened.

Her friends came in but paused when they noticed her standing there, raising her arms in an exaggerated shrug.

"Where have you been?" Roxie exclaimed. "I was worried!"

"Shopping," Toria said, holding up a couple of bags. "We're meeting people for dinner."

"People?" Roxie asked, surprised and curious. "What people? We know people here?"

"People we met at the show last night," Jane said, putting her own bags aside to come over and hug her. "We didn't know you'd be here."

"Why didn't you call?" Toria asked, taking her hair down. "Like I don't know…" Her roommates were more than aware of her proclivity for forgetting to charge her phone. "We have a million things to do before tonight. I'll never be ready in time." It was only three in the afternoon, but Toria liked to linger over getting ready. "We're meeting for dinner and drinks. You should come with."

"Yeah," Roxie said like it was obvious, because, duh, it was. "I've been bored out of my mind all day."

"Bored?" Jane asked, jerking back in surprise. "How could you be bored living with the world's number one playboy? What's he like? Oh my God, you have to tell us everything!"

Managing a smile, Roxie couldn't restrain her sigh. "About whom? Only people I met were an overworked assistant and a cutie errand boy."

Toria rushed over to Jane's side. "You haven't met him?"

Roxie shook her head and backed up to sit on the corner of the bed. "I'm not sure that's a bad thing. Guy seems like an asshole to me."

"You know he's richer than sin, right?" Typical that Toria would use that truth to excuse a multitude of sins. "I'm jealous as all hell… Where did you go last night?"

"A hotel… The Grand."

Jane swung around to sit at her side. "He always stays at The Grand... Unless he's in New York or London."

Toria laughed. "She's like a Lomond encyclopedia."

Laying a hand on her friend's head, Roxie stroked her hair. "This prize is wasted on me. You should totally take my place."

"I wish," Jane scoffed. "I have to be at work next week."

"Yeah, you're the only one of us who can do their job anywhere," Toria said.

Was that why she'd won? She kept stroking Jane's hair. "You're so pretty."

"Would you stop and be serious," Jane said, taking Roxie's hand from its task. "You have to live this for me."

"And me," Toria said. "You're being whisked away across the world by a gorgeous, enigmatic millionaire."

"Billionaire," Jane corrected her.

"Billionaire, excuse me," Toria said, descending to sit at Roxie's other side. "You do deserve this, honey. You've had a crappy year where men are concerned. Forget about Porter trying to tie you down and get back to who you are. Go wild. Embrace the experience."

"How do I do that?"

"You start by showing us the room in your fancy hotel."

That might be fun. "It's a suite."

Jane squealed. "We'll pack up your stuff and take it over there before dinner."

"Good plan," Roxie said, standing up, freeing herself from their flanks. "Now I know you two are alive, I can use the gym downstairs... That should give you a head start, Tor. Think an hour will be enough or should I make it two?"

Her friend sneered, but it was all in good humor. Toria was almost always late even though she'd start to get ready first. Although they teased her about it, Roxie didn't mind waiting for her friend. If preening made her feel good, then who was anyone to judge Toria for that?

A night out with people and alcohol was a perfect recipe for a reset. She'd be optimistic about the prize by the time the morning came.

Their group was a real hoot. Roxie had missed the whole hookup at the show. While she'd been with Astrid and her contracts, Toria and Jane were networking.

The private dining area of the restaurant was filled with strangers. Mostly strangers anyway. Somehow, the range of the group extended to her computer room companions. With so many bodies and the alcohol flowing, they were a boisterous bunch.

The restaurant was a launch pad for an unexpected night on the town. One bar became two, hour piled on hour. They were bumbling down the street, bouncing off each other, singing and shouting. Where they were going was a mystery. But so was the name of the woman holding her hand.

The energy was incredible. Her skin was buzzing, her blood hot, and she couldn't stop smiling. She wanted to dance; there was no better way to show her joy.

"Oh! Oh!" Ron bawled, jumping up and down. "This is it! Who's ready to party?"

As everyone whooped and rushed forward, Roxie noticed where they were: Crimson.

The rest of their group stampeded toward the entrance. Her hand was dropped, so she was left there staring up at the bright red letters that somehow screamed sin.

"How does he do that?" she whispered.

"Come on," Toria said, materializing from the rear of the tight crowd. "You're our way in."

Her friend cajoled her to the front of the group. Ron was spearheading the effort to get inside.

"We'll spend money, a lot of money," Ron was saying to the two guys behind the rope that held back the masses. "Look how many of us there are... and we know Zairn. We *know* him!"

A line of people extended along the side of the building. A line Ron wanted to cut.

"Here's our ticket!" Toria called, pushing her forward.

The moment Ron saw her, his excitement bloomed. "Yeah! Yes! This is Roxie. She's Zairn's buddy! Like his best buddy!" Hooking an arm around her neck, he tugged her to his side, which pulled Toria to him as well. "She's allowed in anywhere."

"Anywhere?" the security guy asked, dragging his gaze from her feet to her face. "Not in here."

"Hey!" The superior ease of his dismissal heated her blood. "Don't look at a woman that way. It's rude!"

"You're not getting in, sweetheart."

"I'm not your sweetheart," she said, shoving Ron aside to put herself in front of the security guy, despite him being three times her size. "Isn't it your job to make patrons feel welcome? We're patrons, right here, all of us."

"Yeah," the security guy said, nodding at the line. "They are too."

"So you couldn't just suggest we wait in line rather than belittling and leering at women?"

"No one was leering, honey."

Infuriated, her affront was bolstered by the alcohol coursing through her system. "I can't believe a guy like you is in charge of anything." She inhaled. "Lomond is a piece of work. I bet he selected you personally."

"Ma'am—"

"No," Roxie said, tossing her hair over her shoulder. "You are a bully. Drunk on your power. Who do you answer to, huh?"

"Ma'am, it's my responsibility to ensure the safety of those inside."

"Are you saying we're dangerous?" someone called out from behind her.

"Yeah!"

A weight of bodies rushed up, tipping her off balance. The security guy grabbed her before she hit the concrete. Everything became sensory overload in a snap. People were everywhere, shouting and pushing. The mass of them closed in on her from every angle. The suffocating crush jostled her; she bounced off one person and then another. Adding to the commotion of shouting and cussing, she screamed. Terror and hilarity warred for control. It didn't matter. No one would hear an individual voice in the melee of madness.

Unable to see through the darkness or hear any guiding voice, moving with the crowd was the only option. A glimmer of space to the side gave her hope until a jolt at her other side propelled her into another body. The shouting and shoving didn't stop; if anything, it intensified. The rising sound of sirens did nothing to calm the free-for-all.

Toria's advice to go wild had been prophetic. It was funny. They were making an impression. Crimson wouldn't forget them in a hurry.

5

Jail wasn't on her sightseeing list.

The cops had their work cut out for them. Dealing with such an influx of people took time. Other than the noise and the sick-scented stale air, the experience was a blur.

Scraping together change took time. Most of it went on tracking down the number of the Grand Hotel and trying to convince the receptionist that she really did know Astrid. Yes, uh huh, she did... even though she was drawing a blank on the young woman's last name.

Talking on the phone wasn't easy in a room of drunks. Especially when she was one of them. By the end of the exhausting episode, Roxie had sobered up some.

The call was easy in comparison to the experience of walking up to the front desk where Astrid waited. The blonde assistant didn't say a word, not a single word while the cop guy took Roxie through the process required to cut her loose.

She put on her necklace and started for the front door, assuming they were leaving, but didn't get more than a couple of steps. Astrid hurried over to urge her in a different direction.

"This way."

Astrid crowded her through a side door, down a blah grey hallway to an exit. It wasn't unlike leaving the studio, except an Escalade awaited them this time... Oh, and it was beginning to get light out.

Bundled inside, the vehicle started to move before Astrid closed the door. Despite the tinted windows, daylight still managed to hurt her eyes.

"I need to get my emergency credit card to bail out—"

"Your friends and their friends will be taken care of."

Astrid's cold, curt tone was expected... justified. They'd only known each other for a day. Great first impression. Hmm. No wiggle room. Astrid was young but already a pro at playing the disapproving principal.

In this production, Roxie was the naughty schoolgirl. "I'm sorry." Apologizing was the right thing to do. "Things got out of hand."

"Crimson is in the press... for all the wrong reasons... again."

Lomond put it to the world that he had nothing to hide and wasn't debauched. Then she'd gone out and started a riot on the doorstep of his club.

Oh, wasn't she a treat?

"It wasn't meant to be... we were going for dinner and drinks... I didn't know there would be so many people."

"Why did you leave the hotel?" Astrid asked. "If I'd known you were going to be slippery, I'd have put security on your door." The woman focused straight ahead. "Usually women have to be torn away from Mr. Lomond's hospitality. They don't leave voluntarily."

"I guess I'm not a usual woman," Roxie said. There were probably a lot of ways in which she wasn't like one of Lomond's women. "I went to see my friends. Did you think I'd just sit around in a hotel room alone all day and all night? What was I supposed to do? I didn't know I was breaking any rules. Winning the contest wasn't supposed to be a jail sentence, was it? I don't do well caged."

Something that had been reinforced to her while "enjoying" last night's accommodation.

"We haven't received your contracts," Astrid said.

"That's not my fault. They're on the table in my room. No one came looking for them. Was I supposed to knock on every door in the hotel until I found whoever wanted them?"

"Og thinks you're going to be trouble."

Roxie sighed and settled back. "I don't know what that means."

"The wrong kind of trouble, he says. Exactly the kind of trouble Mr. Lomond doesn't need."

What kind of an asshole...? Why did people make judgments about those they didn't know? Superior sonofabitch no doubt. Lomond sure liked to surround himself with uptight people.

Folding her arms, Roxie shifted to get a better view of Astrid's profile. "Does this Og plan to say that to my face?"

On glancing her way for the first time, Astrid became a little less severe. "You don't want to talk to Ogilvie. No one messes with him."

"If he doesn't want to mess with me, maybe he shouldn't go around casting aspersions behind my back... Who is he anyway?"

"Mr. Lomond's most trusted advisor."

"Can't be that good at his job if he's telling Lomond I'm trouble. *Og* doesn't do very thorough research, does he? Seems he jumps to conclusions. All the wrong conclusions."

Vacant, Astrid blinked a couple of times. "You refused to sign the contracts—"

"Without reading them. That's sensible."

"Snuck out of the hotel—"

"I walked out like everyone else does," Roxie said. "I'm not Lomond's prisoner."

"You fought with a security guard—"

"I argued with him," Roxie said, raising a straight finger before folding her arms again. "And he was rude."

"You started a riot outside his club."

"I didn't *start* the riot." Roxie waved a dismissive hand. "I was just... an un-instigating, totally passive participant."

"You got arrested."

Filling her lungs, Roxie prepared to fight the charge, except... yeah. "Okay, I'll give you that one." She released the fortifying air. "If I'm that much trouble, why didn't you say to hell with me? You didn't have to come and bail me out. You could've left me there. I'm sure there's something sneaky in the small print, some loophole you could've exploited."

"That's what Og told Mr. Lomond."

Roxie nodded once. "Good. First smart piece of advice I've heard him give... I would've said to hell with me."

"Mr. Lomond doesn't retreat from challenges."

Hit by offense, Roxie forced her arms back to push herself upright. "A challenge? Is that what the asshole called me?"

Astrid squirmed in her seat and averted her gaze.

No way she'd give up just because the assistant was uncomfortable. Being such a hot topic of conversation, there should be plenty to say about it.

"Mr. Lomond isn't... I'd never use that word to describe him."

Roxie scoffed, dragging her attention to the window. "That's 'cause you work for him," she muttered. "He can't fire me."

"He's dedicated to his work. He's a serious person."

"A serious person?" Roxie said, spitting out a burst of laughter. Hilarious! Lomond? A serious person? Yeah, right. "Playboy of the century? Yeah, I can see that about him... Uh huh, totally... He's sure serious about his own hubris." She couldn't resist whispering, "Asshole."

"Mr. Lomond is... he is..."

The pretty assistant puffed up and moved with a little more purpose, though it was clear she didn't know what to do with it. Roxie couldn't see Astrid's face, but the woman was blushing, without a doubt.

Blushing and bluster. They were screwing. Had to be. Playboy of the century probably screwed everything in a skirt that he stumbled across.

Roxie set a discerning eye on Astrid. "It's never a good idea to screw your boss." Astrid's eyes and mouth widened. "Don't worry, honey, we've all done it. It's something about the power... frowned upon these days for sure. As it should be, too many people abuse their power. But when they look like Lomond, I can see how you could get sucked in… You've gotta see past the cut of his fancy suit and the perfect hair. A guy like that isn't capable of loving anything as much as he loves himself."

"Mr. Lomond is a thorough and considerate employer. Why would you accept the prize if you despise him?"

"I don't despise him." Roxie shrugged. "I just know his type."

"So you're putting him in a box… like you think Og did with you."

Their eyes met.

Young and smart. Impressive. Maybe, one day, Lomond would see past the perkiness and give the beautiful woman a little respect too. Except, hmm, yeah, Astrid was right. She'd judged Lomond by his reputation. In her defense, there was more of his than hers. Roxie didn't have internationally renowned status, she was shiny new, and already Lomond's people were putting her in a box.

"Touché." Roxie smiled. "Okay, you think I'm talking out my ass, that's fine. We'll ignore his press, ignore everything that's ever been written about him, ignore every report."

"The media have an agenda."

Sinking back in the seat, Roxie closed her tired eyes. "Everyone has an agenda," she said, opening one eye a little to peek at Astrid. "That's what I was trying to tell you. Men especially, they usually have two motives, and at least one of them will be related to their cock." Her eyes sank closed again as her lips stretched in response to the innuendo. "And, honey, if it's a cock that belongs to you, it's your responsibility to own its priorities."

"There isn't much time for… men." The squirming was back again, it was in Astrid's voice. The woman seriously lacked confidence. "We're on the road a lot."

"You're young though, right?" Roxie wriggled to get more comfortable. Exhaustion was beginning to weigh her down. "Or does Lomond have the secret to eternal youth too?"

"I'm twenty-three," Astrid said. "I've worked for Mr. Lomond since I left college. I interned for Tibbs for two summers before that."

"I don't know who Tibbs is," Roxie said and yawned. "I think I'll sleep for twenty-four hours and then avail myself of the hotel gym… I am allowed to use the gym, right?"

"I think so… We'll have to check with Ballard."

"You keep talking about people I've never met like I should know them."

"We get pretty insular… Sometimes we forget there's a world beyond Crimson."

"A whole universe," Roxie said, almost losing the words to another yawn. Covering her mouth, she exhaled a whine. "Sorry, that was rude."

"Didn't you sleep in jail?"

Roxie was a big believer in the value of experience and wasn't ashamed of her run in with LAPD's finest.

"Never been to jail, have you?" That tease lingered in the air. "You promise my friends will be free?"

"They're already on their way back to their hotel."

Astrid was thorough. Maybe she'd learned that from Lomond or maybe she was eager to maintain her position.

Breathing out, Roxie couldn't think anymore. It had been a strange couple of days. She needed to reboot.

6

In bed, Roxie opened her eyes to darkness. Night. The best time of day. Her body bowed as she pushed her shoulders back and stretched her limbs. Would the gym be open twenty-four hours? Top-rated hotels did that kind of thing, didn't they?

Her stomach grumbled. Okay, no gym. Food or shower? After eating, work would be next. A super quick shower would have to come first. What did she want to eat? Ice-cream, coffee cake... fresh strawberry mousse.

Fantasizing was fun, but when she eventually picked up the phone to room service, steamed chicken and vegetables were the only things on her order. Smart. No indulgence or excess. Not in food anyway.

Her phone was dead again. Like that was a surprise. She dragged out her charger to juice it up and switched on her laptop too. Having slept all day, she'd be up all night. Her body was returning to its regular rhythm.

When someone knocked on the suite door, Roxie sprang up from the dining table where she'd positioned the laptop and hurried over to answer it.

She threw open the door but was in reverse before setting eyes on whoever was there.

"Hold on, I have to find my purse," Roxie said. The uniformed guy with the trolley paused. "You can bring it in, that's fine. I just have to find cash to tip you."

"Thank you, ma'am, but that's not necessary."

Astonished, she stopped and stood silent while he brought the tray in and set a place for her at the table.

"I have to tip you," she said, snapping out of her shock. "I always tip. Hospitality staff deal with some amount of BS."

"Thank you, ma'am," he said, retreating with a smile. "It's unnecessary. You are Mr. Lomond's guest. Enjoy your meal."

What the hell? Her impulse was to argue. What was the opposite of robbery? Why wouldn't he want a gratuity? Her stomach grumbled again, diverting her bewilderment. The food smelled good, really good. She went to sit at the place the guy had set and dragged her laptop over to open her email. If she didn't reply to clients now, their messages would distract her later.

Spam. Nonsense. Client. Client. Bill. Spam. Meme from Toria. Client. Technically, she was on vacation and wasn't supposed to be working. Any work that she got done would be less for next week. Being ahead of the game was never a bad thing.

Stabbing another vegetable, she pulled it from the fork with her teeth. One email caught her eye. Crimson.com, what did they want from her? Recompense for what had happened outside the club? Astrid hadn't said anything about that earlier. Maybe it was decided after she'd been retrieved from jail. The email had come in hours ago, while she was sleeping.

The only way to find out was to open it. The text was straight to the point. First was a link to her dedicated page on the Crimson website. Her own page, fancy. Clicking on the link took her to an admin login screen. Hmm… Returning to the email, she discovered a username and password. Inputting both, she was delighted that they worked.

The actual page was divided into two sections: one for videos and one for chat. Two buttons, one said "upload video," the other "stream." Glancing down at the hotel robe, she pulled the lapels together, laughing. Yeah, streaming would be a bad idea.

People had posted a bunch of comments and questions. Thus far, they went unanswered. It wouldn't hurt to work her way through them while she ate, would it?

Everyone seemed so happy and excited. Ignoring them would be rude.

Before she could do anything else, the system demanded a username and profile picture. Curses. Selfie-time. The laptop told her there wasn't enough light, once, twice and again. No matter how she angled, the lamp wasn't sufficient. Putting on the overhead light worked, though balancing her laptop on a forearm while posing was tricky. As she switched off the ceiling light, she loaded the picture to her profile.

Username was a little more difficult. It had to be something fun... and couldn't link back to her business pages. The Crimson website wasn't hers; it was Lomond's. After the tour was done, her page would be erased and her credentials revoked, as they should be.

Lomond's... What was she to him?

A comment caught her eye.

Smiling, Roxie chose her username: "***Lomond's Delight.**"

He'd get the irony of that, right? It wouldn't matter. Her username wouldn't cross his desk; anyone official would have better things to do.

After the way Astrid had run down her greatest hits, Roxie wouldn't blame Lomond for having a negative opinion of her. Her opinion of him wasn't exactly lofty. When he went around exuding arrogance like he did, he was asking for people to judge him. He couldn't be as good as he thought himself to be. No one was that good.

Reading the questions one at a time, Roxie typed answers under her new username...

Q: *How do you feel about your prize? You must be crazy excited. Going on tour like that, with Zairn Lomond, it would be a delight! Amazing fun.*

A: *It was unexpected. I had no idea there were going to be any contests or prizes the night we went to see Sunset. Just goes to show that anything can happen any time!*

Q: *Who are you? Do you even like to party?*

A: *I love having a good time! Music and lights, what's not to love?*

Q: *Are you a Crimson Queen?*

A: *Uh… I'm not totally sure what that is, but thanks for your question.*

Answering another and another, she worked her way down the never-ending list. A counter in the corner was ticking up… fast. What was it for? She scrolled down to read the words beneath it. "Users online." Cool. People were logging on right in front of her. The positivity and excitement were infectious.

The comments were coming so fast she could hardly read them before three more popped up. The counter kept rising. Her fingers stalled, hovering above the keys. An audience. A huge number of people rushing to read her words.

Hmm, there were two choices: run or give the people what they wanted. Cracking her thumb knuckles, she pushed the food away and sat up straight. The people wanted to talk, and she was never short of something to say.

"*Hello, everyone,*" Roxie typed. "*Wow, you're all so enthusiastic!*"

The cascade of eager greetings blurred the screen for a second.

Lomond was popular. He was in the press for the women he dated and the men he socialized with. He'd appeared as himself on the big screen. Hosted business seminars. Offered commentary in the news. He was the businessman that the paparazzi wouldn't leave alone.

He lived in a world many aspired to. Everyone wanted to be him or date him. Yachts in the Mediterranean. His own Bahamian island. Owner of sports stadiums and concert venues, he epitomized the playboy lifestyle. Always wearing hand-tailored clothes, he was showered with lavish expensive gifts.

The world paid attention to his every word, both in person and in the press. One word from him could make or break a brand. He'd created celebrities and cut them down. Established and extended careers while demolishing and restricting others.

In the know and the primary interest on any scene, Zairn Lomond was idolized all over the globe.

Sitting there, watching question after question pop up, the true scale of what she'd waded into became clear. Most of the questions were about him. What he was like and what he'd said to her. Everyone wanted details.

"*Whoa, beauties,*" she typed. "*I can't answer everyone at once.*"

"*What's he really like?*" was the next question that appeared.

"*Who?*" Roxie typed, adding a laugh emoticon. "*I'm kidding. Lomond, right?*"

A flurry of the word "*yes*" fired onto her screen, filling the page.

These people were brilliant and hilarious. "*You're really into him, aren't you?*"

Typing a question in response to their question was maybe a cop out. The true answer was she couldn't answer.

The questions kept coming. There was begging too. Begging for an answer.

"*Please tell us. Please. Please!*"

"*We're so jealous right now! You have to give us something.*"

"*Anything!*"

"*Yes, please, please, please, anything.*"

"*Did you swoon all over him?*"

"*What does he smell like?*"

"*Please!*"

"*Did he touch you? Like hold your hand or anything? God, I'd melt if he touched me!*"

"*Please tell us something!*"

There was no getting out of it, Roxie had to be honest. *"I'm sorry, beauties,"* she typed. *"I can't dish the dirt. I've never met him."*

For the first time since the droves had joined her, there were no words. A good five seconds passed before the denials came.

"Bullshit!"

"No way!"

"I don't believe you."

"You have met him. You have to have met him."

"We don't believe you!"

"He's the whole prize."

"Uh, yeah, nothing to hide, remember? Don't bullshit us."

"Why are you lying? Why would you lie?"

"I don't get it."

"She's lying! Total liar!"

"Don't lie about him. You shouldn't be there if you're just going to lie about him."

"Tell the truth!"

"I swear it," Roxie typed. *"I wish I could dish every juicy detail. We have never been in the same room, except at the studio when I was in the audience."*

"No way!"

"I don't believe it."

"I thought the whole point was for you to be looking over his shoulder."

"He doesn't actually want someone in his shadow all the time."

"Imagine…" another user typed. *"Being in his shadow 24/7."*

These people were so dedicated to him.

She sighed. *"You are wonderful people,"* Roxie typed, her fingers moving fast. *"He's blessed to have followers like you."*

"I'm pissed off," someone suddenly wrote.

"Yeah, it was supposed to be a dream come true."

"It was a lie."

"We were duped."

"*So much for getting the truth.*"

Horrified, Roxie watched as the group broke down to insults and upset. Some voices jumped in to try tempering the rising anger.

"*How often in life does anything meet expectation?*" Roxie wrote, hoping they could be objective. "*I'm only at the start of my journey, who knows what will happen next? Tell me what you'd look forward to if you'd won the prize.*"

Some people logged off, others continued the negativity. At least a few people answered her.

"*I'd be excited about Japan!*"

"*Italy! Definitely Rome. That's a total dream.*"

"*The hotels, the high life, unlimited spending…*"

"*I should be taking notes,*" Roxie wrote. "*It's going to be fun.*"

"*Aren't you upset you were conned?*" someone asked.

Roxie sighed. The fans were disappointed, so much for the enthusiasm. "*I came into the situation with no expectations. It is what it is. Lomond is one man with his own life. I don't think we'd get along anyway.*"

More comments, questions, everyone seemed so confused.

"*I thought it was the prize of a lifetime,*" someone wrote.

"*You're being way too understanding,*" another person typed. "*You should demand what you're due.*"

"*Yeah. You won fair and square.*"

"*We should message him. All of us.*"

Someone posted an email address, and the users started to discuss bombarding it with demands.

"*Seriously,*" Roxie wrote. "*I don't want to spend a lot of time with him anyway.*"

"*Yeah, 'cause he's a liar.*"

"*He cheated you out of your prize!*"

Someone knocked on her door. Rising from her chair, scanning the comments, Roxie reversed toward the knocking.

The words got too small for her to read as the knock came again. Someone needed to chill out, that knocking was way louder and more insistent. If the building was on fire, someone should pull the alarm… Maybe the server guy was back for his tip.

Opening the door, she revealed the slick errand boy who'd brought her purse the first night.

"What have you brought me this time?" she asked, sure he wouldn't have anything.

"Ms. Kyst," he said, casting a nervous glance down the corridor. "Have you been…? Are you…?"

Roxie frowned. "What's wrong?" She backed up. "Come in. Come in."

He entered and she let go of the door. It dropped toward its frame without the latch clicking into place.

"Where did you get the laptop?"

"My hotel before I went out last night." Roxie had to pause and refigure her timeline. "I think that was just last night. Are we after midnight?" She laughed. "Feels like a lifetime ago. Would you like a drink?"

As Roxie started toward the minibar, her door flew open. Startled, she whirled around to witness a huffing, puffing Zairn Lomond come storming in.

"Where the hell is she?" he demanded of the slick guy. Lomond didn't wait for an answer and adjusted his angle to charge at her. "Who the hell do you think you are?"

"Excuse me?" Roxie responded, cocking a hip. "Who do you think you're talking to?"

"You have no right to say my name to anyone," he barked, looming over her.

Asshole! "I haven't and I won't."

"You won a prize on a talk show, that doesn't open my inner circle to you."

"Zairn," someone said in the background.

It wasn't Slick, which meant others had followed the hotshot in. The asshole was right up close, practically on top of her, so she couldn't see past him.

The audience could go to hell, right along with him. "Good!" she responded. "I couldn't care less about your ridiculous inner circle."

"Oh, so you lie about me for kicks? You think I'd take that shit from someone like you?"

Ha. What a prick! "Someone like me? Who's that? A peasant? A nobody?"

"A charlatan," he snapped. "A lunatic charlatan."

"I'm a lunatic? *I* am?" Roxie couldn't believe her ears and let out a burst of laughter. "You probably spend your whole life surrounded by yes men and babes with really low self-esteem. You might fool them that you're worthy of their adoration, I'm not so easily deceived."

"You don't know a damn thing about me!"

"I could say the same to you about me!"

If he wanted her to acquiesce or pander, he'd be waiting a long time. Roxie would not blink first. No way.

"Mr. Lomond..."

That was Astrid's voice; they definitely weren't alone. Roxie didn't flinch and neither did he.

He smelled good. Why did she notice that? Clean with just a hint of scotch and a whisper of cologne. His tie was gone; his shirt open a couple of buttons. His hair was relaxed, unlike the rest of him. This was Zairn Lomond casual. Angry, no *furious* Zairn Lomond casual, but casual all the same.

"Z, come on," another new voice. "Don't give media whores ammunition. You know better."

Outraged, Roxie closed her eyes in a long, disbelieving blink, then sidestepped to see around the angry bear. "What did you call me?" she asked the older gentleman near the door. Except he was no gentleman if he went around insulting women he'd never met. "You better apologize."

"Why?" he asked, sauntering a couple of steps closer.

There was another guy further away, but she ignored him to focus on the rude dude.

"Because if you're talking about me, it's a lie," she said, going closer to him. "And you shouldn't insult people who have a big microphone."

"Now she's threatening us," the far away guy said.

"What the hell is going on here?" she asked, looking from one person to the next, stalling on Astrid. "Did everyone take crazy pills?"

"You were on the website," Astrid explained. "You've been talking to users."

Unable to believe that a few words could cause so much upset, Roxie was bewildered. "What? That's what got the precious Lord Lomond in a snit?"

Her attention swung back to him. Lomond wasn't any calmer, in fact the tightness in his jaw suggested he was close to breaking a molar.

Though their eyes were again locked, someone else spoke for him. "You were not given permission to—"

"I logged in," Roxie countered. "If you didn't want me there, why give me the logins?"

"We didn't know you had your computer," Slick said.

Tilting her head to the side, she narrowed her focus on Lomond. "Have you got a tongue in your head or do you always let others speak for you?" Licking her lips, she rolled her eyes upward, fake pondering. "Uh, let me help… I think the word you're looking for is 'sorry.'"

"Sorry?" Lomond snapped, marching closer. "You expect me to apologize to you?"

"Yes," she said, matching his pace until they were up close again. "You came in here yelling at me, sent your little posse to scold me and I was only doing what I'm here to do."

"You upset hundreds of people."

"Hundreds?"

"Online," he said, looming closer. "You have no idea the shit-storm you've stirred up. You had no right—"

"To tell the truth?" she asked. "They asked questions and I answered them."

"There's a process—"

"I don't give a damn about your process."

"Stop interrupting me!"

"I'll do whatever I damn well please, Skippy. I am not your employee. I am not beholden to you." She thrust her fists to her hips. "And I am definitely not afraid of you.

Shout. Threaten. Stamp your feet. Whatever. *You* are in the wrong here."

"Wrong?" he said, recoiling a fraction, incredulity written across his expression. "I am not—"

"Bet you're not used to that. Anyone ever tell you you're wrong before? 'Cause you are. Right now. Drink it in, Tough Guy."

"You had no right to talk about me."

"I didn't talk about you," she said. "Your fans wanted me to talk about you, but I told the truth. Did I meet you before tonight?" He didn't respond. "Did I?"

"No," he growled in a deep, steady reply, tension still vibrating through him.

"So that's what I said. I never met you. I told them I never met you. What would you rather I said? That we were best buds? That we were screwing and you're the best I ever had? Would you prefer me to lie? I can make up all kinds of shit. Guarantee it won't paint you in the best light..." She exhaled. "Asshole."

"Your comments have to be approved before—"

"No," Roxie said, shaking her head. "I didn't sign up for that. The point of my position is to tell the truth."

"Your position?"

"Isn't that what you wanted? To show the world you had nothing to hide? Those were your words. Yours."

"Your turn of phrase matters," he said, dialing down a little. "You don't strike me as a woman who considers her words before she uses them."

Guy had some goddamn nerve. "You think I don't know words have power?" she asked, noting the fade of his rage. "I know words have power. I also know the difference between truth and spin. I won't spin my reality for you, I tell the truth. I couldn't answer their questions because we'd never met. I don't know you. And if they asked me that question again right now, I'd say you're an impulsive hothead because that's all I know about you."

"You don't know me."

"No." Roxie folded her arms "I don't think I want to either. You're not the good kind of spontaneous, that much is obvious. What a disappointment."

His tongue moved behind his lower lip.

He took one step back to switch his focus to the others. "Give us the space."

"What?" the older guy by the door said. "Z, we've got—"

"Give us the room, Og."

Mutterings dwindled and the door closed. Everyone was gone. They were alone.

"What now?" she asked. "You going to yell at me some more without witnesses?"

Rather than answer, he held out a hand. "Zairn Lomond."

What was he doing? Introducing himself, why would he be...? "Oh, I get it," Roxie said, catching up to his motivation. "You're trying to erase the last five minutes."

"Trying a different approach. You don't know me; that won't change unless I do it right."

"I am not easily charmed." Or eager to trust his intentions. "Or intimidated."

"I noticed that," he said, raising his hand higher. "And you would be?"

"Roxie Kyst."

Relenting because it was polite, she kept her suspicion locked onto him as his fingers curled around hers. They didn't so much shake as just hold hands; the heat of his began to permeate hers, lighting something intimate in his gaze. Uh-uh. Nope. Dial it down, Cowboy. She took her hand back in a hurry.

"Nice to meet you, Roxie Kyst. Roxie's short for Roxanne?"

"Roxanna," she said. "But close enough."

"It doesn't upset you when people get it wrong?"

A slight smile curved her lips. "There are real, honest to God problems in the world that should upset all of us. A stranger making assumptions about my name isn't on that list."

"That's a good attitude," he said, retreating to the minibar. "Do you want a drink?"

"Do *I* want a drink?" she asked, her eyes widening. This guy had some set on him. "This is my room, shouldn't I be the one offering the hospitality? I haven't invited you to stay… I haven't decided if I want to."

"You have no choice. It's your position, right?" he said, retrieving a shooter bottle of scotch and a couple of others in his opposite hand. "This isn't good enough." Roxie assumed he was talking to himself. He put the bottles down and retrieved a phone from his pocket. A second later, he was talking into it. "We need drinks." Lowering the microphone, he looked at her. "What's your drink?"

"Lime-drop martini."

Back to the phone again. "Vodka, Grand Marnier, sugar, limes and iced martini glasses," he said, then paused to listen. "Yeah… No, I'll mix it." He hung up and put the phone in his jacket before taking it off. "What do you do, Miss Kyst?"

"How did you know the ingredients like that?" she asked. "You know everything about every drink?"

"Everyone starts at the bottom, me included. Entertainment is what I do." That was almost funny. Licking her lips, Roxie tried and failed to hide her amusement. "That's funny?"

"Imagining you behind a bar slinging drinks? Yeah, sorry, but it is."

He didn't seem offended as he walked by to hang his jacket over one of her dining chairs. "I have to be proficient in every position," he said, removing his cufflinks.

When he angled his chin toward his shoulder to glance her way, there was no mistaking the playful glint of flirtation shining on her.

Raising a pointed forefinger, Roxie intended to be clear. "I am not one of those women. You won't get me into bed just because you buy me a drink."

"Or because I pay your living expenses, gift you an around the world trip, provide global exposure, and give you an allowance for anything you want?"

"Yes, even all that won't do it," she said. "I don't care how much you spend. Sex wasn't part of the deal."

"No, because we couldn't put that on national television… and there were men in the mix."

"Were there?" she asked, watching him fold the cuffs of his shirt to reveal his forearms. Tanned and strong and tempting, she'd always had a thing about forearms for some peculiar reason. Don't go there. Divert line of thinking. Roxie tightened the belt of her robe. "We thought Bree would be your pick."

"Bree?"

"She was one of the other potential winners. In the final five."

He bobbed his head. "I didn't make the decision."

Roxie strutted his way. "Bree was young," she teased, sliding in a little innuendo of her own. "Nineteen, innocent, nubile."

"Mm," he said, his chin rising as he turned toward her.

"Corruptible… blonde… great rack."

Observing his interest, Roxie stopped, assuming she'd whetted his appetite for Bree. Always the same. Men couldn't resist hot and perky.

His brows flicked up. "Would you like me to arrange for you and her to have some time alone? Invite her to the hotel while we're still in town. You're allowed to have people in your room, I don't set rules like that… Though I probably should, given you spent last night in jail. A few rules might be exactly what you need, Miss Kyst." Confused, she didn't realize she was frowning until he laughed. "Young and nubile aren't high on my wish list. The phrase 'been there, done that' comes to mind."

"Oh yeah?" she asked, doubting his veracity.

"Yep," he said and bowed to murmur in her hair above her ear. "Nineteen means she can't drink at most of my bars." He straightened to meet her eye. "Not much use to me…" He scanned her figure, sending a quivering chill up her spine. "Would you like to get changed? You didn't finish your dinner, are you still hungry?"

Uneasy, Roxie couldn't figure out his game. "No, I am not hungry," she said, glaring. "I don't like this."

"Like what? Getting to know me?"

"Yes!"

"Why?"

Because he wasn't what she'd thought he'd be. Yes, he projected the expected confidence and ease, but those weren't the source of her agitation. The playfulness was fun. He teased and rose to her challenge: he matched her. She hadn't expected that.

"I *am* going to get changed." Not because he said it, but because she chose to be in more than just a robe. She pointed at him again. "Do not come anywhere near my bedroom."

"Wouldn't dream of it," he said, smirking.

Going to her bedroom, Roxie took the time to reevaluate her position. At Sunset, seated a distance away from him, it was easy to make snap judgments. When he was right there in front of her, it was harder to see him as a thing. A "thing." That's what it was. Celebrities, politicians, businessmen, they didn't feel like real people to the masses consuming them through the media's lens.

She got dressed and combed her hair away from her face. Lomond was a person. Not one like any she'd met, but a person nonetheless. His world view would be skewed by his life experience, everyone's was. That experience wouldn't earn him any credit. She'd give him a chance but wouldn't cut him a break. If someone, anyone, was rude or being unfair, she'd tell it straight. Regardless of his infamy, Zairn Lomond would get the same treatment.

See, all she'd needed was a little pep talk. Now she was prepped to get back out there and out-sass anything he threw her way.

Lomond was on the couch, facing the entertainment unit on the opposite wall. Her computer was closed and the dinner plate gone.

"I told the kitchen to expect feedback," he called without turning around.

How did he know she was there?

"Feedback about what?" she asked, passing the dining table to go around the end of the couch. Their drinks were on the coffee table. Good, she could do with one, except…Why did he look so confused? "What?"

"Hmm?"

He was just looking at her. Not her face. No, her body. But it wasn't a leer, it didn't seem like he was checking her out. The longer she stood there, being scrutinized by him, the more Roxie felt like a science experiment gone wrong.

"Geez, take a picture why don't you?" she said, opening her hands on her hips. "Stop looking at me like that. What is wrong with you?"

"Nothing," he said, shaking his head. "Sorry, please, sit down."

"Again, I remind you…" Roxie said, closing her eyes in a long blink. "This is my room."

"A room I'm paying for."

"I imagine it's a business expense," she said, putting a foot on the couch to climb onto it. Folding her legs against her torso, she rested back on the high arm. "Why were you looking at me funny?"

"I wasn't looking at you funny," he said, leaning forward to pick up their drinks.

Roxie took hers and drank, monitoring his every nuance as he settled in the opposite corner of the couch.

When he squinted at her pants, suddenly it made sense. "You were expecting lingerie."

"No," he said, maybe a little too quickly.

"Yes, you were," she teased and sighed. "Women all over the world throw themselves at you every minute. You expected me to walk out here in something lacy or see-through. Plaid pajama sweats and a Lola Bunny racer-back just aren't a part of your universe, are they?"

"I didn't know the rabbit had a name," he said, glancing down, though he wouldn't see the cartoon character on her shirt with her legs in the way.

"Do you watch a lot of cartoons?"

"No, but if they look like that, I might start."

"Are you lusting after Lola Bunny?"

Tilting his head, he raised a shoulder in a loose shrug. "I wouldn't send her home early."

"From what I know through the media, you wouldn't send any prospective lay home early. What are your criteria exactly? Famous and flashing the fur?"

"In their defense, not many of my exes have had fur."

That was funny and alarming. "Not many?" she asked. "So some of them did?"

"Do those yappy little dogs count?"

Roxie laughed. "I bet you've adopted many of those little fuzzies. Do you pay doggie support?"

"If they could take me to court for it…" he said, enjoying a mouthful of scotch.

"You can afford it, I guess," she said. Something struck her. "I don't even know if you have kids."

"I don't," he said.

"I don't either."

"I know." Her frown was question enough. "The questionnaire you filled out served a purpose. The questions weren't random. We had strict criteria. You met them."

"Me? I met the criteria. What were they?"

"Young, free, and single."

"I wasn't allowed to have a boyfriend?"

"They get jealous."

The arrogance! It was so unbelievable that she couldn't keep the laugh from her voice. "Are you kidding me?" His superiority didn't fade. "Your winner couldn't have a boyfriend because they'd be jealous of you?"

The slow blink and unapologetic expression on his face reminded her of the man he'd been on Talk at Sunset.

She shook her head, completely mystified. "I'm surprised you got through the door with an ego that big. It must be a helluva weight to haul around all the time."

"Look, single's just easier," he said like explaining was an inconvenience. "Our winner couldn't be married or planning a wedding, couldn't have kids or caring duties, those people have responsibilities."

"How tiresome."

"We're spending months on the road. Most nights we'll be in clubs. Places which aren't conducive to calling and catching up with home. *Drama* is tiresome, to use your word."

"So you think there would be drama if your winner had to call home?"

"How would you feel if your boyfriend won and you were left behind?"

Despite breaking up with her last boyfriend a couple of months ago, Roxie still cast him in the hypothetical. Imagining how Porter would respond to her going on the road without him was enough to prove Lomond's point.

She waved it off. "Let's stop talking about partners."

"Raw nerve?" he asked, intrigued.

Coy wasn't a color that suited her. "When I saw you on the show, I thought you were arrogant and smug."

Another slow blink. "I am arrogant and smug. And proud of it."

That he owned it granted him some credit. But she still let out a bold, "Ha-ha."

"I don't pussyfoot, Lola Bunny. We are who we are, right? Isn't that why you came out dressed like that?"

"I came out in my pajamas because it's nighttime, we're chilling, and I couldn't care less about tempting you." Roxie laid it out. "We don't know each other, I get that, and you don't pussyfoot. Love it. But me, I don't do tact or timid. There's a reason I don't do lingerie too."

"I'm looking forward to finding out what that is."

"No, no," she said, wagging a forefinger his way. "Don't flirt with me." He tried innocence, but his eyes were far too guilty in their innuendo. "Do you even know how to connect with a woman who has no interest in your money or your cock?"

"Give it time, sweetheart, you'll want both."

"Oh," she muttered, drawing out the sound. "You are cocky."

"I've got the goods, sweetheart."

"Be careful, a guy called me that last night and it caused a riot."

"Outside my club, I heard… as did the rest of the world," he said. "What's the story?"

Time to take a shot at innocence. "I didn't start it... A bunch of people from the show connected and we went out to eat. Somehow, we ended up at Crimson. I didn't even know we were going there."

"You been to any Crimson before?"

"No," she said. "My roommates, Jane and Toria, are big fans. They spent a small fortune on a special weekend thing in Boston about a year ago. They wanted New York but..."

"Bring them to the opening. Ask Tibbs for whatever you need."

"Which one's Tibbs?"

"Right, you haven't been introduced to anyone."

"I know Astrid," Roxie said. "She said you all get caught up in each other and forget there's a big world beyond your circle... Personally, I think you forget there's a world beyond your ego."

"You're judgmental, aren't you, Lola?"

He shifted to the edge of the couch to pour himself another drink. After his glass was refreshed, he raised the chilled cocktail shaker toward her.

She shook her head. "I'm still working on mine."

"If you want to tail me on the club circuit, you'll have to learn to keep up."

"I have nothing to prove," she said, finishing her drink. "You're so filthy rich that I bet you're used to everyone always trying to impress you."

Just as he settled back and raised his glass to his lips, she held her empty one out. Though he semi-glared, he did sit up to take it from her.

Rather than refill the same glass, he took a clean one to rim the edge with sugar. "Rich does give you license to get away with a lot of bullshit."

She leaned forward a little. "Filthy," Roxie whispered. "Don't forget the filthy." The next look he landed on her was pure swagger. "That won't work either. You're not that smooth, Casanova."

"You're so sure, why don't you kick me out?"

"Because, Casanova, you mix a good martini."

"Imagine what else I might be good at," he murmured, the bass of his voice rumbling through both of them.

"Stop being sleazy," she sang, accepting the fresh drink. "It's never going to happen for you here. My pussy is Casanova non grata."

Everything just bounced right off him. No concern. No doubt. "You wouldn't know how to resist if I turned it on."

"Oh, I think I would. Cocky doesn't do it for me. I'll be the one woman who'll never have a problem resisting you."

"Just proving how little you know me. Don't lay down a challenge unless you want me to pick it up."

"You better stop flirting with me," she said, dropping her knees to cross her legs in front of her. "Talk about something non-sexy, maybe we'll get your mind out of the gutter. Tell me about your mom."

"Dead," he said, just like that.

Her lips puckered, then she exhaled. "That was a short conversation. What about your dad?"

"Not a feature... Nothing you can't find out on Wikipedia. Do better research, Lola."

"Is it some chore to talk about yourself?" she asked. "What about siblings?"

"None of them either."

"So you have no one to spend all your cents on except yourself?"

"And the business."

It seemed his work was his life.

"Where did the cents come from?" she asked. "I mean, how did you get your start?"

"My mom died when I was a child. Her father took responsibility for me after that. He paid my tuition at boarding school. When I was a teenager, he received a terminal diagnosis and sold his business. No one knew about the diagnosis until after he passed. I was the only surviving relative. Started out with just under six mil in the bank."

She could tell he'd given that answer before. "Bet you have more than that today."

He snickered. "Just slightly."

"One of my friends corrected the other when she called you a millionaire."

He inhaled, much more relaxed than he had been upon entering her room. "For someone who's not interested in money, you talk about it a lot."

"We can't talk about sex. All I know about you is sex and money. What do you want to talk about instead? The weather?"

Resting his glass on his thigh, his attention zeroed in. "You. Talk to me about you."

So she did. For hours. They talked about her roommates and how the three of them ended up at the show. Her parents, who were still together, her brother and her sister too. They discussed her work, copyediting and proofreading. Roxie did some copywriting once in a while too and picked up related work here and there as requested or required.

Whether or not he was taking any of the information in, she didn't know. But he nodded along and asked questions, so he seemed to be engaged. The conversation revolved around her. Why wouldn't it? A guy like Zairn Lomond wouldn't trust a stranger. Probably wouldn't trust many people given the media's interest. Good thing Roxie was a talker, she could keep going all night.

Roxie woke up to the sound of a phone ringing.

Confused and discombobulated, she flipped onto her back, fighting off the hair that stifled her.

Bed. She was in bed... How did that happen?

The phone. Right. Phone first.

Sitting up, she snatched the device while shoving at the hair that got in her way again. "Hello," she answered but received no reply. Maybe she'd been too quick. "Hello?"

"Hello? Rox?"

That sounded kind of like her roommate. "Toria?"

"Where the hell have you been?" she screeched. "You yelled at us for being lost. Last time we saw you was jail!"

Closing her eyes tight, Roxie begged clarity to visit. "I fell asleep," she murmured, her gaze drifting to the window. Light. The drapes were shut, but light seeped around their edges. "What time is it?"

Searching for a watch or clock, she got no satisfaction.

"Like noon," Jane said.

Jane. She was on the line too. Speakerphone?

"We're going home tomorrow! We have to make the most of our last day in town."

Clearing her throat, Roxie still couldn't snap to. "What happened with jail? Are you allowed to leave town?"

"No charges were brought against any of us," Toria said. "Thank God!"

"I don't know how I'll face my mom," Jane said, reeking of guilt and shame.

No one did those emotions like Jane.

"Honey," Roxie said. "You didn't do anything terrible. Wrong place, wrong time. Tell your mom that."

"I told her not to say a word to anyone," Toria said. "We could lose our jobs... though it would be worth it. A Crimson riot! How Hollywood!"

Standing might wake her up. "I wonder why they changed their mind about the charges," Roxie said, tossing back her covers.

"Don't you watch the news?" Toria asked.

Although on her feet, she was still dazed enough to glance around for a TV like one might be on somewhere nearby. Entertainment centers in the Grand Hotel suite concealed the televisions.

Roxie inhaled. "I haven't looked at a television in days."

"Zairn made a statement," Jane said.

Toria picked up the tale. "Yeah, he was on TV yesterday. You didn't know?"

"He refused to press charges," Jane said. "And had his lawyers help anyone who needed them."

Lomond. Hmm. Given that she'd slept through the previous day, the damage control passed her by. But last night... Why hadn't he said anything? The bedroom door tempted her across the space. She opened it to look at the empty room beyond.

"We were thinking the Chinese Theatre tonight," Toria said. "Can't get arrested there, right? We haven't done the star tour yet. How do you feel about a day in the sun? Jane's got a couple of tours on standby."

"I, uh..."

"Why do you sound so out of it?"

Running a hand through her hair, Roxie slouched against the doorframe. "I literally just woke up. I'll need a shower and breakfast." Her stomach was empty; she hadn't finished dinner. "Give me an hour?"

"We'll swing by and pick you up," Toria said, giggling. "Never know who we might run into."

Once the call was over, Roxie frowned into the living room recalling their argument and the talking. Later on, she'd surprised him by lying down and dumping her feet in his lap. Lomond, he must have put her in bed. Had she fallen asleep talking to him? Rude much?

There wasn't time to reflect, her girls were on their way. She'd need more than a wash to wake up properly. Time was of the essence.

Coming out of her bedroom wearing two different shoes, Roxie paused to lift one foot then the other.

"Heels or flats," she asked, tucking her hair behind her ear as she went back and forth, hiding one shoe then the other.

"Why do you even ask?" Jane asked.

Toria's amusement was answer enough. "She's right, honey," she said from her perch against the back of the couch. "You always wear heels."

"You're a shoe girl."

"Not that much," Roxie said and kicked off the flat to put on the heel she'd brought with her.

Her girls laughed.

"See!" Toria exclaimed. "You didn't even bring the flat."

"Who cares about flats," she said, fluffing her hair. "Who has my purse?"

As Jane held it up, there was a knock at the door.

"It's open!" Roxie yelled, shuffling across to the breakfast—closer to lunch—tray on the table.

The hotel staff were attentive. She grabbed her juice to down the rest of it, assuming the visitor would take the mess away. But, no, Astrid peeked around the door.

"Mm," Roxie said, swallowing the liquid. "Astrid, honey, come in, come in. You know my roommates?"

The assistant slunk into the room and was particular about closing the door properly.

"We've never met." Her usual forward self, Toria strode over, hand outstretched. "Victoria Lovell, I would trade lives with you in a heartbeat."

The declaration startled Astrid.

Rushing over, Roxie put an arm around Toria to ease her away. "Let's give Astrid some room," she said and squinted at the uncomfortable woman. "I'm sorry about my crazy friends. What do you need?"

"Oh, uh…" Astrid tried to pull back her professionalism. "We don't have a checkout time, we—"

"Because Zairn pays for an extra night wherever he stays, relieving pressure on hotel staff," Jane said, appearing at Roxie's side.

"And leaves at least a four-figure tip to each member of staff who tends to him and his group," Toria added. "Only a limited number of staff are allowed to his floors. He uses people he's had before or those who are recommended."

"Sometimes he brings in his own people," Jane said. "He's really particular about who gets near to him."

"Okay, you two…" Roxie said, hooking an arm around Jane's waist too. "Stop freaking people out. Astrid doesn't care about your fetishes for her boss. What do you need, Astrid? Do you want me to kick these two to the curb? We're going out anyway."

"Oh," Astrid said, apparently surprised. "I came down to find out if your luggage is ready. It goes to the airport ahead of us."

She didn't get it. Neither did her friends.

"We're going out," Toria said.

"Yeah, our flight isn't until tomorrow," Jane said.

Toria gasped. "Oh my God, Rox is not coming home with us! Of course she's not! She's going off into the sunset with Zairn."

"The sunset," Roxie scoffed.

"Did you get an itinerary?" Astrid asked. "Tibbs never drops the ball… We're wheels up in two hours."

"Wherever you're going, I can catch up," Roxie said. "I pay the extra for transferable tickets."

"No!" Toria called. Both roommates rushed around in front of her. "You get to fly on a private plane."

"Not just any private plane, the Zee-Jet!"

Her friends were bubbling with excitement. Being out of the loop was getting to be a familiar sensation. "I don't know what that is."

"Uh…" Astrid said, attracting everyone's attention. "It's not the Zee-Jet. We're travelling on the company—"

"The Crimson Craft?" Toria screeched. "That's where *someone* signed his first Marvel contract and where a certain reality star got impregnated."

"I'm so disappointed you won't see the Zee-Jet," Jane said. "No pictures exist from inside it. It's like super top secret."

"So why did you think he'd let me on it?" Roxie asked.

"Because he's said in interviews like ten times that he prefers his jet over the larger company one… The Boeing Triple Seven is on permanent loan to Crimson."

"Yeah," Toria said. "Because Zairn's network is better than their marketing department."

"Than any marketing department anywhere ever," Jane said, laughing and looping an arm through Toria's. "I wonder if he gets commission."

Their knowledge was incredible. They'd always been Crimson fans, but she had a feeling they'd studied up after getting tickets for Talk at Sunset.

"Okay, now we've figured that out," Roxie said, none the wiser. "Just email me what I need to know, Ast. I'll get a flight tomorrow."

"Let me call Tibbs," Astrid said, plucking her phone from her pocket.

"You do what you gotta do, baby," Roxie said to Astrid then switched to address her friends. "I'm going to grab a jacket and then we'll leave."

Returning to her room, she tried one jacket and settled on another. She tucked her oversized sunglasses into her cleavage to free her hands so she could put on sun protection. That took a good five minutes, but it was necessary, and her friends would understand.

Satisfied, Roxie washed her hands and went to join the others.

"Tibbs says he's on with London," Astrid said.

Roxie took her purse from Jane to loop the long strap across her body. "He who?"

"Who?" Jane said, laughing. "Zairn!"

"Oh, right. That doesn't matter," Roxie said, retrieving her Chapstick from a pocket in her purse. "I don't need him. I just need to know what city you want me in."

Just as she tucked the Chapstick away, her phone began to ring. An unfamiliar number flashed on the screen, but she answered it anyway.

"Hello?"

"It's always trouble," the male on the other end of the line said.

She frowned. "Who is this?"

"Do a lot of random men call you, Lola?"

Oh, well, that answered her question.

"I thought you were a busy bee," she said, sauntering across the living room into her bedroom again. "Being all international GQ businessman."

"I ended the call when I found out there was a kink in travel plans." The deep hum of his words wasn't angry. They were effortless, smooth, like the rest of him. "Do you know how long it's been since I let anyone hold me up?"

"Who's holding you up? I'll follow. You go on, be wherever you need to be."

"You got a date tonight?" he teased.

"No," she droned, rolling her eyes upward. "Not with a guy anyway. It's my last vacation day with my roommates. We're going to catch a star tour and then a movie."

He didn't need all that information, but, hey, she had nothing to hide either.

"You want me to stay in California another night so you can go to the movies?"

Was it possible he was trying to rile her by not listening or did his arrogance cause selective deafness?

"No one told you to stay anywhere, Skippy," she stated. "Look on the bright side, without me on your tail, you can use your top-secret jet instead of your public one."

"My top-secret jet?"

"The one you prefer flying in."

"It's in New York."

"Oh," she said, stopping in the window. "Guess it would take a while to get here then, huh?"

The sun was so bright, everything its light touched glowed. The novelty was fun, Roxie wasn't sure she'd be able to live with it full-time.

"There are movie theatres in Vegas," he said. "Pack your stuff and watch your movie there. What is it you want to see? I can have a private showing arranged—"

"It's not about the movie, it's about the company. I came on vacation with my friends, I want to spend time with them before they have to go back home."

"Bring them." Uh, what? Her wandering thoughts screeched to a halt. "Staff can pack your things and send them to the airport. Staff at your friends' hotel will do the same for them. Give Astrid the name and room number."

"Staff?" she said, equally impressed and amused. "I don't want people packing my stuff, poking around in my underwear. How do I know I'll get all my panties back?"

"You don't do lingerie," he said, proving he'd been listening at one point of the night. "If anything goes missing, I'll replace it, but I only employ people who can be trusted."

"I don't want anyone to pack my things, I can pack my own things. My friends can too." The alternative he'd suggested was more than ludicrous. Obviously, they weren't used to the same lifestyle, but did they live on the same planet? "Did I fall asleep while we were talking last night?"

"Yes."

She cringed. "Sorry, that was rude."

"You made it until around six a.m., nothing to be ashamed about."

"You took me to bed."

"With Astrid, Tibbs, and hotel staff present."

The serious note of that declaration was weird. "Because you need an audience to carry a woman to bed or... you wanted them to point and laugh at me or...?"

"You live the life I do, you learn to cover your ass."

Silent understanding opened her lips. "So I couldn't accuse you of anything..." Like drugging or taking advantage of her. "Wow..." Roxie settled on impressed. "You're smarter than I gave you credit for… Sort of a sad reflection on the society we live in, don't you think?"

"Yeah, but it's a reality of life."

"We were alone for hours," she said, touching the window frame with a fingertip. "I could say we were doing anything, no one would know if I was lying."

"I would know," he said. "But you're in my orbit now, Lola, don't be surprised if people make assumptions."

"What kind of assumptions?" Sex was the answer to that question; she didn't need him to say it. "You'd like that, if the whole world thought I was incapable of resisting you."

"Baby, you are incapable of resisting me." Swagger rolled through his words. "Just wait 'til I give you the opportunity to prove me right."

How was it that the smug jerk from the Talk at Sunset couch could now make her smile with his conceit?

"You want me that bad, roofies are your only option. There's no way you'll get near me otherwise."

"You think I got where I am by giving up at the first obstacle? Count yourself lucky I'm not interested."

"Oh, you're not interested? Uh huh," she said and laughed. "That's why you wanted to see me in my underwear last night."

"I was concerned I'd have to let you down easy. Uncomfortable moments like that can have a lasting effect on a relationship."

"Good thing I'm just your prop then," she said. "When exactly do I start telling the world the truth about you?"

"You'll meet the documentary crew in Boston… and your handler too."

"My handler?" she asked. "The person who watches me and reports back to you?"

"Makes sure you don't get in the way, that sort of thing."

"I said you were the wrong kind of spontaneous, didn't I?"

"Trust me, Lola, in a couple of days, you'll be thrilled I assigned someone to look after you."

This guy thought he was better at everything. Including reading her mind. "This will come as a shock to a man surrounded by sycophants, but us real world people can look after ourselves."

His laugh was short and sinister. "Baby, you don't have a damn clue what you're walking into."

She leaned on the window. "I'm confident."

"Say that to me again in a week."

"I will," she said.

"Okay, Lola," he said. "Don't give this number to anyone and don't save it under my name."

"In case someone steals my phone?"

"Or you lose it."

"All that confidence you have in yourself and you can't spare any for me," she teased. "Why do you think anyone will care about your phone number?"

"Experience," he said. "And it's a pain to change it. There are too many other plates spinning right now. Can you follow simple instructions, Roxanna?"

She licked her lips, aware he was baiting her. "You and your people are quick to order my discretion, but you share my information around amongst yourselves. Who said you could have my phone number? I don't remember checking that box."

"Everything you put on your application is part of our system now," he said. "Just like you."

The thrill. The heat in her belly. Flurry in her head. The rush. When was the last time a guy exhilarated her?

"Lucky me," she said, sucking in a breath. "Is this what you do with your days? Call women up to remind them how cocky you are?"

"The initial call, sure. After that, I let assistants maintain contact."

"I'll remember that. How many more women are on your call list today?"

He snickered. "You wouldn't believe me if I told you, babe."

"Mm hmm, sure. Go call your next target. I have things to do."

"You'll be on the plane?"

"I'll be on the plane."

"Good girl," he said, then the line went dead.

That should patronize her. It didn't. It was all in the delivery. Damn the man should come with a health warning. Danger: Causes spikes in hormone levels that may lead to involuntary episodes of verbal sparring. Good thing she knew the difference between reality and fantasy.

Leaving the window, she opened the bedroom door with a flourish. The three women in the living room turned to her.

"Change of plan," Roxie said. "We're going to Vegas instead."

A chauffeur driven car taxied them around LA, from hotel to hotel, then to the private plane.

Massive. The plane was absolutely massive. Her wonderings about what a man needed such a large plane for were answered after boarding, when she and her girls walked into what could only be described as a nightclub. With a bar, lights and music, it was far from travelling coach.

At their request, Astrid activated the music and lights at a touch panel on the wall. The trio of roommates enjoyed an impromptu party until the captain announced they were making their descent. Damn the flight for being so short.

Despite the notice, Jane continued tidying up at the bar.

Toria paid more heed and dropped into a curved seat in the corner. "I'm buzzed," she said, putting her heels on. "Think the clubs are open now?"

"It's Vegas," Roxie said, poking at the touchscreen on the wall. She'd worked out how to turn the music down, but nothing would go off. "Why are there so many buttons?"

"Roxie?"

Astrid? She whirled around in the direction of her name. Yes, it was the assistant, she was by the door to the next section.

"I don't know how to work anything," Roxie said, hoping her haphazard button pushing wasn't impacting anything else on the plane.

"You have to put on seatbelts," Astrid said.

"Oh no," Jane said, rushing around the bar to jump into the closest seat. "We're sorry."

Toria was already sitting, safety belt secure. "Can we go clubbing like straight away?"

"Uh, I don't—"

"We have to find a hotel," Jane said. "We need somewhere to sleep tonight."

"We'll crash in Roxie's room," Toria said. "Raid her minibar…"

"Better to stop at a liquor store," Roxie said. "Minibar prices are insane."

Toria didn't seem to be listening. "Oh, Astrid, can we be put on the list for Crimson? I've always wanted to go to Crimson, Vegas. Getting on the list is impossible for a mere mortal."

"No!" Roxie exclaimed. "You remember what happened last time we tried to go to a Crimson club? No! I don't want to get arrested again. I can still smell jail in my hair; I wasn't made for a life of crime and no conditioner."

"Zairn took care of that," Toria said. "And this time he can put us on the list. Ergo… no riot."

"I wish you could meet him," Jane said. "I can't believe you haven't."

That *was* what she'd said online. It wasn't true anymore; she and Astrid shared furtive eye contact. For some reason, rather than confess what had happened the previous night, she kept quiet.

"Is he on the plane?" Toria asked. "Maybe we could talk to him as we get off." She laughed. "I sure would if he was around."

Guilt chewed at her conscience. Her girls were her confidantes. They talked about guys, friends and lovers, all the time. But, this time, if she confessed, her friends would ask questions that she didn't want to answer. They'd give her messages to pass along or request an introduction.

"Seatbelts," Roxie said, diverting the conversation. Sitting down, she fastened the safety belt. "Gotta be safe."

"I'll talk to Mr. Lomond," Astrid said. "If he agrees to put you on the list, I'll text and let you know, Roxie."

As the young assistant began to turn, Toria hollered, "I'd trade lives with you in a second!" Astrid left and closed the door again. "You know a part of me hates her guts."

Jane laughed. Toria was joking... sort of.

Roxie's conundrum kept her quiet. Lomond wasn't her friend; she didn't owe him anything. But her instinct had been to protect. Not him, their time. His life belonged to the masses. A few hours of privacy seemed like the least he was owed. She didn't need to account for every minute; the world could live in wonder.

10

Yet another hotel suite. Could be Lomond just wasn't aware regular hotel rooms existed. What a life to live.

Always a planner, Jane transferred their flights to leave from their new location while Toria preened, and Roxie soaked in the tub. Getting those formalities out of the way freed them up to drink and dance to their happy hearts' content.

High on life, the prospect of venturing out in Vegas stoked bubbly anticipation in her belly. Now if only Toria would get her ass out of the restroom, maybe they could get going. Jane wasn't worried, she was buzzing around, tidying up. Wasn't her idea of a good time, but Jane seemed to be enjoying herself.

Just as she finished her drink, her clutch buzzed. She opened it up to retrieve her phone and read a text from Astrid.

> Come to the fiftieth alone. Platinum Suite.

Apparently, everyone had a suite, even the staff. If Lomond was as rich as people said, he could probably reserve the whole hotel if he wanted.

"I'll be back in a minute," Roxie called over the music.

Jane waved at her and continued putting Toria's clothes on hangers.

The Astrid meeting wouldn't take long; she'd bet big that a warning was in her future. *Don't get into trouble. Don't start any more riots.* That kind of thing. The riot was a one-time anomaly, they shouldn't judge her for it forever.

The jaunt in the elevator was quick. Roxie hopped out expecting a floor like hers. Instead, one door stood straight ahead. The nameplate declared it to be the "Platinum Suite." Her stop. She knocked and, a second later, the door opened like someone was waiting on the other side.

Slick.

Roxie smiled, assuming employees shared space. "Astrid texted me."

Slick nodded and stepped aside. "Just go through."

Rather than join her, he departed and closed the door. Hmm, not a good sign. If they needed privacy, the warning would be a big one.

Strolling up the awe-inspiring grey marble foyer, she reminded herself they were in a hotel, not some stately mansion. Last week she'd thought cork bathroom tiles were fancy; life sure had changed fast. To the right, a restroom. The next door was closed. Closet, maybe? Opposite was a bedroom, small, though it opened to something beyond.

The glass wall up ahead showcased an external deck and pool.

"Whoa," she whispered when the foyer gave way to the vast living room.

Sleek and modern with hidden lights scattering their hues on the ceiling, the grey and white space was less majestic mansion and more bachelor pad.

"I have a condition."

Startled by Lomond's voice, Roxie spun around. He was standing behind a bar by the mouth of the foyer.

She gasped. "There's a bar up here?" Rushing over, she spread her hands on the cool marble to hop up onto a stool. "Is this like some secret hang out only the cool kids can access?"

"Hardly," he said, pouring liquid into a sugared, limed martini glass. "You're here, aren't you?"

"Implying I'm not a cool kid," Roxie said, laying her fingers on the base of the glass when he put it in front of her. "You're such a gent."

And if they were fourteen, she might have finished with "*not*." Her sarcasm was in full working order.

"You're welcome," he said, stabbing an olive with a toothpick to snag it in his teeth.

"You went to boarding school," she said, sweeping up the glass while he chewed. "What do you know about the cool kids table?"

He swallowed. "I invented the cool kids table, Lola."

"So you like to think."

Leaving his post, he disappeared out a door and reappeared on her side of the bar. "Are you going to behave yourself tonight?"

"Haven't decided," she said, sipping her lime-drop. "I'm just a drink or two away from wasted… Who knows what fun might happen?"

His brows descended, heating his scrutiny. It lingered, then he took out his phone and began to type.

"I came to see Astrid, is she around?" Roxie asked, telling herself not to peek over the top of his phone despite her curiosity.

"You came to see me. Astrid delivered you."

"Like take out," she said, licking sugar from the rim of her glass. His eyes rose from the phone. Her smile was half hidden by the glass, but her gaze was telling a story all of its own. "Does that mean you plan to eat me?"

A semi-smile joined his slow blink. "We're flirting today?"

"Not me," she said, tipping her head back, arching her body his way. "That's where your mind went, Casanova."

Dipping a fingertip into her drink, Roxie took her time about sucking it clean. He put the phone down and rested his hands on the bar, trapping her between his arms.

"Your mind isn't as clean as you let on," he murmured.

Slanted back, her spine pressed into the rounded edge of the bar. "You'd like that, wouldn't you?" she asked, dipping her finger in the drink again, stirring it slowly. "You'd like to corrupt my innocent mind."

"You're anything but innocent, Miss Kyst."

At the spot her crossed legs rested on his outer thigh, searing awareness began to spread. "No? What am I?"

His smile faded. "You're complex, Roxanna. Smart, sassy, pragmatic yet a dreamer... You're a host of contradictions. Both sensible and wild, aloof yet excitable... You're a beautiful, enticing mix that equals trouble... especially with a mind that's so open."

"Oh," she said, her lips curling. "What is that? You think if you say I'm open-minded, I might be swayed to open my pussy to you?" Her smile grew. "You wouldn't think I was open-minded if you knew the snap judgments I made about you during Talk at Sunset."

Interest arched his brow. "No? Enlighten me. What did you think?"

"That you were too rich and hot for your own good. You know yourself far too well... and know exactly how to use your talents to your advantage."

"You think I'm taking advantage of you?"

"I believed you thought a lot of yourself. Too much."

"And now?"

If only Roxie could answer that question. Being around him was fun. Different to any other casual association, there was something innate about the way they communicated. So much of it was more than words. Her stomach clenched with excitement whenever they were alone. She wanted to smile. To tease and play with him. Not in a sexual way. At least, not in a physical way. Something more existed behind the smug playboy's polished exterior. She didn't know what it was and didn't expect him to show it.

In his super-public life, all sorts of people would cross his path. He couldn't trust all of them. She was just another in a long line of people who'd pass him by. Understanding his reluctance to trust didn't make it any less frustrating.

The intensity of his mysterious gaze tickled her interest. He was right there in front of her, showing complete confidence, like it wouldn't matter what she said or thought. A part of her wanted to push further, to see how open they could get with each other.

"I don't think I should answer that," she said.

"Because you know I am exactly as rich and hot as I think I am."

"Rich and hot maybe," she said, licking her lips slowly. "But you are not God's gift to the world."

"Are you sure about that?"

"Careful," Roxie said, sipping her drink. "Your ego is showing."

11

Something in him beckoned to her. The mystery of it pulled her deeper. Without a doubt, he was one of the most confident men she'd ever met. Befriending arrogance: always a mistake. It stifled her. Eventually, a competitive edge would raise its head and her needs would be marginalized.

Male ego could be fragile. Impugning it in any way wasn't usually well received. None of the men from her past could handle it. Lomond, somehow, was different. She teased him and he didn't back down. He didn't wilt or retort in anger. He didn't fight her, he played with her.

Staying near him, being alone with him, wouldn't be a good idea. Except she didn't have a choice. The contest put her in his path. Her girls would want an explanation if she forfeited. But making friends with an international jet-setting billionaire wouldn't end well.

As though he came to the same conclusion in the same moment, he boosted himself away from the bar, freeing her from his cage.

"This is the last night you'll have to yourself," he said, standing in front of her, absorbing every nuance. "You'll meet the documentary crew tomorrow."

Roxie licked her finger clean. "We're going to Boston?" she asked, low and quiet. They were alone, yet she spoke as though someone might eavesdrop. He nodded. "That's a shame, I haven't seen anything of Vegas yet."

He slid onto the stool next to hers. "We'll be back here."

Twisting her seat to face him, she propped an elbow on the bar to support the fist she lodged under her jaw. "You know, I was thinking, owning a few clubs wouldn't get you this kind of lifestyle."

"The money again."

"If I thought you'd talk about it, I'd ask about how your mom died and how you feel about her. I'd ask about your grandfather's passing… or about your dad. If you knew him, if you ever looked him up, if he knows what you've made of your life—"

"I invest," he said, confirming her assumption that he didn't want to talk about his family. "I own shares in a large number of successful companies. Crimson is the top tier as far as the clubs go. The jewel in the entertainment network crown. We also have interest in liquor companies, make our own whiskey, and have hundreds, thousands of bars and clubs under the Rouge umbrella. Of course, there's the resort. I own a minor record label and we finance movie production."

"Geez…"

"The movie production happened through Collier. I'm not hands on."

Her simple question had a complex and impressive answer. "You couldn't be hands on with that many balls in the air."

"My property portfolio is vast. There's the sports stadiums and concert venues, rent from those makes a mint… and we own a private airline network."

"We?"

"Rouge," he said. "It's the parent company of all my ventures. And the diamonds, I for—"

"Stop," she said. Her fist dropped from her jaw, so her palm came to rest over the back of his hand. "Forget I asked! You're making me feel so unaccomplished."

"Comes with a cost too… A personal cost."

Yeah, she couldn't begin to imagine the complications in his life. He'd called her complex. Compared to him, she was as simple and straightforward as people came.

Her fingers curled, their tips stroking his wrist until her nails met skin. Without breaking eye contact, she straightened her fingers to repeat the action, caressing the same few inches over and over.

As his eyes grew heavier, the light around them seemed to dim.

"Are you going to the club tonight?" she murmured.

"Do you want me to go to the club?"

"Your club, your call. Toria and Jane are excited, but you don't have to put us on the list. If you're going to be there, I would understand why you wouldn't want us to crash. I wouldn't—"

"You're on the list. LA was an oversight on my part."

"You took care of that," she said. "I didn't know that you... I didn't see you on TV or know that you helped everyone out."

"It's not a big deal," he said, reaching over the bar for the cocktail shaker. "Another?"

As he tipped the shaker, she put a hand over her glass, stalling him. "You don't like praise," she said, noticing how he'd tried to change the subject.

"Baby, I drink it up."

"No, you don't," she said, relieved and intrigued to see the more human side of him. "Maybe you drink it up on TV or in your clubs when your fans are around, but here, one on one, you don't like it."

But that swagger wouldn't yield. "I just don't recognize it from you," he said, smirking. "You're not usually so pleasant."

"Must be the alcohol," Roxie said, giving him a break. If he wasn't comfortable, she wouldn't push. He'd shown a glimmer of his human side, it wouldn't hurt to show hers too. "Can I ask you something?"

"Yes, I am God's gift."

She exhaled a quick laugh and pushed his arm. "Okay, but not that."

"What do you want to know?"

When her hand left the glass, he topped it off, diverting his attention.

Studying him was easier while he was occupied. The angle of his jaw, strength of his brow, his warm complexion. People could see him as a thing because the view was so damn good. Those people didn't get close. She could smell his cologne, see individual strands of hair, watch him breathe. He was real and right in front of her.

"What do I tell my friends about you?" The question just came out. He paused, then slowly set down the cocktail shaker. "I didn't tell them that we met. I should have. I don't like being dishonest, but… they like you and I don't want—"

"It's about boundaries," he said, sliding a flat hand along the bar until his fingers twined between hers, their palms on the cool marble. "You set them early and stick to them. Your friends are a good place to start. If they truly are your friends, they won't push you. The docu crew will push you. Decide your boundaries and no matter what, under all circumstances, stick to them."

"You know a lot about this."

"I've been doing it a long time."

"Your whole life is this," she said, glimpsing his perspective. "People, expectation. How do you know who to trust?"

"You get a nose for it," he said. "For those who are insincere, and there are a lot of them. It takes a while and no one is right a hundred percent of the time."

"It's a horrible way to live, to be suspicious of people every minute."

"I think of it more as protecting those who are important to me," he said.

He didn't have family to protect. Talk at Sunset came to mind.

Roxie moistened her lips. "You're friends with Knox Collier."

"Mm hmm."

"Protecting him?"

"And others."

There were people that he cared about. More evidence that there was a human behind the unshakeable suave façade.

"What do boundaries look like?" she asked.

"You decide the limit of what you'll share or facilitate."

"You don't introduce anyone to your famous friends, that sort of thing."

He snickered. "If I didn't introduce people, half the world wouldn't make a living." Flashing his arrogance... again. Calling him on it with a head tilt got only a half-smile response. "I don't introduce the people I care about to anyone I don't care about."

Closing one eye, she tried to figure that out. "So there's a difference, professional and personal, is that what you mean?" He nodded once. "But Drew Harvey on the talk show said you were responsible for some famous marriages."

"My network is complicated, and my rules vary depending on my relationship with a person," he said. "If I think people are suited, I'd speak to both of them individually before introducing them. Likewise, if someone asked to be introduced to another person, I would check before facilitating that meeting. I never give contact details without permission either."

She smiled and leaned a little closer. "Bet you don't give them even with that. You'd have Slick do it."

"Slick?"

Roxie shrugged. "The young guy who works with Astrid, wears too much gel in his hair."

By the twist of his lips, it was clear her observation entertained him. "I get it," he said, chuckling. "That's Tibbs."

She'd sort of guessed that, though it had never been confirmed. "You should leave the house every morning assuming someone will run their fingers through your hair."

"That's your rule?"

"Just smart. Think about it, if a woman's close enough to run her fingers through your hair, you don't want her mind to be on how soon she can wash her hands."

"No," he said. "I guess you don't."

The intriguing slant of his mouth drew her in. "Why do you do that? Look at me like I'm strange."

"Not strange, unique," he said. "You look at things in a way... Sometimes I think I've heard everything."

"You must meet all kinds of people. From all over the place."

"Mm hmm."

The longer they sat there, assessing each other, the more Roxie wished she was in her Lola pajamas. The ease of the intimate mood suited a cozy night in rather than one on the Vegas Strip.

"I should go," she said, but stayed put.

His brows rose. "Mm hmm."

Neither of them moved. "The girls are waiting."

"Yep," he said, waiting another few seconds before sucking in a breath and letting go of her hand to straighten up. "I have a meeting in Henderson."

"A meeting?" she asked as he got to his feet and leaned over the bar to retrieve something from the other side. "At this time of night?"

"In my line of work, more business is done in the dark than by daylight."

He held his hand up and opened his fingers. A shimmer of light cascaded down from his fist, bouncing back on itself, swinging side to side.

Roxie steadied it to identify what it was. A large emerald cut diamond set on a pendant. "I don't think you should call the woman you give this to a 'meeting.' Are you averse to the word 'date'?"

"The guy I'm meeting is a third generation Vegas billionaire. Not a date," he said, opening the chain to loop it over her head. "He can buy his own jewels."

"Wait," Roxie said, startled that he was putting it on her. "You can't give it to me." The cool metal settled against her body as she curled her fingers around the gem hanging over her breasts. "Is it real?"

"Yes," he said, taking her fingers away from the diamond to admire it. "If you lose it, you have to tell Ballard immediately."

"Immediately? So he can have me arrested?"

"No," he said, amused again. "So he can cancel your credentials. It's your security pass."

"I don't... I don't understand."

"There's a chip built into the setting," he said. "We don't want our guests worried about codes or cards. The chip will speak to any protected doorway as you approach."

"If I'm allowed in, the door will work. If I'm not, it won't." He nodded once. "Does that mean I should be careful about standing too close to protected doors? How will I know it's protected?"

"It's smart technology, Lola," he said. "The door literally senses your approach. If you are not the person moving toward it, it won't open. It doesn't work only by proximity; the doors have motion sensitivity... Anything seriously restricted is behind more than one door anyway. Even if someone got through an initial door, they wouldn't get through the second."

"You're a paranoid guy."

"A smart guy," he said and reached over the bar again. He put a small jewelry box on the bar and picked up his phone. "I also happen to have a relationship with Dyce Technologies."

"They invented basically... everything."

"And we have access to their R&D department."

"Because you own part of that company too?" she asked, reading in his expression that he did. "I saw their CEO on the web one time, they were launching something or something."

"Yeah? Couldn't have been a successful launch if you can't remember what it was for."

"He smiles too much," she said. "I got the impression he was counting his money while he talked to a bunch of suckers."

He laughed. "I'll tell Zane you said so," he said, nodding at the box. "Put your thumb on top."

"What?" Roxie asked, still recovering from the whiplash of the last comment. "You don't mean that you'll actually... You're not really going to tell him I—"

"I sit on their board. We have an AGM coming up."

Flicking her hair from her face with a quick head turn, Roxie didn't know whether or not to believe him. "Did I just insult one of your friends?"

"Zane's a serious guy. There's nothing like feedback from the audience. Maybe the next launch will be even more successful."

"I am not his target audience. My phone is like six years old. I'm definitely not an early adopter." His expressive eyes twitched in question. "Yeah, I'm not a complete idiot. I minored in business." He cleared his throat in what she was sure was a disguise for an instinctive laugh. Roxie glared. "You think I'm an idiot because I'm not one of your billionaire buddies?"

"No. I'm sorry, I… I imagine you'd be more of a distraction than an asset in the boardroom."

"Because I'd actually ask questions rather than toe the company line?"

"Toeing the company line is not something you'd ever be accused of, Lola," he said. "You're too honest to make it at the top level, and believe me, that's a compliment." Roxie wasn't so sure, but he kept on smiling and gestured at the box again. "Put your thumb on top."

Still side-glaring at him, she shifted the box to do as he said. "Why are we doing this?"

"Hold it there."

He was doing something on his phone again. This time, Roxie peeked. "Am I your patsy?"

"No," he said, another laugh riding the word.

"You smile too much too," she muttered.

"Only when you're around, Lola," he said without giving pause. "Okay, you're good."

"I can move now?" she asked and got the nod. "What was that for?"

"Just toss the box into your room on your way out."

"I get to keep the box?"

"And the pendant," he said. "Put the pendant in the box if you take it off. It's coded to your thumbprint."

"Wow," she said, picking up the box. It looked like any other jewelry box, an off-the-charts high-end one, but still a jewelry box. "It would be impressive if it wasn't for one major flaw."

"What's that?"

"If someone wants to steal it..." Roxie held up the box. "They can take it in this."

"The chip won't work while it's in the box."

"So they could steal it, but not use it? I guess that gives me time to tell your buddy that it's gone. The diamond is probably worth more than most people make in a year. That's worth selling on its own."

"It's insured," he said, opening an arm. "Your friends are waiting."

Leaving? Yes, she was supposed to leave. Downing the last of her drink, she hopped off the stool, ready to hit the road. The rest of her had a different plan. Dizzy, she caught his arm to balance herself. Heels on marble while her blood was twenty proof wasn't a great combination.

"I'm good," she said, letting go of him in a hurry. "All good."

Staying close, he began to walk her toward the entrance. "Ballard will look after you," he said. "He'll drive you there and take you in the side."

"I can't go in the front? Because you can't show the world you've lowered your standards so far?"

"Gotta keep up appearances, Lola, you understand."

He was hilarious, in his own way.

"Now I won't feel guilty about not drinking all night," she said, head held high. "I won't be lining your pockets."

"You can use any of the facilities and won't pay for your drinks."

News flash! "I won't? Why won't I?"

"Because you're my guest."

"Wish I'd known that before I went to the liquor store."

He frowned. "There weren't drinks in your room?"

"Do you know how expensive those minibar products are?" The pitch of his mouth adjusted again. "Okay, fine, so you can afford it. That doesn't mean I'm interested in spending your money."

He bowed a little lower. "You're on the company dime, Miss Kyst."

"So I can bankrupt it with booze?"

"You can try," he said. "The media might recognize the spending anomaly in our financials. If you're happy to face their scrutiny, have at it. Don't think I'll cover for you, I'll point right at you in public when we start to talk layoffs."

Shaking her head, his enjoyment at her expense was perplexing. He was so different from what she'd first assumed. "Zairn," she whispered, stepping closer when he straightened.

"What?" he asked when she didn't follow his name with anything.

"Nothing, I... don't think I've said it before. In my head, you're Lomond."

"My last name isn't an insult."

"No," she said. Her hand rose of its own volition. When her fingers sank into his hair, she grinned. "I'll keep those to myself."

Stroking his hair, she didn't feel any impetus to stop or apologize.

"Too much gel?"

"No," Roxie breathed, her fingers repeating their motion in his tapered businessman hairstyle.

His soft locks were always perfectly styled. Its length would look just as good relaxed... maybe better. Maybe Zairn wanted the world to believe he didn't do relaxed... her private time with him revealed that wasn't so.

They couldn't stand there all night. She exhaled and lowered her hand.

"Have a good time," he said. "Ballard will get you whatever you need."

"Thank you," she said as he opened the door.

It had been on the tip of her tongue to ask if he was going to be at the club later when she spotted the man in the outer hallway. He came over from the elevator, fixed on Zairn.

"Roxie Kyst, this is Sean Ballard."

"It's a pleasure," Ballard said as a formality. His attention quickly switched back to his boss. "Og going over with you?"

"No, I'll drive."

"Last time you did that in Vegas we didn't see you for three weeks."

"Risk is the way of this city," Zairn said, laying a hand on the small of her back to ease her out. "Enjoy yourself, Lola. Take care of her."

The door closed, sealing her in the hallway with Ballard. About the same height as Zairn, he was bulkier, security must be his usual gig.

"You're the guy who accused me of threatening Zairn."

"Water under the bridge, Miss Kyst," he said, stepping back to press the elevator button. "Shall we go get your friends?"

Despite being in Vegas, she was losing the urge to party. Still, her girls expected it and Roxie couldn't let them down.

12

Okay, so any uncertainty about Crimson was gone. More than simply a nightclub, it was a whole complex of adult fun… Not like porno adult fun, just everything for everyone.

There were quiet bar and lounge areas suited for intimacy or conversation. Of course, being in Vegas, there was a casino as well. A massive, sprawling casino spread across several of the vast floors. People could easily get sucked in and never find their way out again.

Because they were in Vegas, their trio placed a few bets, but they were soon drawn to the nightclub zone. For a group who hadn't expected to be in Vegas, and after being thrifty about their drinking, it didn't make sense to blow their rent money on games they barely understood.

At home, the three of them would go out two or three nights a week. More often than not, they went to a bar and then to a club. Dancing in the mass of others, all inhibitions thrown out, Roxie relished the indulgence.

On the Crimson dancefloor, time disappeared when she gave herself to the music. The sprawling club space had several bars and dance pits. Her friends were super excited and quick to point out the cylindrical glass room suspended from the cavern's ceiling. Large and busy, the glass was braced in a frame of metal girders. Apparently, it was VIPs only up there.

Some guy had been paying her close attention for the last hour. He chose that moment to slide his arms around her waist to pull her body against his. Her girls were occupied dancing with his buddies. How had her party hooked up with theirs? What did it matter? It didn't.

Whatever, he was whatever. Up close, grinding against her, kissing her neck, the guy obviously thought he was on the road to somewhere. Did she care? No. Lust was the furthest thing from her mind.

The Platinum Suite occupied her thoughts. Rather, the man she'd left there.

A light flashed over the glass room above, drawing her eye. That's when she saw him. The man from her thoughts was in the VIP room.

Given the distance between them, it wasn't easy to pick out details. He wasn't paying attention to the twenty or thirty people drinking in the intimately lit space behind him. With a hand on the vertical metal girder that segmented the glass, he stood apart from everyone. A man surveying his kingdom; but not a happy one.

Maybe his meeting hadn't gone well. Maybe he'd got bad news. Question marks everywhere. Why did she even care? Maybe it was the forbidden. Bad ideas didn't seem so bad after a few drinks. He didn't trust her and never would. In his suite earlier, he'd given her some insight. Trust was a commodity he couldn't buy to guarantee.

Geez, the slobbering guy pissed her off. Enough with the tongue already. Backing out of his arms, she showed a smile and gestured off the dancefloor, hoping he'd assume she was going to the restroom.

Instead, Roxie checked her friends to make sure they were okay, and then took her phone from the clutch looped around her wrist to write a text.

> Platinum Suite. Alone. ASAP. X

Roxie sent the message to the number saved under "*Casanova*" and tucked the phone away.

Ballard was standing by the handrail at the top of the half dozen stairs that led to that particular dance pit. From there, he kept an eye on her and hadn't strayed at all. Giving him the slip wasn't possible, so she didn't even try.

Honesty was the best policy anyhow… at least some version of honesty.

Walking right up to him, Roxie raised her voice to be heard. "I'm going back to the hotel!"

He bent down to speak near her ear. "The leech bothering you or joining you?"

"Neither," she said, grateful that he'd remained low for her to speak in his ear. "Will you stay and look after my friends?"

"I'll put you in your room and come back to watch out for them."

Concerned, her fingers curled into his lapels. She shook her head before pulling him back to talk in his ear. "Anything could happen in that time. I don't want them alone in a strange place, especially with those guys around."

"I'll have security watch them while I'm away."

"Why not have security take me back?"

His next words contained a smile. "Because Zairn would have my ass. Won't take long. Come on."

He gripped the back of her neck to weave her through the masses. As promised, he directed security to watch her friends. Roxie couldn't hear Ballard's words as he issued the orders, but his expression was reassurance enough.

The hotel wasn't far; it didn't take long to get there. Just as he'd said, he parked to take her to her room. The escort wasn't really necessary, but it appeared he took his duty seriously.

"You need anything?" Ballard asked.

Roxie unlocked the door to go inside. "No, I'm good."

"I'll tell Z you got back safe."

She nodded, thinking that wasn't really necessary. "Thank you. Goodnight."

"Goodnight."

The night wasn't over yet. Observing through the peephole, Roxie waited for Ballard to walk away before running through her suite. Changing superfast, she grabbed a hotel robe and put it on over her clothes.

Gallivanting around a hotel in bare feet was weird, but they were in Vegas. Everything went in Vegas.

Only a few hours had passed since her first visit to the Platinum Suite. Casanova had been waiting for her then. She knocked on arrival, just in case, but no one responded. Now it was her turn. Leaning on the wall by the door, she waited. Maybe he didn't get her message. Maybe he did and didn't care. Maybe it was his plan to bring company back to the suite. Even if he didn't, he still might have Tibbs or Astrid with him. If she was standing there in a robe when the elevator doors opened…

The elevator doors began to open. Like actually right then, in that second.

Pushing off the wall to stand on her own two feet, Roxie's heart raced. Who was in the elevator? Was it him? How many people were there?

Zairn.

Alone.

He stopped just outside the elevator to look at her. Just to look. His expression gave nothing away.

"Are you going to keep a lady waiting?" Roxie asked.

Snapping to it, he crossed the hall to use his fingerprint to open the door. He went inside first, she followed. The rigid line of his broad shoulders was tense.

Roxie closed the door and trailed after him. "What?" she called to him. "No quip about waiting for a real lady to show up?"

He stopped at the bar, dropping a hand onto it as the other loosened his tie.

It wasn't like him to put his back to her or to hesitate.

Could he be mad?

She asked, "Did I pull you away from something important?"

The moment her fingertips made contact with his back, he spun around, stealing her breath.

"Babe, you're a beautiful woman. You're sexy, you're sassy, you're amazing." What was going on now?

"Under any other circumstances, I would lay you down in my bed. Without hesitation."

"Zairn—"

"We flirt, I know, we have fun. You're fun, but…" He took hold of her shoulders, bracing his arms straight as he crouched to level their eyes. "I gave you a diamond, you think you owe me something. You don't. That's not how this works. You read too much into it. It didn't mean anything; it doesn't mean what you thought it meant. The contest is PR. God knows we need good publicity right now and if I screw you… It can't be like we picked the winner based on which woman was best suited to ride my cock."

"I know."

"And you'll say we won't tell anyone." He carried on like she hadn't uttered a word. "I'd love to believe that, but my experience tells me—"

"Z," she said, putting a finger on his lips. "Would you quit digging a hole for yourself? I didn't message you for sex."

Her hand fell from his mouth as she stepped back, reaching for the belt of her robe. The horrified trepidation that seized him was funny. Revealing her Lola Bunny pajamas wouldn't help him understand why she'd summoned him.

"You didn't message me for sex."

"Nope," she said, holding a hand out for his. "Though I'm not surprised that's where your mind went. You're crazy about me. You're probably thinking about having sex with me day and night. I'm surprised you haven't sprained your wrist already."

"Hmm," was all he said as he put his hand in hers.

She led him across the room. "We are going to sit on your unbelievably massive couch and watch movies."

"What?" he asked, surprised all over again when she pushed him onto the couch. "You pulled me away from the club because you want to watch a movie? An adult movie? If you're trying to shock me, you'll be disappointed."

"I beg to differ," she said, sitting next to him. "You look pretty shocked right now, Casanova."

"Yeah, because no one's ever…" Leaning back, his scrutiny of her intensified. "What's going on? What is this about?"

"What happens in Vegas stays in Vegas, right? Maybe for just one night, you don't have to worry about being Mr. Insanely-Gorgeous-International-Playboy. Maybe tonight you're just a guy vegging out. I love to party, I really do, but there are other ways to have fun. We've only known each other a couple of days, but I can tell you'll benefit from my tutelage."

"Oh, yeah, how's that?"

Unfastening his tie, she tossed it away and began to unbutton his shirt. "I'm going to find the remote and a movie for us. You are going to change into your pajamas."

"I don't own pajamas."

"Mr. Billionaire can't spring for nightwear? Do you have sweats? A tee-shirt?"

"For the gym, yeah."

"Okay, go put them on." She pushed at his shoulder. "The longer you take, the more likely it is I'll pick something really cheesy. Go."

There hadn't been a plan when she texted him. If she thought he'd open up to her, she'd spend the night talking to him like they had before. But he wasn't ready to talk about himself and perhaps never would be. That didn't mean she couldn't help him.

He'd lived in the dark for a long time. Partying, being Mr. Social, was his lifestyle and maybe he loved it. But there were times when everyone could benefit from kicking back, releasing themselves from the pressure they were under. That was where she came in. Fun, not sex, she definitely wasn't offering that.

13

A contented kind of peace weighed her lashes. Even though Roxie was technically awake, she hadn't yet mustered the will to open her eyes. Something smelled good. Hot. Like the kind of hot that took her awareness to her pussy. That tingling corner was much more awake than the rest of her. Like ready to go awake. Need heated the pulse between her thighs, moving her hips. Instinct rocked her against the solid body beneath hers.

Huh.

Still without opening her eyes, a frown creased her brows. A body in her bed? It wasn't either of her roommates.

Hair. Her fingers were in his hair and yes, it was a guy because her forehead was against scratchy stubble. Damn, she loved the way men felt in the morning.

Men. She smiled. Zairn. He was the only one she could be curled against. She'd shifted to lie down during the second movie and told him to lie with her. No guy had ever been so safe, which was maybe why she hadn't minded taking his hand to coil his arm around her. Directing and arranging them was harmless because he couldn't read into it. Movies was the agenda. Just movies.

Not that she would boast about it, but Roxie had woken up with her share of guys. Yet, somehow, she and Zairn had discovered a unique position she'd never experienced before. One of her legs was curled up over his torso, but she was so high up on his body that only her calf came into contact with his good stuff. And, yes, hello, his good stuff rose with the sun... Both of his arms were wrapped around her; his hands filled with her ass. Yep, apparently, he was an ass man. Even in his sleep, he managed a strong grip. Impressive.

If he got to grab her ass, then she got to do something fun too. Without opening her eyes, Roxie tipped her head back and opened her mouth to drag her teeth through his stubble until it settled on his jaw.

The sound he made was half groan, half moan. His grip tightened. Either he was awake and figuring out what was going on, or he was still in his dream and her real-world actions were transferring to his subconscious.

Under her leg, the line of his cock grew harder and thicker. Whoever he thought she was, his body sure didn't mind her taking liberties. Pursing her lips against the square corner of his jaw, she hummed, teasing him with the vibration.

Tucking her head deeper, she rubbed her nose in the arousing scent of his hair before letting her lips tickle his ear. "This is your early morning wake-up call, Mr. Lomond," she purred in her deepest seduction voice. With her leg, she stroked his dick through his sweats. "You've taken care of rise. I'll take care of shine, if you ask nicely."

Instantly his head shifted away, not far, just enough that he could turn to focus on her. "Rox," he exhaled and relaxed, letting go of her ass to drop his fist on his forehead. "Shit."

"Who'd you think it would be?" she said, her leg still sliding up and down. "I was the last woman you lay down with."

"I thought you were a nightmare," he said and dropped his hand to stall her knee. "Stop that."

"You don't like it?" she teased, propping her fist on her temple to support her head.

"No, I do..." His eyes were closed again. "I shouldn't."

Those last two words were muttered with disdain, but it wasn't aimed at her.

"Oh, cut yourself some slack," she said, boosting herself on top of him. "You're a guy with morning wood."

The glare in his gaze roused her smile. Bowing to touch her forehead to his for a second, she rose to sit on him, trailing her hands down his torso. Her hips did their own thing again, rolling in varying patterns to grind against him. "It doesn't mean anything."

The glare was still there although the hue of it altered. "No?" he asked, curling his fingers around her hips. His digits straightened to insinuate themselves under the hem of her Lola top. When they curled again, they wormed their way under the elastic waistband of her plaid cotton pants. "If you take that shirt off, it still won't mean anything."

"Yeah?" she asked, amazed that he hadn't yet learned not to play chicken with her.

Demure just wasn't her. Gathering the hem of her top, implying that she might... His eyes flared. Oh, he was anticipating it. Yeah, right, how many millions of pairs of tits had he seen? Letting go of the fabric, she dropped to plant both hands on the couch at either side of his head, suspending herself over him. He adjusted to the disappointment fast, driving his fingers deeper into her pants to hold her ass without the inconvenience of clothes in the way.

Releasing the lock of her elbows, Roxie descended, her eyes growing heavier in response to his doing the same. Her lips hung barely an inch above his. The heat of their breath mingled, intensifying the morning humidity that was absolutely all them.

"It wouldn't be fair," she murmured, rolling her hips to respond to his kneading hands. "To tease you with the one thing you can't have."

"You're not unattainable, Lola."

"Money can't buy you love, Casanova," she said, angling her head to take her mouth even closer. "Didn't you hear?"

"I'll hear you when you tell the truth. You're wild for me, baby... It's 'cause I said no. Ever since then, it's been the only thing on your mind."

"Oh, I wondered where my cocky friend had gone," she said, searching his expression with a smile.

His hips surged up and he forced her ass down, clamping their bodies tight together. "Mm?"

"You want it bad," she teased, brushing her nose across his. "Are you thinking about it, baby? About sliding yourself into me?"

"If I took control of this, I'd fuck you anyway I wanted. You'd be begging for it, baby."

"You think?"

"I know."

"Mm," she hummed.

"Shit, you feel good, baby," he admitted in a rush of breath, forcing his head far back.

Their bodies raced each other. Hands weren't required; instinct led the way. Excitement of intuitive animal stimulation fired her with blazing fury.

The exposed column of his throat was too tempting to ignore. After kissing and licking his Adam's apple, her mouth trailed to the side of his neck. The pressure behind her clit began to build. Damn, she was close. Coming only minutes after waking up with him would dent the credibility of her aloof taunting.

Oh, who the hell cared? "Z," she whimpered, pressing her mouth to the underside of his jaw.

"Fuck it," he hissed, yanking his hand from her pants to drive it under her top up the route of her spine.

Just as his fist clenched in her hair, both of them heard the same sound: the door opening. For a breath, they froze, eyes locked, then in frantic unison, they fought to extricate themselves from each other. Despite movement in the long foyer, she didn't pause to check who was about to join them.

Dashing around the chairs, Roxie snatched her robe from the floor and tied the belt in the same second Ballard appeared. His scowl went from her to the man she'd left by the couch, back and forth a couple of times.

"Been years since you pulled this kind of shit," Ballard said, focusing on Zairn. "No, I take that back. This? You've never been *this* stupid."

"Bal—"

"Og is on his way," Ballard said, cutting off his boss: ballsy choice. "He's finished downstairs."

"We're not buying," Zairn said.

"On Balfour's word?"

"We'll talk about this later."

"Right," Ballard said, punctuating the word with a judgmental snicker. "You trust her to suck your cock but are smart enough not to talk business in front of her. And you wonder why I'm glaring at you."

"I don't wonder," Zairn said. "Did you hear me ask your permission?"

"I'm gonna go," Roxie mumbled, pointing at the hallway.

Ballard spoke before she got more than a step. "Your friends are on their way back."

That startled her. "Back from where?"

"They stayed at the club last night," he said. "At the private lock-in lounge."

At the whosy, what-now? "That sounds like a super-secret, top-level something... Why were they invited there? The leech guys?"

"Staff notice when the owner's head of security and logistics singles out two particular women."

And who asked him to do that? No one, mm hmm... Though that wouldn't be the best moment to climb onto her high horse.

"Did you know?" she asked instead.

"That you snuck off early for a booty call with my boss? No," he said and drew his eyes past her to Zairn again. "Not until I got back to the club and found out he'd left too."

"We don't have time for this. Rox—"

"I'm going," she said, throwing up her hands, returning to her escape route.

If her friends were on their way back from the club, she didn't have much time to get to her room. They'd have some tales to tell, hopefully giving Roxie a reprieve from telling hers.

"Oh, it was incredible! Amazing!"

For the better part of an hour, Toria and Jane told tales of their fun at Crimson. The excitement kept on going and going like the Energizer Bunny.

The fact that she'd been in the shower when they returned didn't slow them down. They'd burst into the bathroom, talking over each other, trying to say everything at once. The talking continued through to the bedroom. Dressed, made-up, ready for the day, they were still telling stories.

"I'm thrilled you had such a good time," Roxie called over their chattering, silencing them both. "But shouldn't we... you know? Get you ready for your flight?"

"That's more good news," Jane exclaimed, grabbing her hand. "We're flying with you!"

"With me?"

Toria nodded fast. "Astrid said it was arranged in California and thought we knew. You're dropping us off on your way to the east coast."

Dropping them off in a Boeing Triple Seven. "Oh, okay," Roxie said.

"Yeah, Astrid said Zairn would be totally cool with us tagging along if it wasn't for the documentary crew."

"Yeah," Jane added. "And the fact we'd lose our jobs."

Toria scoffed. "Who cares about work? If I got the chance to follow Zairn Lomond around, I'd do it for the rest of my life. He'd never get rid of me."

Both roommates laughed.

Uneasy, Roxie sank down to sit on the chaise at the end of the bed. The documentary would show that she and Zairn had met. In the long-term, it wouldn't matter that her girls didn't get real-time details. Once the documentary aired, they could bombard her with questions, and she'd answer them… if she could.

Zairn was like two different men. The Talk at Sunset guy, idolized by her friends, and the man who'd slept under her on a couch. They'd only known each other a couple of days. Roxie had known herself for twenty-six years and was still figuring herself out. That didn't bode well for her future with Zairn.

They didn't see Zairn before or during the flight. Jane and Toria ran out of fuel and spent most of it sleeping. Saying goodbye wasn't easy. Before Sunset, the plan was for them to go home together, back to their lives together.

The sleek limo awaiting them on the tarmac outside the plane was some consolation, for her friends anyway. After a lot of hugs, some tears, and promises to keep in touch no matter what, Roxie watched their frantic waving through the back window as the car drove away. Still on the concrete, she lingered so long that Astrid had to come out and remind her that their journey wasn't over.

On the plane, Astrid showed her into the room beyond the party zone. It was more private-jet-like, as per her stereotypical imaginings at least. Sumptuous leather recliners, recessed accent lighting, a sweet scent mingled in the air… It was like a movie.

She gave up on the idea of accomplishing anything on her laptop and went to a window seat to listen to music. Messing around on her phone kept her distracted from what may lie ahead.

Someone touched her shoulder.

"Zairn," she said, taking out her AirPods as he sat opposite her.

"What are you listening to?"

"Music," she said, offering him one of the earbuds.

He took it and put it in his ear. After a second, he registered the music and gave her one of his looks. She was getting used to him thinking she was strange.

"That's Haddaway."

"Yep," she said, putting the phone and AirPods on the narrow table by her chair.

"Nineties dance. You like nineties dance music?"

"So what?" Roxie asked, taking the AirPod when he offered it back. "I like happy music. I like dancing."

"Hey," he said. Holding up his hands in surrender, he sank back in the luxurious seat. "Not my place to judge. Just, you know, let me know when you get to this century."

"Oh, ha ha," she said. "You're one to talk. You own the most premium dance venues in the world, and I haven't seen you listen to music even one time. Too busy counting your money?"

"That's me, Scrooge McDuck."

Her eyes narrowed. "Thought you didn't watch cartoons."

"He's less of a cartoon and more of an idol in my circles," he said. "He's who we aspired to be when we were kids. We worship him."

After just a few seconds in her vicinity, he'd put a smile on her face. "Sacrifice virgins in his name or would that be a waste of a virgin?" His shoulder rose in a minute shrug. "Role playing with you in the bedroom must be a lot of fun. I should warn you that Lola Bunny wouldn't go with Scrooge McDuck, not in a million years... Not unless she was really, really drunk."

And it would require a Disney, Warner Bros crossover; that was unlikely... Yeah, corporate competition, that's why it wouldn't happen.

Rather than tease or flash those suggestive eyes her way, Zairn shifted and cleared his throat. "I'm glad you brought that up."

"Brought what up? Sex? Doesn't take long for you to steer the conversation in that direction."

This was where he'd point out that she'd been the one to bring it up. Being in opposition was what they did for fun.

"Right," he said. "I apologize."

Apologize? Okay, not the way she'd expected him to go. Keeping her on her toes? Interesting.

Dampening her impulse to laugh, Roxie needed more from him to figure out the aim of their new game. "Do you?"

"Yes, I've been unprofessional. For that, I apologize."

Serious? Solemn? Respectful? It wasn't a game; it was hilarious. His affect morphed right in front of her. Rather than being his usual self, lacing every glance and word with innuendo, he carried an air of aloof authority.

"Oh, this is good," she said, lapping up the faux detachment. "I love this."

Zairn continued. "I should've shown more decorum. It wasn't appropriate to spend the evening in your suite… or for you to spend it in mine."

"The night," she said. "We spent the night together. Twice. In a row."

"Roxanna…"

How many women had heard that compassionate note in his voice? Hundreds? Maybe thousands.

The gentle let down of his pitying tone didn't patronize her, though she did lose the battle against damming her laugh. "I'm sorry," Roxie said, noticing his offense. "It's just funny."

"It's funny?"

"Yeah," she said, sliding her feet from her shoes to tuck her heels on the front edge of the seat. "It is funny. This morning you were all, 'Fuck it.'" Her impression of him didn't do anything to ingratiate her; his expression soured even further. Leaning over her knees, she lowered her volume. "You would've fucked me this morning if your buddy hadn't walked in."

"Doesn't make it right," he said. "We've gone about this all wrong."

"You'd prefer to do it properly? Moonlight and roses? Come on, Zairn, that's not what you do. You're a 'wham, bam, thank you, ma'am' kind of guy."

"You think so?"

"Oh, I know so," she said, exaggerating her movement when looking around the room. "Don't see any wife or girlfriend around to suggest otherwise. You're not known for your lasting relationships. You're known for sticking around until it suits you and then disappearing."

"You spent the night with me anyway."

Roxie shrugged, settling back in the seat. "Not because I was looking to change you. I was never in any danger of falling in love with you... And nothing you say will convince me there would ever be any chance of you falling in love with me. You were fun... or I thought you were."

For a beat, he assessed her. "Do you grasp the scrutiny we'll be under during this tour? Do you have any clue...? The documentary crew have carte blanche. They're CollCom affiliates, but that doesn't necessarily buy me loyalty."

CollCom was the name of Knox Collier's family business. Strange that a multibillion-dollar multinational could be called a family company, but what did she know about it?

"So walk in here and tell me the truth," Roxie said, smirking at him while gesturing up and down at him. "Don't come in here with this ridiculous sympathy act."

"The truth?"

"Yeah," she said. "Either your buddy guilted you into this or you're not at all the man the press makes you out to be."

"And who's that?"

"Fun, independent, arrogant, entitled, the kind of guy who does what feels good and doesn't give a damn what the world thinks. I'd have more respect if you told me the truth that I don't fit the image. Makes sense to me. I'm not a glamorous actress or dazzling supermodel." She shrugged. "I don't give a shit, Zairn. I don't live and die by the click of the paparazzi lens. You do. So, walk in here, tell me it's been fun, but you have to concern yourself with your professional image."

The clamp of his jaw took its time to loosen, reminding her of their first meeting. "I told you this was PR."

"Yes, you did. I won't embarrass you by approaching you or pretending to *know* you. Can't say I planned to throw myself on you the moment the camera was turned on, but that's what you wanted to make clear, right? We don't know each other, we're strangers. Hands-off. It's clear."

With her knees tucked against the arm of the chair, she leaned closer to the window, trying to see the ground beneath them. Down there was life, and love, and action. The world always kept on turning.

"You don't care?"

She glanced his way. "About what?"

"About this."

Roxie smiled. "There is no this. There never was a this… What is it you want exactly? Tears? You want me to beg for your attention? You've got the wrong woman for that, Mr. Lomond. My self-esteem is fine. I don't define myself by the relationships I have with men. Now or ever.

"As for this? No trust means no this. You'd never be able to trust me and that's cool. I only got out of a serious relationship a couple of months ago. I am not in the market for another one." Sliding her feet from the seat, Roxie scooched to the edge and leaned all the way forward to rest a hand on his knee. "I'm sorry you got hurt." He recoiled in sync with the jolt of surprise that went through him. "That you thought there was a chance of anything happening between us. We can still be friends just… with a little more distance."

"I… Roxanna, I don't…"

Speechless didn't look like part of his regularly scheduled programming.

"I'll stay away from you as much as I can," she said. "I don't want to send mixed signals."

He kicked into gear. "You were the one dry humping me this morning, you were right fucking there."

"Yeah," she said without any embarrassment or intention of denying it. "We were messing around. We both said it didn't mean anything." Grabbing her own knees, she straightened her arms. "Did you think it meant something?"

"No, I—"

"Did you want it to mean something?"

"No! I…" When he didn't come up with anything else to say, she widened her eyes, anticipating an explanation. "Fine. Okay. Forget it." He shot to his feet. "We keep our distance. That's it."

"Okay," she said, sliding back in her seat. "Works for me."

Movement in his jaw suggested there was something else in his throat. The scowl darkening his expression formed clouds in his brooding eyes. Roxie waited, but nothing came of it. He marched off, slamming the door at the other end of the cabin.

She blew out a breath. The captain's voice rose from the speaker to tell them they were beginning their descent. They were going down, wasn't that just the perfect metaphor for her life?

15

Roxie rode to the hotel with Astrid and Tibbs. She hadn't seen her luggage. Apparently, that was the norm. Tibbs gave her the run-down of the schedule. A week in every city. Sometimes it would take them a day or two to travel between destinations. The Triple Seven would be a constant companion, home away from home. It would literally take them around the globe.

Being on tour had to be lived to be understood. She guessed. Her brain was too exhausted to envision it. When Astrid said they were going to the hotel to eat and sleep, gratitude prevailed. Thank God for a little breathing space. Work wouldn't begin until they met the documentary crew the following day.

By the time she closed the door on her suite, her head hurt. Maybe it was the adjustment to a new schedule. She was nauseous and forewent dinner in lieu of working. Her heart wasn't in it. According to texts, Toria and Jane were out at a bar. It wouldn't be fair to distract them from their fun. In truth, returning home was the only thing she wanted to discuss. Her girls wouldn't understand.

Later on, Porter called. She let it go to voicemail, proving there was a limit to her desperation to stay occupied. He left a message asking her to call him back. Maybe she would. Maybe she wouldn't. Her decision making wasn't in the best form.

Figuring that a new day would bring a new attitude, she went to bed, prepared to be optimistic in the daylight.

Feeling brighter, Roxie woke early enough to locate the gym and to soak in the tub.

Astrid knocked on her door a minute or two after one p.m. Apparently, it was time for the meeting with the documentary crew.

"Who are they?" Roxie asked Astrid as they walked out of the elevator.

"I don't know," Astrid said. "The director's name is Greg. That's about as much as I know."

"Hmm," Roxie said. Maybe she should've done some research of her own. Though with only a first name, she wouldn't have gotten far. "Is he cute?"

They reached their destination.

With a hand on the door handle, Astrid paused, shock in her countenance. "Roxie!" she exclaimed, following the surprise with a laugh.

The gal needed to relax and open herself to new experiences.

As Astrid opened the door to go inside, Roxie squeezed her shoulders. "Hello, all," she announced.

Ballard and Tibbs stood in the middle of the windowless conference room with three men she didn't know.

One of the guys broke away to come over. "Greg Hatfield," he said, offering his hand.

"The director," Roxie said, bumping Astrid with a hip.

"That's right," he said, casting a glance back and forth between them. Astrid was first to shake his hand. "And you are?"

"Astrid Ballard."

Struck instantly by the name, Roxie planted her shock on the young assistant. "You're married to…" Keeping her eyes set on the squirming Astrid, she extended a not-so-discreet finger in the direction of the male Ballard. "Oh my God."

"He's my cousin," Astrid mumbled.

"Ah, nepotism," Roxie said, putting her hand in Greg's to shake. "Roxanna Kyst."

"Yes." A smile spread on Greg's face. "Your reputation precedes you." She didn't get it. "I knew we had the perfect candidate when news of your arrest hit the wires."

Oh, yeah, she got it now. "Happy to accommodate," Roxie said, though the icy response of the Crimson crew chilled the air a few degrees.

Astrid left her side to go over and join her cousin and Tibbs.

"We can begin," Tibbs said. "Messrs. Lomond and Ogilvie will be along as soon as they're free."

"Okay," Greg said, going to the two unknown men. "These are my guys…" Greg stood behind them to slap a hand on each of their shoulders. "Carl Glover is sound. Tevin Lind is our cameraman. We might have other people dropping in and out on the journey, but we'll be with you every step of the way."

"You won't need anything from us, from, like, the staff," Astrid said, "will you?"

"We'll need all of you to sign releases and be open to whatever happens. If something goes down and you guys are in shot, you'll be included. We will want to interview as and when. Miss Kyst…" Her name snapped her into the moment. Her mind must have been wandering, though where it went was anyone's guess. "You're going to be key. I'm the director and I'll ask questions, but you will be the face we see most."

"I will?" she asked, resting a hip on the end of a desk.

"Yes. We'll do your interview first. And it will be important to get you streaming on the website as soon as possible. We'll aim for at least one feed a day while we're in each city. We'll judge how much to stream during travel hours. We want to keep our audience engaged, but the stream has to be entertaining."

"Right, yeah," Roxie said. One a day sounded like a lot. "Don't you want to keep some stuff for the documentary?"

"Sure, of course," Greg said, wandering to the head of the room. "Contest winners have been announced. There will be three each night. One who gets the full VIP experience. Two who get a meet and greet... It'll be informal. We'll bring them in together, have a conversation, a few drinks. It's easier for us to light and film if we can control the environment."

"And you want me to stream that?" Roxie asked.

Did these people know she wasn't a tech whizz?

"No, no," Greg said, laughing off the question as though it was ridiculous. "Your streams won't take place in the clubs. Strictly in the hotel or out and about in the city we're in. You'll serve as a teaser for the documentary. We'll film in each city and at the daily briefs, where winner details will be discussed. We're going for a casual fluid feel. Today will be the first of the formal interviews."

"There will be some boundaries," Astrid said.

"Yes, we were discussing that with Tibbs," Greg said, becoming more serious. "The first thing we have to get everyone clear on is that this is not reality television. That's not the essence we're going for at all. I'm sure there will be drama and tears. We definitely want to get all of that. But no one will be set up. No conniving. No plotting. No lash inserts here."

Roxie got that. It was funny, so she laughed, but she was the only one.

"No what?" Ballard asked, not amused.

"Like in mascara ads," Roxie said, delighting Greg with her understanding. "They do the close up of the lashes and in the bottom corner of the screen somewhere it says something about the model wearing lash inserts. It's basically another way of telling the audience that the fabulous mascara they're trying to hawk doesn't do what they're claiming it does."

"Yes, thank you," Greg said, visibly pleased that someone was on his wavelength.

His eyes met hers and lingered. Someone had a sense of humor, finally! Her track record for the last few days was bleak on that score. Maybe the trip wouldn't be a complete loss if the documentary guys were easier going than the Crimson crew.

The door behind her opened, though she didn't turn around to see who'd joined them.

"What's going on?" Zairn's voice filled in that blank for her.

"Roxie and Greg are bonding over eyelashes," Astrid said.

"What's wrong with her eyelashes?" Zairn asked, glancing in the direction of her lashes as he strode on past to shake Greg's hand. "Zairn Lomond."

"It's an honor," Greg said, shaking hard. "We were just getting started."

"What are we doing in here?" Zairn asked, scanning the environment with disdain.

"This is the conference room the hotel had available."

"No," Zairn said as a phone began to ring. His as it turned out; he retrieved the device from his inside pocket. Hitting answer, he raised it to his ear. "One second…" He used the phone to gesture up. "We'll do it upstairs. Tibbs?"

"Sir," Tibbs said, jumping to attention. "Everyone follow me."

"We were going to start interviews down here," Greg said to Zairn, who'd been about to put the phone to his ear again.

On a short, irritated exhale, Zairn's phone hand dropped. "I don't like it. We'll get you a backdrop, you can do it anywhere…" The men stared each other down. "You choosing this battle?"

"No, sir."

Greg backed down. Fast. No way he'd intended that exchange to be so hostile. Someone must've peed in Zairn's cornflakes, his mood was awful.

"Okay," Zairn said. "Tibbs."

"I'm on it," Tibbs said, hurrying over to open the door and gesture everyone out.

She'd never been in Zairn's vicinity while he was doing the urgent CEO thing. It was hot and hilarious at the same time. Seeing the guy take charge: hot. Anyone being afraid of him: hilarious.

Everyone went toward the door. Everyone except Zairn. As the others passed by, she lingered, looking at the man she hadn't seen since the plane the previous day. Funny thing was, his expression hadn't changed all that much, he was still growling at the world.

Poor guy had a lot on his plate. Spinning around, she started for the door.

"Hatfield," Zairn called out to the man holding the door. Curious—some might say nosey—Roxie paused to look back, Z was focused on the director. "Kesley, was that you?"

Kesley? Searching her recollection, the only reference Roxie came up with was the actress. It didn't come as a surprise that Zairn was connected to such a renowned beauty.

"I didn't—"

"If I need help with a hookup, I'll call you. Got it?"

"Sure thing," Greg said.

Departing the room, she fell into step with Greg. Everyone else was still a little ahead.

"He's talking about Kesley Walsh, the actress?" Roxie asked.

"She's in town. Gonna be at the club tonight. They used to date."

And Zairn obviously hadn't known that his ex was around.

"It's a week for exes, I guess."

"Yours been in touch?"

"Yep," she said. "Haven't called him back yet."

"He'll have heard about your win," Greg said. "Have you been broken up long?"

The rest of their group waited at the elevator.

"Couple of months," she said.

"Because…"

Casting her attention to him, she smiled. "Are you always looking for an angle?"

He laughed. "Sorry. I wasn't interviewing you. Not yet anyway."

They reached the others. Going upstairs, she was sure, meant going to Zairn's suite. It was a different space and a different city, but still his private zone. He'd said they should keep their distance and then invited her into his room. With a bunch of people, but still it was his and she definitely was not.

16

At a loose end while the documentary guys did a bunch of coordinating with Zairn's staff, Roxie spent time on the terrace texting her girls.

Once they were ready, Greg called her in, declaring it time to do her interview.

The backdrop, which came from goodness knew where, was set up in the corner of a bedroom. Zairn's? Maybe. She didn't dwell too much on that likelihood, he had invited her there after all. To his suite, not his bedroom.

For what felt like ever, she answered questions. Perched on the edge of a high stool, with nothing to lean on, the position wasn't at all comfortable. She'd joked a few times that they intended the discomfort to distract her from her answers.

Most of the questions were standard biography stuff, of the same hue as those she'd received online from Crimson website users. Greg wanted her reaction to winning and quizzed her on what she knew about Zairn. Not much was the answer to the latter. Yes, she'd met him, but couldn't say anything other than that.

"We're almost done, Roxie," Greg said.

The camera was aimed at her and the furry microphone thing was on a stand that kept it stable off to the side, out of shot.

"Good. I'm losing feeling in my feet."

Greg laughed. "We'd like to know more about the people in your life."

They'd covered her parents and siblings, none of whom knew about her win yet. Yeah, she'd have to make that call soon.

"Who else is there?" she asked. Who else was there? "I told you I live with two of my best friends and they're the reason I was at Talk at Sunset."

"What about love?"

Suspicious, Roxie raised her chin. "What about it?"

"Do you have a romantic interest in your life?"

"Not currently."

"No one, old or new, been in touch about—"

"I don't want to talk about that," she said, hopping off the stool.

"Okay," Greg said, jumping up from his seat. "I'm sorry, I thought I'd—"

"No, it's okay," she said. "I'm not angry. I just won't talk about that. He didn't sign up for this, so… no."

"Okay."

Movement by the door attracted everyone's attention.

Zairn stood there, targeting Greg with his glare. "Everything okay in here?"

"Yeah, we're good," Greg said. "Just wrapping up.

"Good," Roxie said, sidestepping around the microphone.

Noticing that her trajectory would take her to the door, Zairn stepped into the room, freeing up the exit.

"There's one thing I want to talk to both of you about together," Greg said. "Just a really quick logistical thing."

"Okay," Roxie said, sensing tension reverberating from Zairn only three feet away. "What is it?"

Greg took his time about inhaling after his mouth opened. "Fans aren't in the best frame of mind about this experience. There's a sort of impression that it's false."

Because of her comments online. Sweet of him not to be direct. Obviously, Greg didn't know Zairn that well if he thought the CEO wasn't thinking of exactly that.

Roxie owned her mistakes. "I'll go online and—"

"Make it worse?" Zairn asked. "No. You don't get to talk to people."

"Excuse me," she said, raising her hands to her hips. "I can talk to anyone I like. You don't own my voice."

"I own the website," he said. "So no more talking to people for you."

"Hey!" Roxie exclaimed. "Those people liked me. I told the truth. That's the whole damn point."

"Truth is a fluid concept."

"No, actually, truth is truth. You're the one fuzzy on its definition," Roxie said, setting her annoyance on Greg. "I'm sorry, as you can see, he's not the easiest person to get along with."

"I get along with everyone else on the planet," Zairn said. "And don't do that, don't apologize to him for me. I'm not sorry. You hear me? I'm not sorry!"

His volume grew in those last words, changing the aura of the room. They weren't talking about the website or the public anymore.

"It's okay," Greg said. "Nothing to argue about. We decided it would be better if you two shared a suite."

Standing there, the world slowed down as those words filtered in. Roxie could see the same incredulity creep through Zairn. They'd just promised to keep their distance and there was this guy...

In unison, they both laid their disbelief on Greg. Paling under the scrutiny, the director only shrank for a few seconds. In his expression, Roxie witnessed the exact moment curiosity crept in.

In that same second, she smiled. "That's a great idea!" Shrieking in delight, she jumped forward to grab Zairn's upper arm, keeping her focus on Greg. "Why don't you get setup for Zairn's interview and I'll go downstairs to pack... again!" She laughed. "Something I'll have to get used to." Patting Zairn's arm, Roxie got his attention. "You can't wear that tie. I'll find a better one for you."

Marching into the closet at the other side of the room, Roxie glanced back to check the documentary guys were distracted. She gestured at Zairn to follow and, without waiting, went to the furthest corner of the closet.

The sight of Zairn's ties hanging on the rack in perfect alignment took her aback. She was still ogling it when Zairn approached.

"What are you doing?" he hissed.

"Look at this," Roxie said, stepping back to open her arms at the ties. "How do you do this? I was so tired last night that I couldn't even eat dinner. Yet, somehow, you had the wherewithal to arrange your ties in like color gradient order, how do you do that?"

"I don't," he said. "The staff do it."

"Oh, the staff do it," she mocked, snatching the darkest blue tie to toss it over her shoulder.

"We can't share a suite," he said, dutifully raising his chin when she loosened his tie and turned up his shirt collar.

Roxie discarded one tie to replace it with another. "Yes, we can. No mixed signals," she said, focusing on the Windsor knot at hand. "You can't argue with me in front of people. Not like we argue."

"Who was arguing, Lola?"

"And no Lola either, not in front of people."

"You gave me the 'I'm sorry you got hurt' speech," he grumbled. "I walked in there to show you I had the reins… I never had the reins, did I?"

"No," she said, fixing his collar then smoothing his lapels while she checked out her handiwork. Happy with it, Roxie turned him to face the mirror. "That's why you were in a snit? You take life too seriously."

"No one ever accused me of that before." He admired the knot on the tie. "Good job."

"I have many talents…" Roxie stepped between him and the mirror to talk to his reflection. "Hatfield is not benign. You said just because he was CollCom you couldn't buy his loyalty. Don't forget that when you're talking to him."

"What was he trying to push you on?"

"Forget that. You won't get into my pants by making a fool of yourself out there. Answer the man's questions. Be suave. Charming. Like you're good at."

"I have your permission?"

Roxie heard the mocking smile in his voice. It was an odd relief to see him relaxed again. "Stop thinking about sleeping with me."

"I'm not thinking about sleeping with you," he said, crouching lower to murmur in her hair. "I'm thinking about bending you over the tie rack and looking for those reins."

"You have a one-track mind," she said, pushing him. "How is it you're responsible for so many thousands of social lives?"

"I'm responsible for yours tonight," he said, running his palms down her bare arms. "Any requests?"

"I request that you stop touching me," she said, leaving her post to peek past him at the door, checking no one was spying on them. "They want us to share a room and that's no big deal, you can't make a big deal of it. Your fans want someone looking over your shoulder. That's what you signed up for. He said it earlier, he wants the documentary to be entertaining. How entertaining is it to film you or me alone in a room? They'll want as many people together as possible… They want to see your playboy lifestyle."

Yeah. Exactly. Where were the naked women bathing in booze, taking turns to mount the loaded party guy anyway?

"Do you have a girlfriend?" she asked.

"No."

Taking hold of his lapels, she bent a knee and leaned back groaning. "You're supposed to say yes! Tell me you have a woman in every port."

"I don't need to string them along, Lola. I pick 'em up and put 'em down as I want."

Good. Better. "Thank you," she exhaled in relief.

"It would make you happy if I was a promiscuous womanizer?"

When he said it that way, it sounded bad. "Why did you and Kesley Walsh break up?"

"She wanted something I couldn't give her."

"Fidelity?"

"No, attention," he said, pretty deadpan. "Twenty-four hours a day, seven days a week, three hundred and sixty-five days a year."

"Oh…" Roxie pondered. "Hmm… that doesn't sound like fun. Was it fun?"

"If it was fun, I wouldn't have broken up with her."

Pleased, the pursuit of fun was something that fitted with her original assumptions about him.

Flattening her hands under his lapels, Roxie stroked him gently. "She called you?"

"Yes."

"Are you going to see her?"

"She'll be at the club," he said. "I can't bar her… Do you want me to bar her? It'll make headlines."

On blogs and in gossip rags, but it never took the mainstream media long to catch up with the drama.

"I didn't say that."

"You're jealous," he said, relaxing into his arrogance. "It's okay, Lola, it's a natural reaction."

She swiped at his chest. "I am not jealous."

"It's okay," he said, his swagger in full bloom. "I forgive you. You just have to breathe through it. The pain will get easier in time."

"Do you want me to show you pain?"

"Mr. Lomond?" Astrid called from the doorway.

From the sheepish look on her face, the assistant wouldn't have chosen to intrude, but the reason for it became apparent when Greg popped in behind her.

"Can we split your interview in two, Mr. Lomond? Do some now and the rest later?" Greg asked. "Astrid plans to take Roxie shopping. We'd love to follow."

"Shopping where?" Zairn asked.

"Ah! My Pretty Woman moment," Roxie exclaimed, bouncing around Zairn to pat his chest. "We need a credit card."

"What?" he asked, looking at each of the three faces in the room like he didn't have a clue what was going on. His hands went to his chest and pants pockets. "My wallet's on the bar."

"Astrid!" Roxie called spinning around, but she didn't get far. Zairn caught her wrist to pull her back. She tried to twist it free. "Let me go, I want to go spend your money… Maybe I'll buy you a tie."

Greg laughed. "That's something I'd definitely like to film."

"Only if it's an R-rated documentary," she said, still trying to free her wrist from the confused Zairn who didn't get the reference. Astrid hadn't gone anywhere yet. How frustrating! "Girl, go get his wallet so he can tell us which card to use... unless we're going to use them all."

Astrid giggled, but quickly covered her mouth to hide it. "I have a company card."

Roxie perked up. "That's right, we're bankrupting Rouge."

"Shopping's better in New York," Zairn said.

"We're not in New York, Skippy," Roxie said. Fixating on Zairn's grip, she gave up the struggle. "It's probably better in Milan too. Maybe in London or Paris as well."

"The plane's just sitting there."

Was he suggesting that they take the plane to go shopping? "You know humanity is trashing this planet, right?" she asked. "It's dying because of people like you, with your private planes and casual attitude to the detriment caused by flight. Have you ever worked out your carbon footprint? Bet it's worse than a small, industrialized nation... maybe even a big one... They should've demanded your signature on Kyoto and the Paris Agreement, the planet's doomed otherwise."

"A simple 'no, thank you' would've been enough," Zairn said, releasing his hold.

Her head dropped to the side. "When have you ever heard me use one word when I can use fifteen instead?" She patted his chest and raised an arm as she headed for the door. "I have to go shopping now!"

17

As if streaming for the first time wasn't pressure enough, Roxie then had to deal with her first real meet and greet at Crimson. No one paid much attention to her. The contest winners were ecstatic to be in the private VIP lounge with Zairn and his people. Kesley Walsh's attendance took even more of the heat off. The actress and Zairn greeted each other like old friends. Fond ex-lovers who held no grudges.

Whether that was true or not was anyone's guess.

Turned out the Crimson Experience winners were allowed to bring a friend. Made sense, sharing their experience would enhance the joy. So rather than three, there were six people seated on the raised platform in the VIP lounge. Zairn had his own couch at the head of the group. His usual posse were behind him, Astrid, Tibbs, and Ballard. A couple of servers floated around. Security agents congregated by the door. Maybe those guys belonged to Kesley Walsh... or the club expected trouble with newbies around.

Greg and his colleagues were filming everything around Zairn as it unfolded. Despite not being an actor, Zairn was aloof and didn't acknowledge them or appear irritated by their presence.

With everyone otherwise occupied, Roxie ebbed from the throng of people baying for Zairn's attention and went to sit elsewhere. A rise of noise at the doorway heralded the arrival of a new group. All guys. Hot guys too... mostly. The host left his couch to go greet them. She didn't know who they were, though they did look familiar. Sports maybe?

"It must be strange." Roxie hadn't noticed Kesley approach, but there she was standing at the end of the couch. "Can I join you?"

"Oh, uh… Sure, yes."

It was a free country. Roxie didn't own the club… or the couch. She moved her clutch off the seat and Kesley sat down, leaving little space between them. Hollywood was touchy, feely, lovey; were they gal pals now?

"I still wonder how he does it," Kesley said, fixated on Zairn shaking hands with the half dozen new guys before introducing them to the Experience winners. "He remembers everyone's name. Have you noticed that?"

"Oh, this is my first night out like… this."

"Really?" Kesley asked, glancing her way. "And you're not in the thick of it?"

Roxie laughed. "I have enough to worry about without stepping on any toes… I just came here to dance."

"You're the winner, the woman from the Sunset prize."

"Yep," Roxie said. How did she reciprocate the acknowledgement? "You do movies."

The beauty exhaled a laugh and cast her attention back to Zairn. "Yes, I do."

Damn. Cringe. Great, so the fabulous, talented actress thought she was a fool. Fantastic.

"It was lucky you were in town," Roxie said, trying to salvage the conversation. "At the same time as Zairn being here, I mean. And that you're still on good terms."

"Z is on good terms with everyone. Even those he isn't on good terms with." Kesley enjoyed her own comment; Roxie wasn't sure she understood it. "He has this knack for making everyone feel special." The actress swayed closer, pointing at Zairn. "Look at that… you see the way he put his hand on her back."

The group was returning to the couches. Kesley was right, Zairn was guiding one of the winners across the room, his hand on her back.

"Yeah," Roxie said, shrugging it off. "What does that mean?"

"You see how he keeps it just under her shoulder blades? He won't touch any woman below the waist... on the back. On the front, it's below the neck."

"I don't know what—"

"He's so aware." Kesley's awe was palpable. It dripped from her words and shone from her skin. "He never wants any woman to be uncomfortable and is so careful not to do anything that could be misconstrued."

Hmm, maybe they weren't talking about the same Zairn. "Misconstrued?" Roxie asked. "Like that he's coming onto them?"

"Yes," Kesley said. "He keeps his touches light and in the most appropriate places. He won't sit next to a woman; he lets them come to him and boy, do they." She laughed, still watching the focal crowd as they sat and settled into their groove. "It took me a long time to notice... It's incredible... I think it's the respect that does it. He gives women all the power... in the approach anyway. Once the wheels are in motion, it's all him. Every woman could benefit from a Zairn Lomond courtship."

Finishing her drink, Roxie leaned forward to put the empty glass on the low table in front of them. Less than a full breath later, a server appeared to put new drinks down. What the...? Where had she come from?

"Thank you... very much," Roxie said. A smile was all she got from the blonde picking up the used glasses. "I don't even have any cash."

Kesley laughed as the server departed. "You don't have to tip here. Zairn takes care of all that." The guy took care of a lot. "The drinks are him too. People are taken care of when he's around; hosting is what he does."

"I suppose he wouldn't have got far in his business without mastering that skill."

"It's amazing, he's so good at knowing what everyone else needs," Kesley said, concentrating on him as she picked up the fresh drink. "But has no clue what *he* wants."

"We're all guilty of that."

Although happy in life in a general sense, she wasn't aiming to hit any specific objective. Zairn had to be goal-driven, right? Wasn't that how successful people achieved their potential?

"I would never wish bad things for him," Kesley said and sighed. "I would never say it to him, but I miss him every day… Life after Zairn Lomond is never the same as it was before. There's something so… secure about being with him. Not in fidelity, I was always hyperaware of the hundreds of women in his life. About how they offer themselves to him. I've seen it. Some of them did it right in front of me. They have no shame… He has this way of putting women at ease. Like bees to honey."

"He's an attractive guy," Roxie said, conceding a shrug. "There's appeal."

"Yes, like the money and the connections. That's why he avoids LA so much. Just walking down the street can be a minefield. People think if they can be granted VIP access to Crimson that they'll rub shoulders with key players with the power to make their careers. Zairn could do that, if he wanted to, but that's not what he's about." A lingering silence stretched the moment. "I think that's why he felt safe with Dayah."

"Dayah?" Roxie asked, recalling Talk at Sunset. "Dayah Lynn?"

"Yes, her career was on the rise. So young and she received the Oscar nomination… He went to the ceremony with her."

"They were together?"

"No one knows that for sure," Kesley said. "They were pictured together several times and Dayah was a Crimson Queen."

Shifting to angle toward the actress, Roxie seized the opportunity. "What exactly is a Crimson Queen?"

"Often a woman who's slept with Zairn," Kesley said. He really highlighted the notches on his bedpost by titling them "Queen" in his clubs? Was that creepy or sentimental? The actress turned away from Zairn to witness Roxie's confusion. "That's not a hard and fast rule. They're women with access to all Crimson sites."

"Don't all his friends have access?"

"Most people only access one or two clubs. Queens can show up whenever, wherever. Anyone else has to clear their VIP admission with the club in advance... Them or a representative anyway. Crimson Queens don't need to do that. We each get..." Reaching up, she pointed to a red gem on a hair slide. "It's a ruby."

"Was Dayah a Crimson Queen?"

"Zairn and I broke up a few weeks before he and Dayah started to be photographed together. I always assumed there was overlap. Things weren't good between us for a while... His life is so busy, and he meets new gorgeous people all the time. The courtship is amazing, but he just can't sustain it." A laugh warmed her breath. "Ironic to say that given what he can sustain elsewhere, right?"

Kesley returned to gazing across the room at Zairn. That question implied... Not that Zairn was good in bed. Weird, but even in her limited experience that seemed like a given. No, the implication was that she and Zairn were sleeping together. He'd said people would make assumptions. She'd shrugged off that warning and sure hadn't expected anyone to be so explicit in their presumption.

Switching focus, she wracked her memory for details of Dayah Lynn's death. At the time, it was on the news. Her girls chattered about it. The glamorous Dayah Lynn died in LA. As to how Zairn was connected... Dayah had been at Crimson with him on the night of her death. Wasn't that what her girls said? Damn, if only she'd paid more attention.

The chance to converse with Kesley had come out of the blue. If she had anticipated the conversation, she'd have done research. Not about Zairn and Dayah, about Kesley. The woman was way more personable than she'd imagined a famous person would be.

"How have you been getting along with Ogilvie?" Kesley asked, interrupting Roxie's thoughts.

"I haven't spent any time with him."

Her prevailing memory was him calling her a media whore. That wasn't fading any time soon.

"Believe me, that's a good thing," Kesley said. "He'll literally walk into a room and talk to Zairn as if you don't exist. He's a serious guy. All business. Difficult to get to know. I don't know anyone who's done it. He keeps Zairn's mind on business… usually when I didn't want him to… Og likes to have influence at the top."

"Are they family?"

"Zairn doesn't have family, not blood family. Ogilvie dated Z's mom before she died. They didn't see each other for years, but Og got in touch somehow after his grandfather died."

And the young Zairn received his six million inheritance. Coincidence? She chose to reserve judgment.

"Ballard is important to him," Roxie said.

That was evident from the way they talked to each other. Zairn was employing Ballard's young cousin too.

"They go way back. I don't really know the story. I never asked," Kesley said, suddenly bouncing around to face her. "Gosh, listen to me, he'd hate me spilling all. I don't suppose it counts among Queens. And you'll be one of us soon."

"The plan is to visit all of the Crimson venues. No one said anything about being a Queen."

"Zairn never gives warning of it. He just slips the pin in your hair while you're getting dressed." Not getting dressed in his vicinity was a good indication of the likelihood it would happen to her. "We'll invite you to the dinner," Kesley said, shocking Roxie again.

"There's a dinner?"

"Welcome to the lifestyle, honey," Kesley said, throwing out an extravagant hand. "You're going to love it. Any excuse for a get together. I'm sure you'll fit right in."

Kind and optimistic. Kesley knew next to nothing about her yet was warm and welcoming. Maybe it was just the way of people in the entertainment industry. She had no idea.

"Now," Kesley said, sliding to the edge of her seat. "Grab your drink and come with me. There are some Bruins I am desperate for you to meet."

Roxie hesitated. Bruins? That could be a problem. "I'm from Chicago."

Kesley laughed. "That's okay. I won't let them hold it against you."

The lifestyle: drinking, schmoozing, staying up late. Roxie could do that. She could have fun. What was so difficult about that?

18

"Okay, thank you," Roxie said at the door of the hotel suite. "Goodnight."

Finally, after like twenty minutes of saying goodbye, Greg and his colleagues made it to the elevator. Every time they took a step that way, one of them would say something else and they'd go through the whole palaver all over again.

Closing the suite door, she made a point of locking it before dropping back against it, exhaling her exhaustion.

"I'd have closed the door in their faces nineteen and a half minutes ago."

She peeked at Zairn out of one eye, then pushed away from the door to head in his direction. "That's the difference between me and you," Roxie said as she passed. "I'm nice."

The bedroom designated hers offered hope in the form of a bed. Ah, the prospect of rejuvenation. Last she'd looked at a clock was around two a.m. Despite the hour, none of the guests had been in any hurry to leave the club. VIPs liked to get the most out of their time at Crimson.

The immersing intimacy of darkness was her natural habitat. Being out and social, switched on, gave her a buzz. Even alone, working at home, she chose the night over any other time. But, man, was she tired. The previous day had started earlier and was busier than her regular life. Burning the candle at both ends was going to take some getting used to. In her college days, no problem. She was out of practice.

Shoes away. Dress unzipped and... ah. She paused. Her Lola pajamas went out with the laundry. What else could she wear? Nothing? An option. Not one she should embrace with no idea what might happen in the morning. There was nothing in the closet that… Twisting around, she sought the door. Not in her closet anyway.

Traipsing to Zairn's room opposite hers, she didn't ask permission to go in or to continue to his closet. He'd been standing by the bed on his phone anyway, so it was doubtful he even registered her.

At least that's what she thought until he appeared at the threshold. "Scavenging?"

"For a shirt," she replied, selecting one from a hanger. Pushing the straps of her dress and bra from her arms, she managed to put the shirt on and shimmy out of her clothes without flaunting too much flesh. A perplexed frown formed on his face, so she explained. "I'm not cruel… or stupid." She used her toe to flick the dress up from the floor to toss it at him, though it didn't get that far. "You have a thing for women in their underwear."

"Do I?" he asked, sauntering deeper into the room to scoop up her dress.

"Yes. That's why you asked me to wear lingerie for you."

One side of his mouth tipped higher. "We remember that moment differently."

"Sure, because you skew everything to your advantage," she teased, her chin rising to maintain eye contact when he invited himself into her personal space. "A woman remembers when a man makes predatory advances."

"I seem to have missed that too."

Yet, still wearing the semi-smirk, he lifted her discarded dress to breathe in her scent.

Oh, mocking him for that would be easy and so much fun, but she couldn't bring herself to do it. Because his body heat was mingling with hers in the private closet where they stood alone? Maybe. Probably. Or it could just be that the move was predatory and he owned it. Being the prey never felt so nice.

"We're doing really good at the distance thing."

"Mm hmm," he said, dropping her dress. He scooped a hand under her hair to cradle the side of her head. "You and Kes spent a lot of time together tonight."

"I like her," Roxie said, undoing another couple of buttons on his shirt. "I didn't think I would."

"Because you're jealous of her."

Stating it like a fact didn't make it true. "Jealous that you dumped her? No, if you were ever lucky enough to be with me, you'd never want to end it... You'd give up every cent and all your credibility to pursue me."

"Why would I be pursuing you? You wouldn't go anywhere. I'd just keep providing the high life."

"Oh, you would?"

"Mm hmm," he said, pulling her higher. "You look good in Crimson."

"There should be more dancing in the VIP areas... I don't think I'm cut out to be a VIP if there's no dancing."

He took her arms from her sides to drape them against his chest, drawing her into his embrace to begin dancing. "You can dance anywhere, Lola."

"This is not the kind of dancing I meant," she said. Envisioning them doing the same thing in Crimson roused her smile. "Can you imagine if we did this at one of your clubs?"

"I can dance with women at work. It's allowed. Guaranteeing you a good time is my job."

"I am not your job, Casanova," she said, shaking her hair away from her cheeks. "You better be careful, you're falling for me."

"Think maybe I should come to that conclusion myself?"

"You need me, Lomond," Roxie said, sliding her hands higher to tuck them beneath the fabric of his shirt onto the warmth of his chest. "You can't stay away."

"You're in my closet, in my suite. I'm not the pursuer here."

"Oh, I know you bribed Hatfield to set this up for you," she said, showing him a glimpse of humor. "You think you're so suave, Casanova. In the long term, you'll thank me for being the strong one."

Exhaling, Roxie wrapped her arms around him to rest her head on his chest. He felt so damn good. Hot and hard, steady and stable, there was safety there in his arms.

"Yeah," he murmured. "You're a real stalwart."

She did smile, even though he couldn't see her face. His hands wandered up and down her back, reminding her of what Kesley had said earlier in the night. The actress asserted that Zairn was a stickler for never acting in a way that could be misconstrued as interest. Apparently, he was happy, eager even, to convey that message to her.

The security that Kesley mentioned circled Roxie. Relaxing her, soothing her, he definitely had a knack for looking after people.

"What do you want, Z?" she asked, thinking of another comment from the club.

"Right now?" he asked, crouching lower to hold her tighter.

The innuendo was forgiven; it was their norm. He didn't know where her head was at... neither did she. Flirting back would be the safest path. Without trust, there could never be a this. Weren't those her words to him? Except they'd be spending the next few months together. Forging a friendship was necessary, especially while living in such close quarters.

"In life," she said. "Do you know what you want?"

His next comment was laced with confusion. "There are always developing plans in the business for—"

"Not business, in your personal life." Getting no reply, she looked up at him. "You don't have a clue, do you?" His blank affect said it all. He had no words. "That's okay..." Sighing, she tucked herself against him again. "Neither do I."

In silence, they kept on dancing. Breathing together. Peace and calm. Until the contest experience, she'd never considered herself a creature of habit. Usual routines were out the window. Workwise, she'd complete the contracts already on her books but wouldn't set up anything new. Rouge was taking care of her typical overheads anyway, which took the pressure off.

"Where did that question come from?" he asked, tangling his fingers in her hair.

"Just something me and Kesley were talking about."

Confusion reigned in him. "About what I want?"

Having opened that particular vein, it was her duty to seal it again. Flirtation came in handy.

"Yeah, we thought about hijacking your bedroom and slathering each other's naked bodies in something edible to tempt you," she said. "But we couldn't decide which you'd like better, whipped cream or chocolate body paint."

"We'll get both. You and me we'll figure out the answer together. I don't want you to lose sleep wondering."

Tightening her hold, Roxie breathed him in. "Shame I don't have either whipped cream or chocolate body paint with me."

"Want to see how fast I can get both here?"

Roxie peeked up. "Show off."

"Just facilitating your fantasy, baby. Your good time is my vocation."

Dancing with him was a comfort she could sink into. For a minute anyway. With the prospect of the documentary hanging over them, alone time wasn't guaranteed. Bearing that in mind, while she had the chance, she had to ask…

"Were you and Dayah Lynn together?" He stopped. "Kesley was talking about her. She didn't know if—"

When he took her shoulders to part their bodies, Roxie stopped talking to look into him. What was he thinking? What was in his head? Interpreting what could be any of a dozen emotions in his expression was impossible.

"Are you asking me that?"

Confidence came easy. Whether or not the question would put an end to their friendship before it began was another matter.

"Yes," she said.

"Why?"

"Because I'm curious."

Zairn let her go to back up a few steps. "Babe, that's a complicated question."

"Because you weren't together and you wanted to be, or because you were and you didn't want to be?"

"Neither," he said, running a hand through his hair. "It's complicated because talking about it... It causes problems."

From her vantage point, she got a clear view of his shutters going down. There was no trust. It didn't matter how many times she reminded herself that his lack of trust came from a lifetime of conditioning, the confirmation was still a blow. It was his right to refuse answering. His right to keep his private matters private.

She shook her head. "I completely understand why you don't want to talk about it... Whatever your relationship, you knew each other. Her passing can't have been easy... especially with everything that followed."

Okay, so she couldn't remember many details of Dayah's death. Her hazy interest at the time had been absorbent enough to notice Zairn's frequent appearance in the press. Every time his name was mentioned, her girls would wave around newspapers, phones, tablets, whatever. The headlines were always related to stories about police and investigations.

His gaze left hers. He moistened his lips and took a steadying breath. "I can't involve you in that."

"It was a simple question. The answer wouldn't involve me in anything."

"Yes, it would," he said, his patience fraying. "Because the more people I talk to, the more people there are to talk to the media, the more people the cops will want to talk to."

"And if I repeat what you say to me, it could be bad for you."

"Dayah's family have been through enough. They don't need everything churned up in the media again."

And he obviously believed that discussing it would lead to her recounting his words to the press. Maybe not now, but at the end of the tour, there would undoubtedly be a book deal in it for her to share any salacious details that weren't shown on film.

It hurt. Of course it hurt. But, damn, she couldn't put that on him. He couldn't trust her. He couldn't trust anyone new in his life. Just because that truth was manifesting itself now didn't mean she should suddenly be bowled over by it.

"Okay," Roxie said, accepting his position.

"Babe," he said as she began to walk away. "Lola." He bounded over to snag her wrist, stalling her. "Stay. Lie down with me."

"No."

"We don't have to talk about that, about the drama and the spectacle. We have fun, can't we just have fun?"

"We can have fun," she said, showing a smile. "I'm not mad. But I'm not sharing a bed with you either."

He dropped her wrist. "Because I won't talk about Dayah? You're using sex to manipulate me."

"First," she said, raising a forefinger. "You said 'lie down' not 'sleep' with. You and I both know that we can sleep in the same space just fine. It gets complicated when we wake up together. Distance was the agreement. If we don't stick to that while they've got us locked up together, it will come back to bite both of us on the ass. You're the one who said experience told you it would never stay a secret."

"It's different now."

"It's different for you because I'm here and convenient," she said. "We can be friends, but you know it can't go any further than that while we're doing this PR exercise."

Casual sex wasn't a problem in itself. Casual sex with the guy she'd be living with for three months would be insane. If the world got wind of it, as they eventually would, the bad publicity Crimson were trying to combat would go from grenade to global nuclear strike.

From the conflict apparent in his stance, it was like he couldn't decide whether to be angry or apologize. Giving him a break, she went over to curve a hand around his neck to pull him down and kiss his cheek.

"Goodnight," she said, wearing a simple smile.

Conflict joined her on the walk back to her room. Being a prop was what she'd signed up for. The journey, with a friend, could be fun. If Zairn kept reminding her that she was, and always would be, an outsider, it could turn out to be a long three months.

19

Roxie didn't look at the time when she woke up the next day. What was the point? Her only commitments came when darkness fell. There was nothing to rush around getting ready for, not in the daylight.

Still yawning, she rounded into the living room and paused at the sight of Ogilvie standing in the middle of the space.

Unfortunately, he spotted her too. Damn, reversing out to slink away was tempting... if only they hadn't made eye contact.

"Good morning," Roxie said, catching her hair in a finger comb to toss it back over her head.

"It's afternoon."

Oh, well, that didn't matter. If he was going to be pernickety, she wasn't in the mood.

A subtle shrug was her response. This Og wouldn't be impressed no matter what she said. The balcony would be a better way to greet the day.

"Is that Zairn's?"

Ogilvie's question stopped her. What was he talking about? The whole suite was Zairn's. A look his way revealed he was sneering at her apparel.

The shirt. Right. She'd forgotten about that. "Yes," she said, lifting the corner to drop it again.

"And you think that's appropriate?"

Folding her arms, she couldn't prevent the angle of her hip from sliding into impudent. "I just woke up, I'm wearing what I slept in." No apology. No less judgment in that leer. "What is your problem with me?"

"You're trouble." Thank God the guy didn't insult her with denials. "We wanted a contest winner who would improve our image. You have a pretty face, but you're going to be a detriment to us."

One of her hands landed on her cocked hip. "I'm sorry, is Rouge your company?" His expression grew more disgusted. "I haven't knowingly done anything to hurt Rouge or Zairn. And, just so you know, Zairn is a big boy. He can make his own decisions."

"It's my job to protect him."

The guy didn't strike her as the type to back down. Maybe it was her gender or her economic sphere... or maybe he was just an asshole.

"He doesn't need protecting," she said. "Not from someone who magically found their way back to him right when he discovered he was a multimillionaire."

Direct hit. Ha! Take that.

Taken aback, Ogilvie blustered. "What did you...? How do you...?"

Anyone who expected her to pull her punches would be disappointed. She was more than capable of standing up for herself and would prove it any time. Fear didn't factor. Yeah, she could be a sasspot, but it was no less than Ogilvie deserved in that minute.

Zairn appeared in her peripheral vision.

Ogilvie stared her out. His determination would be funny if hers wasn't so fierce. No matter if it took all damn day and night, she'd still be there glaring right back.

"What's going on?" Zairn asked.

She waited a few beats, giving Ogilvie a chance to speak first.

When he didn't take advantage of the opportunity, Roxie spoke up. "Your friend wants me to strip for him."

"What?" Zairn barked, as confused as he was offended.

"I didn't say that!"

"Oh, so you were accusing me of stealing?" she asked. "It's not your shirt. I didn't steal from you."

"I don't care about the shirt," Zairn said, approaching. He put an arm around her and kissed the top of her head. "We good, Lola?"

Her eyes rose to his. "We're good."

Last night wasn't an argument. She hadn't gone to bed mad or holding a grudge. Had he been worried about that? Did it disrupt his sleep?

"Ogilvie doesn't have a sense of humor," Zairn said, tucking her hair behind her ear. "He doesn't have a good ear for sarcasm either."

"Who was being sarcastic?"

The door opened, offering a reprieve. Tibbs entered with Astrid and Greg not far behind.

Was she the last person awake in the whole city or just in their group? Ogilvie was there and Zairn was dressed. If they'd had a "morning" she'd missed it.

"Mr. Hatfield would like a few moments," Tibbs said.

"What for?" Zairn asked. "We're due to meet this afternoon, I'm busy now."

He didn't look busy. He was just standing there next to her. Not doing anything.

"No, uh, with Roxie," a sheepish Tibbs said. "He wants a few moments with her."

She pointed at herself. "With me?"

"If you don't mind," Greg said, passing Tibbs. "Thought I could take you to lunch."

"Sure," she said. It wasn't like the invitations were stacking up. "I have to shower and change."

"I can wait."

"Okay," she said. Zairn didn't move when she turned. Rude. He was in her way. Adjusting her path to go around him, she gestured Greg over. "Come wait in my room. I only need ten minutes."

"He can wait out here," Zairn said in a weird kind of guttural voice.

Roxie groaned. "Oh, Greg doesn't care about seeing me naked. Even if he did, what's it to you? You should know better than anyone that one pair of tits is just like any other."

"I don't know that, thanks," Zairn said, laying a glare on her. "And he's still waiting out here."

"Interrupting your secret meeting?" she said, spinning around to walk backwards toward her room. "What if that leads to Armageddon?"

"Then I'll see you in Hell. That's where the party's going to be, right?"

Yes, Zairn was overstepping to think he could dictate what she did and didn't do. But he was funny, even when he was angry, that covered a multitude of sins.

Raising her arms, Roxie sighed at Greg. "Guess you're waiting out here. I'll be as quick as I can."

Zairn and Ogilvie were in the dining area on the other side of the room when she emerged again. Tibbs and Ballard were nowhere around. They'd probably been sent on errands.

Everyone else was going about their day, it was time to get hers started.

Greg loitered in the balcony doorway. When he noticed her, he started to walk, but she shooed him back.

"Go outside, we'll get privacy there."

"I can take you out somewhere."

"We'll go out after you've apologized," she said, looping an arm through his to take the lead in guiding them outside.

"How do you know I'm going to apologize?"

Sitting him down first, Roxie perched herself on the edge of the patio chair angled toward him. "Because we got off on the wrong foot. We hit it off with the lash thing and then it fell apart when you used the first thing I confided in you in front of the camera. You were snivelly last night, did a lot of brownnosing. A straight apology works better with me. Groveling is less effective."

"We try to go where the story takes us," Greg said, holding up a hand when her expression grew more severe. "I'm sorry, you're right. I apologize."

"It's okay," she said, resting her shoulders on the chair back. "You did me a favor."

"I did?"

"Yeah," she said, draping her wrists on the arms of the chair. "Now I know who you are. Better to know that sooner than later."

"And it's my fault that you think I'm that way. I got too excited."

"And shot your load too soon," she said, examining her nails on one hand. "I tend to avoid men like that."

"I hope you won't avoid me. I shouldn't have been so heavy-handed. Like I said, this is not reality TV. I'm not trying to trap you. I apologize if it came off that way."

"It did come off that way. You forget this isn't my world. Someone screws me over, it's personal, not professional."

"I hope you'll give me the opportunity to make it up to you."

"How are you gonna do that? I like chocolate and heels... and compliments."

He laughed, seeming to enjoy her. Although his apology was appreciated, she would remain wary until he proved that his faux pas was a unique misstep... if he proved it.

"Do you want to spend a day at the spa?" he asked. "On us."

"I was thinking about seeing some sights. There's so much history here."

"We can arrange that. Astrid said your handler was due to join us today."

"I don't need a handler," Roxie said, standing up. "You get your guys setup downstairs and I'll meet you in the lobby."

"I can wait if you—"

"I need to make a call," she said, sweeping her hair away from her shoulder.

While in the shower, she'd missed a call from her folks. Rather, she'd missed *another* call from her folks. Yes, she'd been avoiding the conversation. With the frequency of their attempts to get through to her growing, putting it off any longer wasn't an option.

Greg rose. "Calling the ex back?"

Maybe that was a joke. Maybe not. She narrowed the evil eye on him. "Not yet, docu guy. Not yet."

His laugh joined her on the walk back inside. Without checking what was happening in the dining area, she strode to her room.

Confident. Bold. Two of her specialties.

Dialing her parents, she closed her bedroom door and strolled to the window to get a boost from the sun. Although it wasn't California bright, Roxie appreciated the familiarity of the warmth on her cheeks.

"Yeah?"

Her father's abrupt voice startled her.

"Dad, you hate talking on the phone. Put mom on."

"Your mom's doing something with her flowers out back. Wait a sec." Scuffles and creaks carried down the line. "Your mom called your apartment. Jane said you were still out of town."

So the "*wait a sec*" didn't actually offer her a reprieve. Great. "Yes, Dad, I'm still out of town."

"Thought you girls were coming back from LA together."

Her mom's voice echoed in the background. "Who's on the phone?"

"The middle one."

Exhaling, Roxie rolled her eyes. "I have a name. You should know, you gave it to me. I'm in Boston."

"She's in Boston," her father said, presumably to her mom.

"Why?" her mother's voice was distant.

"Why?" her dad asked.

"Dad, if I'm having this conversation with mom, put her on the phone."

"She's got her gloves on," he said. "She's busy."

"Okay, well I'm in Boston, I'm safe. I'll call you when I can."

"Is this about a boy?" her mom asked, closer to the microphone but still not on the phone.

"A boy?" Roxie asked, tucking an arm under her breasts. "I'm twenty-six. Tell Mom I'm twenty-six and date men. Not boys."

"Who is this boy?" her father asked, suddenly concerned. "Does he have a job?"

What the…? "Yes! He has a job."

"Jane said they were in Las Vegas," her mom said, more likely to her dad than her.

"Did you get yourself hitched?" her father asked. "Are you pregnant?"

And they wondered why she resisted calling them. "I'm not pregnant or married, Dad. I won a contest. I'm going on a trip."

"What kind of contest?" her father asked. "Is that what this boy told you? Is it a scam?"

"No, it's not a scam, Dad. It happened when we went to see a show. A TV talk show. We were in the audience."

"And you won a prize. She won a prize."

"What prize?" her mom asked.

"I'm going on a tour of some places, Dad," Roxie answered before he could relay what she'd already heard. "A trip around the world."

"Alone?" he asked. "I don't want you going to strange places by yourself."

"I'm not by myself, Dad. I'm traveling with a group."

"I don't know if that makes me feel better."

She sighed. "Geez, Dad, make up your mind."

"Who's in charge? I want to talk to him."

Her arm dropped. "No!" she squealed. "Why would you—"

"Who's in charge of your safety? Are these sensible people? How do I know they're not going to marry you off to some cult?"

"Dad, what the hell are you reading these days? It's harmless. I'm with a business guy, he owns some nightclubs and stuff."

"A womanizer?" her father barked. "She's with a sex pest."

Parents could be infuriating. Hers especially. "He's not a sex pest."

"What's his name?" her dad asked. Another scuffle, a breeze, the screen on the back door creaked—he was going back inside. "Sonia's at work. I'll have her look him up… our laptop's busted."

"How did that happen? Blayne looking up porn on your network again?"

Her younger sister's not-too-bright boyfriend had been a part of their lives for a couple of years.

"They're on the outs too," her dad said.

"Oh, God," Roxie groaned. "They're always on the outs, Dad. Learn a lesson."

"Okay, I have a pen. What's his name?"

"I'm not telling you anyone's name."

If he tracked down the show, he'd see her. One call to Toria would be enough. Her friend would have no hesitation in revealing all about Zairn.

"I don't trust anyone I don't know to look after my little girl."

"Sonia is your little girl, I'm the loud one who always embarrassed you at parties."

"Put him on the phone."

Her father had a great way of being in his own head and sticking to his guns.

"No!" Roxie asserted. "Dad, you can't talk to him, he's busy."

"If he's too busy to talk to me, he's too busy to keep you safe. I'm gonna get on a plane—"

"No," Roxie said, the word deep in its simple, definite syllable. "You are not getting on a plane." Talk about picking the lesser of two evils. "Wait. Just hold on."

Putting the phone against her shoulder, she went over to peek out of her room. Zairn was on his own at the dining table. Yes! Small victory, but she'd take it. Her scampering over there didn't distract him from the laptop he was working on.

She prodded his shoulder half a dozen quick times to get his attention. Pasting a wide smile onto her face, she went for gracious.

A twitch at the corner of his eyes screamed suspicion. "Lola…" he drawled. "What do you need?"

"My dad wants to talk to you," Roxie said, thrusting the phone his way.

"Your father?"

This wasn't her finest moment, he didn't need to rub salt into her humiliation. "We'll argue about it and then you'll just do it anyway," she said through gritted teeth, thrusting the handset again. "Talk to him… Casanova."

An almost tsk came from him as he inhaled and took the phone. "Mr. Kyst? Zairn Lomond."

Roxie sat in the seat perpendicular to his, resting her jaw on the heels of her hands. She expected to listen, but Zairn got up and walked away.

"Yes, sir, I understand," Zairn said.

His bedroom door closed. Stunned, she pushed her shoulders back. What the hell did he plan to talk about that she couldn't eavesdrop?

Roxie pounced to her feet. "Asshole," she whispered but didn't mean it.

Talking to her father went above and beyond, she owed him, and eventually he'd figure that out.

Didn't take him long to figure it out. Almost half an hour later, Zairn appeared in her bedroom doorway.

"You owe me."

Exasperation spiked her adrenaline. Patience was not her strong suit at the best of times.

"Half an hour!" Roxie exclaimed, leaping off the bed to rush over to him. "What the hell were you talking about for half an hour? You don't even talk to me for a half hour and you're trying to get in my pants!"

"Guess you told your dad I already did," he said, handing over the phone. "He asked if we were married."

Her affect flattened. Trust them to compound her humiliation. "That's my family." She was not impressed. "He heard Vegas and thought I'd lost my mind."

"He asked if you were pregnant."

"Because my word wasn't good enough," she said, her fists jumping to her hips. "And I'll bet you told him yes since that is, like, your ideal scenario."

"Knocking you up *is* high on my list of priorities," he said with no sincerity. "I'll tell you more about my conversation, if you tell me what Hatfield wanted."

Ha! Her chin rose in defiance. "None of your business."

"Good, then you won't want to know about the call. You need to give Tibbs your parents' address."

Her eyes rolled side to side. "Why do I need to do that?"

"We're sending them a laptop… You think they'd prefer a desktop? We'll send both."

She didn't know who was trying to kill her fastest, her dad or Zairn. Frustration came out in a growling groan. "He wants to look you up."

"And he's entitled to, I'm responsible for his daughter's safety. What are you doing today? You haven't worked out yet."

"Which makes absolutely no difference to my rack," she said, gesturing at her breasts. "Keep your eyes on these and ignore the caboose."

She turned to go back to her purse on the bed.

"I like your caboose."

"I know. Your subconscious told me the first time we woke up together."

"My subconscious worked out that it would be best to take you from behind… far away from that fresh mouth."

"I can mock and jeer in any position, Skippy," she said, throwing her phone into her purse. "I'm a level above expert. You're way down there in the vaguely proficient region."

Tossing the strap of her purse over her shoulder, Roxie intended to go out, except Zairn didn't move out the way.

"You need to tell me where you're going. Your father tasked me with looking after you."

"Like you weren't already tasked with that." She mock gasped and slapped both hands to her cheeks. "Imagine the PR nightmare if something bad happened to your contest winner!" She tried to go past, but he didn't budge. "Sheesh, okay, since you're so adamant I'll tell you.

I'm going out to look at wedding venues. Obviously, that's what you want to hear since you're already daydreaming about impregnating me."

"You have to meet your handler today. I have someone special lined up."

"I don't need special or a handler."

"Someone to take care of your needs."

"I take care of my needs," she said, noticing the tilt of his lips. "Yes, that too. You don't need to hire anyone to do it."

"Your handler can liaise with my team. Ensure your requests are fulfilled."

"An assistant? Astrid does all that and she needs me. That girl needs to loosen up and have a good time."

"You want Astrid?"

"Yes."

"Done," he said. "She'll be with you from now on."

"Okay," Roxie said. "Now are you going to get out of my way? You can't get me pregnant just through sheer will, it would require far more effort... on your part. I'd just lie there thinking about china patterns."

"You're unique, Lola Bunny," he said, enjoying her again.

"Get out of the way or you'll be unique too. The only one-balled billionaire in the world."

"You'd have to check them all."

Shaking her hair down her back, she hitched her chin higher. "I will. I will check them all and I'll keep hacking at you until I reach my goal. You wanna test me or move out of my way?"

"You don't want to hear what I want to do right now."

His amusement was laced with innuendo, but at least he stepped aside.

"Sex pest," she mumbled, pausing at his side to tap her cheekbone.

He bowed to kiss her offered cheek. "I'll send Ballard with you to keep you safe."

"Whatever floats your boat, Casanova."

Looking after her was his remit, she didn't know how talking to her father changed that. Still, Zairn had been a sport about the call. Anyone who treated her family with respect scored points. If he hadn't been respectful, her father would've called back the minute they hung up and told her to pack her bags. No, her father was happy, which was odd, but Roxie wouldn't fly in the face of good fortune. She'd take the win. She needed the win.

20

Boston became Montreal became Miami became Buenos Aires. They made it all the way to Sydney and got through four nights at the Australian Crimson. Whether it was jetlag or just sheer exhaustion, Roxie was fighting a headache. Her usually rosy demeanor was difficult to maintain under the pulsing weight of the dull pain.

"Are you sure you don't want me to come in with you?" Greg asked as they wandered along the hotel corridor toward her suite.

"I've been streaming to the masses for weeks now," Roxie said. "I can handle it alone."

Over the past couple of days, fatigue clawed at her every minute. That was what she got for not being an international jetsetter. The sucker punch of jetlag was a real bitch.

Still, she was doing her best to maintain the routine, which meant going to dinner with Greg. Unless there was something else going on, they tended to eat together. The documentary director was good fun, as were his buddies when they weren't in work mode.

She slipped her keycard into the door. Usually their hotels were more high-tech. Their Sydney suite was smaller than normal too, but Zairn had his reasons for everything.

She popped the door open before turning back to Greg.

"Thanks for dinner," she said because it was polite.

Being on Rouge's dime and that of Greg's CollCom production company, Roxie was grateful for everything they gave.

"You didn't eat anything," Greg said, coming closer to slide his hand up the doorframe next to her. "Want to invite me in for a drink?"

"I have to stream and get ready for tonight," she said, laying a consoling hand on his shoulder. "You're low on the list, docu guy." She boosted the door further open with her hip and caught it on a flat hand when it swung back. "You have time to console yourself though, look for the bonus."

She gave him a pat, then went into the suite. The door clicked shut. Relief. Except Zairn was in the living room. If it wasn't for him, she might have lay down and taken a nap right there.

"From one guy to the next," she murmured, forcing herself to smile. "I know it's your first instinct to get me drunk, but I would kill for a gallon of the strongest caffeine in the hemisphere."

"Hatfield wouldn't pay for coffee?"

"I can buy my own coffee," she said, intending to go to her room, though that did mean walking past him. "I only wanted to stroke your ego by playing pretend damsel in distress."

"You've been tired the past couple of days—"

"I'm going to work!"

Roxie traced her middle finger across his chest as she walked by. Anything to keep him quiet. If she stopped or let him express her failings, she would drag all night. The only remedy was to keep going.

Hmm, a kink in the plan: streaming meant sitting down. Getting setup on autopilot, Roxie logged in and went to the streaming section. When the user numbers picked up, she'd be glittering and personable. Just for a second, she surrendered to weakness. Folding her arms on the desk in front of her laptop, she dropped her forehead to them. Why was she so tired? Her whole body ached and trembled, she couldn't remember ever experiencing lethargy like this.

"You're broken."

Zairn's voice. No surprise. They wandered in and out of each other's bedrooms all the time.

"Damaged is the word," Roxie said without lifting her head. "And if I am it's because you're dragging me around the world, subjecting me to your indulgent life of luxury... Come rub my shoulders."

Her exhaustion was so potent that she couldn't even muster a smile when his strong, satisfying fingers slid onto her skin.

"I can have a professional come here to do this."

"Why?" she asked. "Is it too much like hard work? This is not high-intensity labor. Work for a living, Z. Just for a minute."

"Your skin is clammy," he said, concern embedded in his words.

"So what? Wash your hands when you're done."

He wasn't listening. "You're burning up," he said, laying a horizontal hand on the back of her neck.

Any other time that grip would be hot for a whole other reason.

She stayed still when his hands left their task. The power to object or jeer wasn't in her. When she was scooped up out of her chair and carried to the bed, all she did was moan pathetic sounds of objection.

"Stay there," Zairn said, pushing her hair away from her face. "Jesus, you're sweating. What the hell was Hatfield thinking?"

He didn't expect an answer, which was just as well. Talking was beyond her ability; bed felt too good to contemplate concentrating. He went into her bathroom. The offensive glare of the light intruded even through her closed eyes. Recoiling, Roxie turned away from it.

A second later Zairn was back, scooping up her head to lay a cold, damp compress on the back of her neck and another on her forehead.

"How's that?" he asked, stroking her cheek while holding the forehead compress in place.

Tipping her face up in the direction of his voice, she showed him a smile. "Good..." she said, trying to sit up, except he caught her shoulders to hold her down. "I don't need it. I'll be—"

"Stay put."

"I am not your employee. I don't have to do what you tell me," she said, shoving his hands away to sit up. But not for long. Her head spun and nausea flared in her belly, so she flopped back down. "Maybe for a minute."

"Yeah," he said, putting the compress back on her head.

The cool, soothing weight tried to lull her to sleep right there.

She snapped awake when his hand left her head. "Where are you going?"

"Nowhere," he said, returning his hand to the compress. "I'm right here, baby."

"Stay… Just for a minute… until I have to get ready for tonight."

"Yeah, baby, you aren't going anywhere tonight," he said. Before she could object, he spoke again, although not to her. "We need a doctor… For Rox… No, bring someone here… I don't care."

His hand left her head again, but it didn't leave her body. He skimmed it down the length of her, as though assuring her that he wasn't going anywhere.

When he took off her shoes, she smiled at the relief. "You've been looking for an excuse to strip me naked for weeks, Mr. Lomond."

"Hold on a sec," Zairn said, probably into the phone. "I'm paying the doctor who's coming to see you, Lo. If he says we have to sew your mouth shut…"

She smiled again and as his hand rested on her knee, she bent it into the caress. "Maybe the doctor will say I require full body massages every hour on the hour, will you hire someone to do that too? Someone hunky and hot. I want final approval."

"You get grandma or I do it myself—yeah… okay and—good man."

"Was that Tibbs?"

"Yes," he said. The bed moved as his hand withdrew; she whimpered in protest. "Taking off my jacket, babe."

After inhaling, she exhaled a pathetic blub. "I'm too tired to even sass you."

"Damn, you must be dying."

"Z," she whined.

"If you weren't wiped, you'd tell me to take off anything I like, to get more comfortable. You'd comment how I might use this situation to my advantage and how it won't make a damn bit of difference. I'll never be lucky enough to have you."

It was sweet of him to tease himself in her place. His kindness highlighted her selfishness. "You should go," she said, slipping her phone from her pocket. "If you stay, I'll get you sick. I'll call Jane and she'll talk about making me chicken noodle soup."

The phone was plucked from her hand. "No phones, you're going to rest. And I'm not going anywhere."

The bed moved again. He settled closer. Sitting semi-upright, he scooped her up to rest her against him.

"You'll get sick," Roxie said.

"I don't get sick."

"Your arrogance applies to germs too?" she asked and tried to peek up at him, but he stroked her hair, using the motion to settle her again. "I thought you said everyone on the planet liked you. Why would germs be exempt? You don't appeal to that audience?"

"They like me, so they don't slow me down."

She was vaguely aware of him doing something with a phone. Hers or his, she had no idea and didn't care.

"It's so sad," Roxie mumbled. "I really like Australia."

"Good. It likes you."

"It made me sick."

"The dancing made you sick," he said. "I tell you every time we hit the club that you have the run of Crimson. You could turn the most private of VIP areas into your own little Haddaway den. You still insist on going down to dance with the masses."

"It's part of the experience, party boy," she said, shifting her head to undo a couple of the shirt buttons over his abdomen. Sliding her hand into the slot, she relaxed further when her fingers loosened against his skin. "Being ill will do me one favor. All the icky mucus should put you off. Maybe I caught a break."

"I've never wanted you more, Hot Stuff," he said, distracted by whatever he was doing on the phone.

Roxie sighed. "It's your hero complex… that or you like your women weak."

"Mine or not, Lola, you will never be weak."

"Don't you forget it, Casanova."

Lying there, breathing him in, he'd granted her permission to feel as lousy as she did. Something she'd never have done on her own. Her throat ached, her head throbbed, and despite being on top of another person, it felt like someone was sitting on her.

Moving of her own accord wouldn't be happening any time soon. She wanted to stay there, against him, slipping into slumber. His fingers combed through her hair, over and over in a rhythm that sent her to sleep.

His next words startled her awake.

"Doctor's here, baby," he murmured, taking her hand out of his shirt to kiss her knuckles. "Let me go talk to him."

The way he laid her down was so gentle. She snuggled against the pillows and opened her eyes to watch him leave, but the glare of the laptop on the table by the door stung her eyes.

"Z—"

"I'm on it." The click of the laptop lid closing betrayed that he'd read her mind. "Close your eyes, babe. I'll be back in a minute."

A minute, a day, a week, Roxie wasn't sure she'd ever move from the bed again. She'd planned to go to Crimson and do her job, but Zairn had overruled her stubbornness. In truth, him cutting her some slack was the greatest gift ever.

21

Rather than slack, Roxie was given free rein. It wasn't like she went crazy partying or disappeared in a heady whirl of psychedelia or anything. Nope, she stayed in bed. With the drapes closed and her head buried in a pillow. Reality didn't seep back in until whatever was wrong with her began to wane.

What day was it? She'd definitely missed some of the tour. How much? Two days? Three? Five? It was anyone's guess. Dragging herself into the bathroom took herculean effort. Hmm... the tub... Not a good idea. There was a good chance she'd fall asleep and drown herself.

Setting the shower temperature lower than normal, she used all of the pressures to work her muscles. By the time she got out, Roxie was human again. Impressing herself, she even managed to blow-dry her hair and put makeup on.

Would it be terrible to go to all that effort just to go back to bed? No! No. She'd spent enough time in bed. Though there was nothing else exactly pressing, sleeping should be avoided. Definitely avoided.

A few steps out of the bathroom, the bedroom door opened. Zairn came in, but paused when he noticed her standing outside the bathroom rather than in bed.

"You're up."

"You're observant," Roxie said, crossing the room, past the bed, intending to open the drapes. "I brushed my teeth, flossed, used mouthwash and everything." She threw open the drapes as far as they'd go with one thrust then spun on the spot to smile at him. "So we can make out."

"Tempting," he said. "But it's not even noon."

Zips of mischief rippled in her belly. This man lit her lifeblood. Proximity to Zairn Lomond was the most potent medicine. Yes, Roxie Kyst was back. For sure.

With a sway in her hips, she sashayed toward him. "Is there a designated time window for foreplay? Would you rather do businessy things?"

As if on cue, his phone buzzed, Zairn retrieved it just as she stopped in front of him.

He read the screen but didn't answer it. "How do you feel?"

After exerting herself to return to the land of the living, that question should answer itself. "How do I feel?"

He bent his knees to align their eyes, resting a hand on her shoulder. "You're on your feet, but that doesn't tell me you're better," he said. "Should I get the doctor?"

The doctor had been to see her like three times. All she'd heard was rest and fluid, rest and fluid. For some unknown reason, Zairn always took it upon himself to talk to the dude for too long. Using a deep, commanding voice, he'd grilled the doc like it was a point of pride. Sleep had been her highest priority. Her only priority.

Sucking up all her gusto, she projected it out. "I'm up, Zairn. I'm ready." Her optimism faded to a cringe. "I'm sorry I screwed up all the plans. I didn't do my job. If you want to kick me out—"

"Babe," he said, tightening his grip to pull her to him. "Your health is the only thing I care about. If you need to go home, I'll take you back, right now. Not the first time I've said that since you've been laid up."

Of which she had little memory. Hmm, what nonsense might she have spouted?

"I don't want to go home; I want to keep going," she said, tipping her head back to look up at him. "Can we keep going?" Smoothing his hand down her hair, he bowed to kiss her forehead. "I don't even know what day it is. How much time did we miss?"

"It's been nine days."

The shock could've bowled her over.

Roxie grabbed the edges of his jacket. "Nine days! Zairn! Why didn't you drag me out of bed? Oh my…"

"What kind of playboy would I be if I forced a beautiful woman out of bed?"

Her parted fingers went from her temples back into her hair. "I haven't streamed or anything!"

The exhale of his gruff laugh was curious, but there was no time to question it.

He stroked her arm. "If you're feeling up to it, we could get on a plane today."

"Absolutely!" No way would she hold up the tour for another minute. "I'll start packing right now."

He caught her shoulders after one step. "The only way I let you get on that plane is if you take it easy. We'll get your things packed—"

"Z, I don't want random people going through my stuff. I told you that already."

"Astrid will do it, while I get you something to eat."

Suspicious, she hitched her chin to peer at him. "Is this a test?"

"Of your stomach? Yes."

He turned her in the direction of the door. From behind, his hands on her shoulders, he steered her a few steps forward.

"Who's out there?" she asked, pushing back to stall his momentum. "I don't want to deal with Hatfield and his—"

"No one's out there, it's just us," he said, unlocking his elbows so her shoulder blades dropped against his torso. "I'll order room service. Everything will be prepared for departure while you eat what you can." He kissed her crown. "You don't have to deal with anyone until you're ready."

Her focus slid to the side. "What if that's never?"

"Then never it is."

"What if it's when I'm naked in the shower?"

A beat went by. "Then never it is."

He kissed her head again and opened the bedroom door. Over the last nine days, her bed and room were the only things that existed. With Zairn's support, which he seemed to be giving in spades, it wouldn't take long to find her groove.

If Roxie expected the documentary guys to be chomping at the bit to speak to her, she'd have been wrong. In fact, as she sat there sipping coffee and nibbling on toast, it seemed like no one was interested in speaking to her at all.

The vast pocket doors to the balcony behind her were open, providing a pleasant breeze. Her position was the perfect vantage point to survey the scope of the living room.

Astrid had arrived, received quiet instructions from Zairn, and disappeared into Roxie's bedroom. A while later, the assistant left without a word.

Zairn's behavior was the most curious. Rather than get on with his own stuff or sit with her at the circular table, he'd remained standing behind the chair next to hers. She couldn't quite work out if he was trying to keep her away from people or people away from her.

Ballard had just been in with the bellhops and taken the luggage away.

The door clicked shut, sealing her and Zairn in the room alone. "Did you and Ballard trade jobs?"

Zairn turned like he'd forgotten she was there. "What?"

"Usually it's him you task with protecting me," she said, picking up her coffee cup. "You've left me sitting here alone like a naughty child or contagious leper. What's going on, Casanova?"

"Are you ready to go? Do you need anything else?"

"Oh, yeah, nothing is going on in here," Roxie muttered to herself. If he was entrenched in whatever was bugging him, it was personal. Personal wasn't her business. Discarding the cup, she rose to her feet. "I need to find my purse. I haven't seen my phone since you stole it from me."

"Everything will be on the plane."

"This super-efficient organizing thing won't fly," she said, swerving around him. "You're covering for something, Skippy." As she passed, Roxie caught his arm to twine it around her. The embrace forced him to stoop when she guided his hand onto her ass. "You miss this?"

"The ass or the sass?"

"Can't handle all of me at once?"

The corner of his mouth curled. "Thought I wasn't supposed to handle you at all."

She shrugged. "You took care of me," Roxie said, curling her fingers around the edges of his jacket to pull him closer. Zairn didn't need her guidance now that he had permission. He was happy to take control of squeezing her ass all by himself. "I've gotta give you something."

"Payment for my kindness?"

Licking her lips, her teasing mouth danced just out of reach of his even when he angled closer. "Ah, ah," she said, chastising him despite her hips easing nearer his. "Don't want to catch my nasty germs."

"You're not contagious."

That was hilarious, though she kept a lid on her laugh. "You asked the doctor?"

"Every day."

The possibility of contagion wouldn't matter if he planned to stay away. Obviously, his agenda didn't involve distance.

He grabbed her hips and swooped her around to back her against the table. Pushing her ass into the edge, he was seeking something, definitely seeking something. They didn't get to specifics.

Ballard came barreling into the suite. "They got tipped off we were moving out," he said to his boss.

"Damnit," Zairn said and caught whatever Ballard threw at him.

A dark hoodie. That's what it was. Zairn swept it around her shoulders and fed her arms into the sleeves.

"This isn't mine," she said as he zipped it up.

Not a leap given how the material swamped her.

"It's mine," he said, putting the hood over her hair and pulling the drawstrings to tighten it so it wouldn't fall. "Listen…" Ballard was right beside them, but Zairn took her face in both hands to lock his eyes on hers. "You're going to stay behind Ballard, take his hand and let him lead you. No matter what."

"I—"

"I'll be behind you. You'll feel my hands on you. Just mine. Anyone else's, you squeeze Ballard's hand three times."

"How will she know it's you?" Ballard asked.

"I'll know," Roxie said, reading Zairn's intense sincerity. "I know something's happened, and we don't have time to talk about it, but nobody's dead, right?"

Zairn stroked her cheek. "Nobody's dead."

He seemed almost lost in his admiration of her.

"It's fixable?" Roxie asked. "I mean, you'll fix it."

"Somehow."

That was reassurance enough. "Okay."

Zairn guided her in behind Ballard and stayed at her back, just like he'd said.

"Your right hand in his right hand," Zairn said into the top of her head. "Three squeezes if anything doesn't feel right."

Her chin arced toward her shoulder. "I never pictured you as a cuckold," she said, taking Ballard's hand. "Passing me off to other men."

"Only so I can protect the caboose," he murmured into her hair.

Ballard might have heard that. Either way, he was glaring when he turned. "We don't have time to wait around."

"Then get moving, Cowboy," Roxie said. "Sheesh, talk about Chatty Cathy dragging ass."

Her comment darkened Ballard's scowl, but she couldn't restrain her grin, she just couldn't. Apparently, he was in no mood to joke. When he strode off, he almost jerked her arm right out of its socket. Guy got his own back, she respected that. Prick could slow down just a little though. Damn. Despite a desire to pull him back, they were out of the suite and in the elevator before she got a full breath in her lungs.

"Elson and Fuller en route?" Zairn asked.

"Yep."

He and Ballard watched the numbers count down. One flashed then the next, down and down, increasing the oppressive atmosphere like they were heading to some terrible doom.

Nine days. That was all it took for the world to fall apart. Created in seven. To hell in nine.

"I told you Armageddon would come if you didn't let Hatfield into my bedroom," Roxie muttered, remaining focused on the numbers when both men looked at her.

"This wasn't caused by *Hatfield* in your bedroom," Ballard said, stepping in front of her and reaching back to grab her hand. "Believe me."

Again, Roxie was jolted forward. So much for taking it easy. It took all her effort just to keep up. Scurrying across a marble floor, she only just noticed they were going out some side door when Ballard shoved it open and took them into the glare of too bright sunshine.

22

Having been indoors for over a week, the sudden change of light on their exit was jarring. Still locked in the adjustment, Roxie didn't notice anyone was around until a cacophony of voices rose. Her name. They were calling her name. Who? Why? A blow of shock tried to stop her feet, but Ballard tugged hard. Someone was behind her, Zairn, his body was literally against her back, propelling her forward.

People. There were people all around. Behind metal barriers that had been set up on either side of their straight path, but why?

Ballard stepped aside and Zairn kept on going. The former pushed her head down. The latter fed her into the car she hadn't noticed waiting for them.

Stunned, Roxie fought with the hood. Escapee sections of hair were getting in her way. She'd just managed to loosen it and toss her hair back when she was jerked again, this time by the car moving forward.

Taking stock, Ogilvie and Astrid were seated facing her and Zairn. Damnit. Zairn.

Unsure if she should scream or laugh, exasperation reigned. "What the hell is going on?" she exclaimed.

The black screen behind Astrid and Ogilvie's heads descended to reveal Tibbs was up front, next to Ballard in the driving seat.

"Did I win the lottery?" Roxie asked, expecting someone to fill her in.

"Some would say," Zairn said.

Astounding. Jokes? After what they'd just been through? "Z!"

"We'll be in the air in little more than half an hour."

"I don't care," Roxie said, pouncing to the edge of the seat, adjusting her angle to face him. "Tell me what is going on!"

He cleared his throat; there was something about the twist of his lips that she couldn't figure out. "It was broadcast."

That didn't help. "I don't understand."

"It's everywhere. Everyone's seen it," Astrid said. "You went viral."

Sucking in a breath, she released it in one, dropping her hands in her lap. "Still no idea what you're talking about."

"The day I put you in bed," Zairn said, looking straight ahead. "When I called the doctor."

Broadcast. Viral. Wait, they were... Did that suggest...? Shit! How? It couldn't be. No way. No goddamn way.

Replaying it, she went step by step. "I... I left Hatfield in the hallway... I sassed you..." A side-nod. "Interrupted you... went into the bedroom and..." She shook her head, recalling sitting at the laptop next to the door. Yes, the camera angle took in most of the room, but nothing to fucking hide was the damn point. Nothing to hide! Did it have to bite her on the goddamn ass? Why her? "I didn't hit the stream button."

"Evidently, you did," Zairn said. "It's on screens across the world."

"Oh, God," Roxie groaned, her fingers disappearing beneath her long bangs to cradle her forehead. She slid back in her seat, curling forward into the brace position. "Oh, God, this is awful." Hope, no doubt misplaced, struck her. "What did we do?" Springing up, she grabbed Zairn's forearm in both hands. "It wasn't that bad, was it?" Memories were fuzzy. Her voice deepened and volume dropped. "I mean, we've done worse, right?"

"Which everyone in the car now knows."

What did…? They didn't know before? No, everything was a secret. Except now… it wasn't.

"I can undo this. I can fix it." Though she didn't have a clue how. "I'll tell them it was all me. I'm the villain. You're not the villain. You took care of me. They can hate me. That's okay. That will make everything okay, won't it?" No one had a chance of getting a word in despite the questioning. "I won't let you take any kind of fall for anything. They can't make you out to be the bad guy if I was just an evil, whatever, temptress. It was me. Tell them it was me. Your reputation can't take a hit because of this, because of my stupidity. Oh, Zairn, I'm sorry. I'm so sorry, I had no idea. I would never have… You don't have to believe me, of course you won't, but I really didn't mean for any of this to happen. Is it awful? Are the media attacking you? I called you a sex pest that one time, but I didn't mean it. You know I didn't mean it. I'm the pest. Me. And I'll tell them that."

Except with every second and word that passed it seemed his amusement was growing. What the hell was wrong with him?

"They ship you," Astrid said, smiling.

None the wiser, Roxie shook her head. "I'm sorry? Who? What?"

Zairn leaned in to speak above her ear. "They ship us."

"I don't know what that means," Roxie said. Both Toria and Jane would know; her girls would get it. And, oh, if it was everywhere, they must have seen the stream too. Her gut clenched. "Oh my God, everybody knows." Not only that they'd met, but that they'd… what? "Are we talking about sex?"

"You are," Zairn said. "You always are. Gotta get that mind out the gutter, baby."

How the tables had turned.

Roxie set a glare on him, though it wasn't very fierce. "Have you seen it?"

"Didn't need to," Zairn said. "I was there."

"So was I and I don't remember the details."

"He carried you to bed and called the doctor," Astrid said with a thread of glee Jane would be proud of.

"I remember that much," Roxie said. "I remember falling asleep on you." Something else she'd done before. "Did you take my clothes off?"

"I took your shoes off," Zairn said. "If I'd stripped you down, I'd be in cuffs right now."

That sad truth was sobering.

Dropping against the backrest, Roxie exhaled. "I should've stayed in bed."

Or drowned herself in the tub. Maybe choosing the shower hadn't been such a great idea after all.

Everything up to and including the airport was a haze. Still stunned in her reflection, Roxie couldn't believe she'd done something so careless. At least on the airfield they had control over the screaming and camera flashes. Zairn took care of everything and navigated her onto the plane, guiding her from behind.

In the party room, she slowed. He hooked an arm around her to boost their speed. "Where are we going?" Roxie asked.

Staff stood ready to greet their boss, but he kept her going, through the party space, the main lounge, dining area, restrooms, seating... Any doors that might have impeded them were open. A never-ending plane. Well, if anyone would have one, it was Zairn Lomond. Another door to... a sleek boardroom. Nice. Shiny. Masculine.

They carried on past the long table and stopped in front of the next door. For the first time, it was closed. An obstacle. Zairn reached around her and opened the door to push her inside.

And it was... another lounge. Huh. Smaller than the previous rooms, but nice. Cozy. A couch and couple of recliners faced the focal fire feature with TV above.

Zairn still wasn't satisfied and strengthened his grip to take her through one of the openings that flanked the center feature and into... a bedroom. Beautiful and modern with crisp white linens and dark grey furnishings.

"Wow," she said, leaving his grasp to approach the bed. "Who knew you had a love nest?"

The typical shape of the plane windows was the only hint of the master suite's roving location. The wide room was dominated by the central bed. Beyond the fixed nightstands were gaps in the wall, which she guessed led to closets or bathrooms.

"Love nest is on the 737," Zairn said. "Thank you."

She turned just in time to see Zairn taking a leather hold-all from an attendant. The guy was quick to scurry away, then the suite door closed. When Zairn dumped it on the bed, Roxie leaned closer trying to sneak a peek at whatever was inside.

"You ever hear what curiosity did to the cat?" he murmured while searching inside.

"Did you lose something?"

"No, you did," he said. "Strip for me."

"Since you asked so nicely," she said, only raising a brow when he drew his eyes up to her. Just because the world wanted them to get horizontal, didn't mean they should... not for the world's sake anyway. So she changed the subject. "I'm looking forward to Tokyo. I had been excited about going out to eat, but I guess that's off the cards now... unless you provide me with my own squad of action heroes for protection."

"Tokyo's off the cards."

Off the... "What?" she asked, disappointed. "Are you punishing me for ruining your sex life?"

"You'll find a way to make it up to me."

He put some folded apparel into her line of sight.

Roxie recognized it immediately. "My Lola pajamas!" Taking them from him, she hugged them to her décolletage. "Want me to dress up for you?"

"Would you?" he asked in a rumbling purr.

Uh, no... definitely not... Don't react like a bitch in heat, Roxie. Breathe. Just breathe. Ignore the hormones. Since Porter, she'd been going through a dry spell. That's all it was, hunger after depravity... Wait, no, not depravity... what was the word? Damnit. Her mind was mush... deprivation... that was it. Hunger after deprivation.

But, shit, seriously, did he have to look at her that way? The intensity of that focus, so sure, so narrow, right on her. No, not on her, through her. Somehow, he exposed her every atom, her whole self became transparent, like she was just another part of him. Crackles of invisible heat scorched and bounced across her skin like nuclear popping candy. Standing next to a bed with him was a bad idea. Didn't he remember she was responsible for blowing up his life?

"I'm sorry," she said, genuine in her contrition. "My head was a mess, it's no excuse. I hope you know I'd never knowingly do anything to hurt you."

He took the pajamas and tossed them over the hold-all onto the bed, then grabbed her wrist to pull her closer.

"There were two of us in that room, Lo," he said, combing his fingers through her hair. "If I'd been thinking, I would've checked. I know you usually hit the button and wait a minute to give people time to login."

"How do you know that?" she asked, skimming her fingers up his chest to push his jacket from his shoulders.

"Because I watch you," he said. His other hand combed through her hair to hold it in his fist at the back of her head. "Every minute I can." The heavy hollowness of unfulfilled need pulled at her. Them together, in any way, was more wrong than ever. It had been their private game, now it was a viral sensation. Sense wouldn't kick in while her hormones were waking and growing, vibrating and bubbling. "Not going to tease me for wanting you?"

"Inappropriate time for that," she said, unbuttoning his shirt one button at a time. "The whole world knows how desperate you are to take me to bed."

"We're in my bedroom this time," he said.

"You brought me here."

"You came."

Smiling, Roxie raised her arms to drape them over his shoulders. "Not yet."

Defaulting to their teasing kept the barriers up. As long as it was just a flirtation, it was harmless... To her anyway. His reputation was held for ransom by the court of public opinion. Ultimately, they were his judge, jury... and, if need be, executioner.

His fingers loosened and his arms sank around her. "I told you to take it easy," he murmured.

With their height difference, when he straightened some, he took her to the tips of her toes, assuming control of her balance.

"We've been on the road for a month and a half," Roxie said, coiling her arms around his neck. "Have you ever known me to be easy?"

"I haven't turned it on yet, baby," he said, ignoring her gaze to admire her mouth. "I'm waiting until you're at full strength. Reaching the summit will be so much more satisfying then."

"Don't start a climb you can't complete."

"Don't you worry about my stamina, baby. Lie down in here and sleep. I'll go do my businessy stuff, you can come through when you wake up."

His stubble tempted her to nip at his jaw. "You don't want to lie down with me, Casanova?"

She didn't expect him to, the tease just took their minds off all the BS.

"Lying down with you is easy," he said, loosening his embrace. "Getting up again is where we hit a problem." A reinterpretation of words she'd already said. "There is some of your soup left, if you want it."

"My soup?"

"Soup is the only thing you've eaten for the last nine days. If you want it, pick up the phone and press one, you'll get the galley."

Soup, yes, the soup. She remembered sitting up while Zairn fed it to her. "Tastes just like Jane's," she murmured, repeating her words from the time.

"Yeah, there's a good reason for that. She made it."

"What? But she'd have to... where is she?"

"Chicago... I told you we own planes," he said like it was no big deal.

Left alone at the end of the bed, Roxie sank down to sit on the edge. He'd shipped in soup from the other side of the planet? The logistics of that... how did that even work? It was dumbfounding.

The hold-all moved on the bed. A familiar sparkle swung into her eyeline; Zairn was putting it over her head.

"My pendant."

"Keep it on. Things happen fast when the media are hyped. The bag…" He nodded in the direction of the hold-all behind her. "It's our jump bag. Essentials only. Anything goes down, we grab the bag and go."

"Where?"

"Anywhere you want," he said, tracing a fingertip down her temple to tuck her hair back behind her ear. "Anywhere in the world, Roxanna Kyst."

Showing him a grateful smile, she took his hand to kiss his palm. "Thank goodness for businessy stuff."

His hand dropped away as he retreated. "Won't save you forever. Get your strength back, Lola."

"Ah," she said, leaping up to button his shirt again. "Wouldn't want to set tongues wagging."

"I think we're past the point of no return on that, babe."

He winked and wandered away to leave the room.

Inhaling a deep breath, Roxie exhaled as she reversed and fell backward onto the bed, flopping her arms out at her sides. Viral. Shipping. Accidental streaming. Roxie could get herself into trouble even passed out in a dark room. Everyone had to have a talent.

23

The shades were pulled down over the windows when Roxie woke up. If some creep came in to do that while she slept, management would receive a serious complaint letter.

Sitting up, she scanned the space. No one was around. Not anymore anyway. She got up and checked in the closet and the bathroom, still nothing... other than her mind blown by the incredible setup. The shower was a circular stall in the middle of the grey bathroom. In the middle! And the toilet had a room all of its own. There was literally a restroom in the bathroom. Wow, how the other half lived.

On getting into bed, the air had been warm. Now there was a chill across her shoulders. She picked up Zairn's hoodie from the bench in the closet where she'd dumped her things.

Yawning, Roxie was still threading her arms into the sleeves when she opened the suite door. The boardroom. Right. Ah. Five people sat around the long table. She paused. All very professional looking. Hmm.

"Uh... morning," she said, only recognizing three people.

Zairn was at the head of the table with his back to her. Three of the four faces she could see, Ogilvie and the two strangers, were happy to see her. Too happy. Again with the creepy.

"Evening," Ballard said from the other end of the table.

"How would I know? All the shades are closed," Roxie said, going to put a hand on Zairn's shoulder. He turned the fixed-base chair her way enough that she could sink down onto his thigh. "Please tell me you put the shades down and I wasn't perved on by airline staff."

"The airline staff are my airline's staff," he said. "They don't have clearance to get into the bedroom. I leave the door open when we disembark if cleaning is needed."

"You could've just said yes," she said, glancing at the papers on the table. "What time is it?"

"Local or your body clock?"

"Who even knows anymore," she said. "We're probably mid-time-zone over some ocean anyway. What time do we land?"

"We just did," he said, startling her.

"We landed?" she asked. He nodded. On pause, she tried to get a sense of her surroundings. "Feels like we're flying."

Zairn stroked her hair down her back. "We are. We landed, got supplies, and took off again."

"And I slept through it? Where did we land?"

"Sri Lanka."

Her mouth opened and she bounced around to better look at him. "Oh my God, I want to go to Sri Lanka!"

His smirk grew. "You just did."

"Z!"

He laughed and hooked a hand around her head to pull her temple to his lips. "I'll take you to Sri Lanka."

"And Tokyo," she said, pointing a forefinger at him. "I can't believe we're skipping over it." Which led her to what should've been an obvious question. "Where are we going anyway?"

"Rome."

Squeezing her lips together, excitement wasn't easy to contain. "Can we go out to eat in Rome?"

"Yes," he said, sweeping her hair back over her shoulder. "I'll have to pay them to close down the restaurant, but, sure."

"Nothing you haven't done before," she said and received a shrug in reply. "How long until we get there?"

"About ten hours."

"So we can go out for breakfast as soon as we get there?"

He cast a look to the top corner of the room. A bunch of wall clocks with city names beneath them showed different times. One glaring omission stood out. Where was the Chicago clock?

"We can," Zairn said. "But it will still be the middle of the night. We'll land around one thirty… a.m."

She pointed at Ballard. "He just said it's evening. Evening plus ten hours is morning."

"It will be morning. Just very early morning… It's another switch in time zones."

"Oh, God," Roxie said. Dizzied by it all, she laid her head on his shoulder. "You don't need drugs to subdue a woman, just take her on one of your planes and her brain will melt."

"Your brain's at a disadvantage. You've been ill this week. How do you feel?"

"Good," she said, tempted to open his shirt buttons. Thank goodness she stopped that thought before it became an action. Groping him wasn't very appropriate in company. It probably wasn't appropriate at all, but hey-ho. "Or I was good until we got sucked into the space-time continuum paradox. What are you guys doing? Businessy stuff? I don't even know those guys."

Ogilvie sat to one side of Zairn, the two men opposite were strangers to her. "Roxanna Kyst, meet Terry Elson, our head of public relations, and Kael Fuller, press liaison."

"Kael, like the vegetable?" she asked, lifting her head.

"It's uh… not spelled the same."

Switching the angle of her head, she talked to Zairn while eyeing the new duo. "Why do you need these guys?"

A smile was audible in his voice. "Among other things, they deal with crisis events that impact Rouge."

"Crisis events," she said. "Like me."

"Like you."

"I am my very own crisis event."

"That's hardly a news flash," Zairn said, coiling his fingers into her locks.

Relaxing further, Roxie rested her head on him again. "If my streaming accident was nine days ago. Why are they just catching up to us now? Out of the loop?"

"They flew out the same day it happened. We had to suspend the documentary filming until we had a strategy."

"And do you have a strategy?"

"We're getting there," Zairn said.

"It's been online for nine days," Ogilvie said. "Interest has been growing since. The media are getting hungrier."

"As are the public," Kael said. "We need to give them something."

Blond and wearing a sharp suit, Kael had one of those unthreatening faces. Given his job, it was no doubt an advantage to disarm people without even opening his mouth.

"It would be easier if we could make an announcement," Ogilvie said, just as the door behind Ballard opened.

Astrid and Tibbs came in. Roxie smiled at the blonde who'd been with her since the start of the Crimson adventure. Astrid did smile in return but seemed subdued, which was sort of confusing. The two assistants went to less opulent seats in opposite corners.

"Make what announcement?" Roxie asked.

Why had Astrid reverted to timid? Something must have happened. She'd neglected her duties while holed up in bed but would get to the bottom of it.

"That you're together."

Ogilvie was answering her question. Yes, her question. The announcement that they were—

"That we're toget—wait, what?" Roxie asked, snapping into the moment, sitting up straight. "Who's together?" Her finger swung back and forth between her and Zairn. "We're not together. Why would you think we're together?" Everyone just looked at them, which made her reevaluate her choice of seat. "No." Roxie leaped to her feet. "We're not together."

"You just came out of his bedroom," Kael said.

"In your underwear," Ogilvie said.

"No," Roxie asserted and pointed at her shorts. "These are his." She pointed at Zairn again but rethought what she'd just said. "Not because I lost my pants in some quick, rough frenzy of fucking, because I was hot and didn't want to wear long pants... I don't even have my luggage; I've worn his clothes plenty..." None of the faces in the room were convinced. "Why are you all looking at me like that?" Zairn's lips were the first to quirk. "Did you pay them to look at me weird? Like you do when you think I'm crazy... like right now."

"Babe, no one would ever suggest something so outrageous."

"As what? Us being together? Because your buddy just did. You didn't tell them we weren't together?"

Even though he pursed his lips, she could still read his amusement.

"Mr. Lomond has refused to comment," Astrid said, her voice quiet.

"Even in private."

That came from Tibbs and it put another frown on Roxie's face.

She turned to Zairn again. "We need to talk."

"Yep," he said, surging out of his seat. "The rest of you talk amongst yourselves."

He took her shoulder to urge her in the direction of the master suite and reached around to open the door.

Shaking her head, Roxie was trying to take it all in. "I can't believe this."

Zairn closed the door. "That anyone could believe we might have a romantic interest in each other?"

She went through the lounge into the bedroom, then turned to face him, raising her arms at her sides. "That the whole world wants to climb into bed with us. Jesus..." Roxie dropped to sit on the end of the bed. "How do you live like this?"

"Boundaries," he said, like he had in the past.

"Why the hell should we be coerced and cajoled into putting labels on what we might or might not be?"

"We shouldn't be," he said, propping a shoulder on the column of central wall and crossing his ankles. "Boundaries, Lola."

Confused, it was difficult for her to understand why he was so calm. Experience was perhaps the answer. He was used to the world and everyone in it picking his life apart. No one, at least not such a vast amount of people, had been interested in her love life in the past.

"I have to call Toria and Jane," she said. "Did you talk to them?"

His head shake was slow. "Your phone is off. Has been since I took it from you. I spoke to your father."

Which he told her without an ounce of shame even though it was the last thing Roxie expected.

"You..." she started, half a step behind while he stood there, at ease, completely relaxed. "Why did you do that? How did you do that?"

"He's listed," Zairn said, following the words with a side-nod. "He *was* listed. We changed everyone's number and made sure their details were inaccessible. I wasn't able to suppress address information in time. We didn't know the stream was out there to preempt the spread. We mobilized fast and got everyone in hotels. They're being taken care of."

"Everyone?"

"Parents, siblings, roommates. Everything is under control. Tibbs deals with your parents and brother. Astrid takes care of your roommates and sister. Anyone needs anything, it's provided. And, yes, I spoke to your father. You were ill and I took responsibility for you. Passing that news through an assistant would've been disrespectful."

Her family, her friends, they'd been going through a hell much worse than any she'd had to deal with. Being rushed to a car while the media bayed for her was nothing to how terrifying it must have been to have strangers calling and showing up, demanding details they didn't have.

"I should call them."

"Your phone's in the jump bag," he said, his attention dropping to her bare legs. "In the closet, which I see you found."

"I'm sorry," she said, pulling her legs up onto the bed to fold them in front of her. "You never cared when I wore your clothes before."

"I don't care now."

"But I shouldn't do it in front of people... I didn't know you'd all be in there." Although, the plane had other passengers. Coming across them wasn't a leap. "I'm used to being me, Z. I'm not used to analyzing and second guessing my every move."

"Do you think that's what I'm asking you to do?"

Over the last few hours, the only thing he'd asked of her was to take it easy.

"Why aren't you mad?" she asked. "Aren't you livid about their entitlement over your life?"

"There's a difference," he said. "Between what they're entitled to and what they think they're entitled to."

"How can you be so chill? I don't feel right about being forced by strangers to explain myself... for their entertainment."

"Babe," he said, boosting his shoulder off the wall to cross and sit on the bed with her. "You will never, ever be forced to do anything, much less discuss what's going on between you and me."

"But that's what they want. Ogilvie wants—"

"Boundaries," he said and took her hand. "You decide yours just as I decide mine. The together part, our boundaries for us, we figure that out together."

With suspicion, she peered at him. "You're good at this."

He shrugged. "I've got the tee-shirt, many times over."

"You've done this with a lot of women?"

"Most women are happy to defer to me and my staff..." Wearing a smile, Zairn drew a fingertip down her jaw. "You are not a defer type of woman, Lola Bunny."

"And don't forget that. Just because I was sick, and you took care of business—"

"It was my pleasure. I only followed through on what I believed you'd want. You're protective of the people you care about."

"Yes, I am." Which may be why the world's intrusion was so frustrating. Whether he admitted it or not, the media were hurting him and had the potential to do worse. "Just like you care about the people in yours."

"Tell me how you want me to deal with this."

That didn't sound much like them making decisions together. "You didn't tell them we weren't together," she said, taking the time to mentally step back and appreciate what that meant. "You didn't tell them."

"What we are is not their business."

"Never," she said, curling her hand over his. "It may not always have felt like it, I may not have made it clear, but I always understood and respected why you weren't able to trust me."

"Why I wasn't able to trust you," he muttered.

"Yes, I would be exactly the same if I was in your position. You are an incredible guy, smart and funny and sexy as hell." She released his hand to lay both of hers on his face and pulled him down until their foreheads touched. "We have a lot of fun, which doesn't leave a lot of room for the serious." She let him go and leaned back to show her smile. "Let's not pretend I'm any good at sedate. There's nothing wrong with having fun, staying cool and casual… If you say we'll get through this stupid viral mishap, I'll trust that we will. Keep hitting them with the no comment. We're for us, not for them. They'll get bored eventually." Roxie took a deep breath and climbed off the bed. "I better find my phone and face the music. Toria and Jane will be going crazy!"

They would be climbing the walls. Roxie withdrew to the closet to locate the jump bag. While raking through it, she heard the suite door close. Zairn must've gone to tie up the conversation in the other room. Much more important business would be pressing. She'd inconvenienced him enough over the previous nine or ten days, depending on time zone. The quicker he could get back to business as usual, the better. She couldn't blame him for wanting that.

"I'm not sleeping with him," Roxie said for the two hundredth time. Her friends kept on chattering without hearing her. "I'm not sleeping with him. I'm not sleeping with him." Her voice droned as she repeated it over and over. "I'm not sleeping with him. I'm not sleeping with him." She wasn't listening to them and they weren't listening to her. "Hey!" Slamming her hand onto the bed, Roxie shoved her torso up. Her roommates quieted. "Victoria, Jane, I love you, ladies, I really do, but you have to hear me. I, Roxanna Amelia Kyst, am not sleeping with Zairn Lomond."

Silence. One second. Two, three, four. They were absorbing, she'd give them a minute. Roxie flopped onto her back again and waited.

"What about sex?" Toria asked. "Are you having sex with him?"

"Oh, yeah, I'm totally doing that," Roxie said. Both women inhaled in a prelude to another tirade, so she quickly laughed. "I'm kidding! I'm kidding. No. No sex, no sleep, I promise."

"I don't know whether to believe you or not," Jane said. "No one's ever seen him like that with anyone. Like he was with you."

"The video was an accident. It was my fault," Roxie said. "I was sick. I was loopy."

"He carried you to bed," Jane said, swooning, maybe even tearing up. Woman couldn't keep her tear ducts under control. "It was so romantic."

"I'm more interested in the abs. Your hand was in his shirt."

"You told us you hardly spend any time with him," Jane said, innocence confused.

"Yeah, six weeks in the same suite. We should never have fallen for that."

"We don't," Roxie said. "I mean, it's not like quality time. The documentary guys are there all the time. And there's people around. Astrid, and Zairn's security guy, his advisors, there's always people. We don't go on dates or enjoy hours of moonlight and champagne."

"You go to the clubs with him, every night."

"Yeah, but not like together," Roxie said. "Sometimes we're in the same car on the way there, sometimes we're not. Even in the vehicles there are still people around. Trust me, we're not together, in any way. I dance and he sits on his private couch brooding. That's it."

"You're so comfortable with him," Jane said. "And he shipped my soup across the world for you. That's like… amazing. When Astrid called to ask, I got her to say it three times before I realized it was real. Incredible!"

Agreed. The Crimson people must have been way worried about their contest winner falling ill if they'd gone to those lengths.

"Thank you for the soup, honey," Roxie said.

"You're a lucky bitch," Toria said. "Sick or not, if Zairn Lomond carried me to bed, I'd mount him there and then." She snorted out a laugh. "Hell, if I was in the same room as Zairn Lomond, I'd climb right up him."

Just at that, the suite door opened.

A second went by then Zairn appeared on the right. "You hungry?" he asked.

Roxie lifted her head from the bed. "It's dinner time?"

"If you're hungry. You haven't eaten much the last couple of weeks."

Except the soup. Yeah, he'd already mentioned that. "Did you—"

"Pick up fresh tuna before we left Sri Lanka? Yes, I did."

Roxie smiled. "You did not go into a store and buy something."

"No, I ordered ahead, and someone brought it to the plane."

"*You* ordered ahead?"

He rolled his eyes. "I told Tibbs, who told someone else. I say things out loud and they happen. It's details, babe."

"Details are where it all happens."

One corner of his mouth lifted. "I know. Why do you think I pay such close attention? Fish is always your first choice. Now you know I noticed that, bet you're soaking through your panties."

"Who are you talking to?" Jane whispered in her ear. "We can't hear right."

"Is that him?" Toria asked.

"Yes," Roxie said and held the phone out toward Zairn. "Tell them we're not having sex."

"Why would you be on the phone if we were having sex?" he asked. "Do you need instructions? There are videos you can watch that give you an idea."

"That how you get dates? Porn?"

"Better than your way of just hanging around the bar waiting for an offer."

"Uh, I don't have to wait, baby. There's a line around the block for me."

"Sure, because once you've given it up, there's no reason to hang around, so the next guy is up at bat. You're not a conversationalist."

"Says the guy who made his living seducing women in dark, noisy rooms."

"I'm rich, Lo," he said, flashing a little smolder. "I don't even have to say please." The suave mask dropped. "Now you want the fish or not?"

"Yes, please," she sang like butter-wouldn't-melt. He'd never buy the prim and innocent act, certainly not when her smirk gave him a glimpse of her real thoughts. "Can I have wine?"

"One step at a time," he said, backing away. "One step at a time."

He disappeared and the door closed.

Roxie brought the phone back to her ear. "Sorry, that was the dinner guy."

"I think I'm in love," Toria said.

"Me too," Jane agreed.

Both roommates sighed in sync.

"Okay, I'm going to hang up and give you both a chance to come to your senses. I have to put on some clothes anyway."

"You're naked?"

"I'm in my pajamas and apparently, we're about to have dinner."

Roxie didn't know the particulars of what had been decided in the boardroom after her and Zairn's quick, private caucus. Anything crazy, he'd have found a way to tell her. Other than that, if she heard nothing else, Roxie would just be her usual self. She was who she was and that was that.

24

Dinner was eaten either in the designated area by the main lounge or in the boardroom. The designated area was more like a restaurant than any dining room. Her food was brought to the board room, maybe because Zairn ate there with Ogilvie and the two new guys.

Throughout the meal, she worked on her phone. Rude? Maybe. But everyone else was discussing business. Talks about opening another Crimson venue were ongoing. The location of that venue was a bone of contention. Paris? Too pretentious. Seoul? Too K-pop. Ibiza? Cliché. South Africa? Berlin? Amsterdam? Brazil? No one could agree.

While they debated, Roxie had plenty to do. Zillions of emails from strangers awaited, some fans, some not. Figuring out priorities in the overcrowded inbox wasn't easy. Hence the concentration that distracted her from dinner conversation.

Picking out client messages, she replied to those, separating out the others as she went up the list. The new Crimson folder was filled with sub-folders: one for nice fan messages, one for not so nice, one for job offers, and the last for press queries.

Not long after Zairn excused himself to the master suite, everyone else departed too. Their host deserved privacy in his own bedroom, which provided the time to take care of a responsibility she'd been putting off: checking in with the documentary guys.

Abandoning her phone in the boardroom, Roxie headed off in search of them. Ogilvie was in the lounge with the two Rouge guys chilling around a low table. Ballard was on his own, reading something. Interesting. Tibbs and Astrid worked opposite each other in chairs she and Zairn had once sat in. Both assistants looked up when she reached them.

"Do you need something?" Astrid asked, closing her binder to slide forward.

"No," Roxie said, laying a hand on the top of Tibbs' chair. Since her path had crossed theirs, it seemed like a good time to find out what was going on. "Why are you so weird?"

Astrid blinked from her to Tibbs. "Weird? I—"

"Not weird, weird," Roxie said, rolling her wrist. "Not weird like I'm weird. You're weird, like, for you weird. Nervous and timid."

"Astrid has always been quiet," Tibbs said.

Her hand slid further across the leather. "Not quiet," Roxie said, raising a knee to the arm of Tibbs's chair.

"Would you like this seat?" Tibbs asked, shutting his laptop as though to get up.

Intent on Astrid, Roxie put her hand on Tibbs's shoulder to prevent him getting up. "You were flourishing before I got sick, Astrid. Something happened while I was out of action."

"Nothing," Astrid said. The color in her cheeks told a different story. "I'm sorry that you were ill."

"Wasn't your fault," Roxie said. "I'm sorry I wasn't around to encourage an attitude. You own the world, don't let anyone tell you different." She stood up. It wouldn't be right to push Astrid in front of an audience. If something had happened, maybe the young woman didn't want the world to know her business. "Where are the docu guys?"

"In there," Tibbs said, pointing at the door she was sure led to the party room.

The documentary crew were as entitled to kick back as anyone. Maybe joining them would require a wardrobe change. If they were partying, the plane's soundproofing was excellent. Rather than lights and music, she walked into a sorry scene. The three docu guys were strewn around the room, all lying down, all worse for wear.

"What happened to you guys?"

Tevin was the only one to react. Gripping the backrest, he hauled himself into a seated position. "Roxie."

"What happened?" she asked. The door swung back to its frame, bumping her forward a few steps. "You guys look terrible."

"We look better than we did a week ago," Tevin said.

Their pallor and lack of movement clued her in. "Oh, you're sick."

"Getting over it," Tevin said, rubbing his forehead. "How are you doing?"

"Back in the land of the living," she said. "I'm sorry, I didn't know you guys got it too. Take the time to relax. You can have a few hours of peace." She reached behind her for the door handle. "Sleep. Trust me, it helps."

"When Greg wakes up, I'll tell him you came by."

Tevin was already sinking onto his back when Roxie retreated into the lounge. Completely focused, she didn't pay attention to anyone else as she traversed the length of the plane.

Ideas of Zairn deserving privacy evaporated. She needed answers and patience wasn't in her repertoire. He wasn't in the suite's lounge or bedroom, so she sought him in the closet. The second she entered, he appeared from the steam of the bathroom, a fluffy white towel slung around his hips.

"Why didn't you tell me Greg was sick?"

He went to the recessed mirror above the vanity and opened the top drawer. "Hatfield? 'Cause I didn't want to get into it with you," he said, pushing his wet hair back from his forehead.

At least he wasn't denying the omission.

Agitation woke in her belly, sending her over to his side. "Get into what with me?"

"How he got your illness."

Zairn took a heavy, no doubt expensive, watch from the drawer to slip it on over his hand.

"He didn't get it from eating my pussy," she said. "If that's what you're thinking."

After clicking the watch clasp into place, he set a deadpan look on her. "Were you kissing him?"

"Kiss, I—" Roxie huffed. "What do you care who I'm kissing?"

Grumpy Pants' attention went back to the drawer to examine cufflinks. "It's unprofessional."

Dude wasn't even wearing a shirt; he didn't need cufflinks. "Unprofessional to kiss?" she asked. "Are we having another Pretty Woman moment?"

"I wouldn't know," he muttered.

She slammed the distracting drawer. "Zairn!"

Her abrupt move startled him, but he quickly recovered and grabbed control. Snatching her hips, he picked her up to dump her on the counter in front of the mirror. She didn't resist when he parted her legs to move between them. He was only wearing a towel. Whoa, boy, probably would've been smart to let that sink in before opening her legs for him.

"This is your bedroom," Roxie said, touching his pec. "Your private space."

"Mm hmm."

"I shouldn't come in here and give you attitude."

"I wouldn't recognize you if you held back on me, Lola," he said, drawing his fingertip down the strap on her shoulder. "You're over dressed for our private space."

"Our?"

"No one else has the authority to enter here." Leaning back, she crossed her arms over her abdomen to pick up the hem of her shirt and pull it off over her head. He admired his view of her plunge bra for a few seconds before a feral smile rose on his lips. "I didn't think that would work."

"You should know by now I'm not afraid of you."

"I've known that since the minute we met," he said, skimming his hands down her sides and around to her ass to drag her closer to the edge of the shelf.

"And I'm hot, Skippy. No reason to hide what I've got."

"Mm hmm."

His smug satisfaction was either rooted in triumphing he'd won or imagining what he might goad her into next.

"You'll just have to restrain your urges. I know seeing women in their underwear regresses your hormones to adolescence."

"This woman in underwear," he murmured, tightening his grip. "What happened to you being the strong one?"

"I'm not the one doing anything," she said, trailing her fingernails across his shoulders toward his chest. "You came out here without clothes and picked me up."

"What's a girl to do?"

"A girl's to do whatever she wants. Haven't you heard? Women are in charge in the bedroom now."

That provoked his smile again. "That right?"

"Mm hmm," she said, using his line, nodding even as he loomed closer. "Easy, tiger." She eased him back just a little. "I came in here to talk about your omission."

Turned out he hadn't forgotten. "Hatfield is not high on my priority list."

"He got his crew sick," she said, stroking his arms, appreciating their definition. "If you'd told me they were ill, I wouldn't have pushed to get on the plane. They'll need more time to recover."

"I don't care about their recovery."

"You cared about mine. The whole world saw that."

"Mm hmm."

"And you're not mad about it," she said, struggling to subdue her smile. "That the whole world knows how Scroogey is owned by his Lola Bunny."

Zairn planted his flat hands on the counter behind her to lean in, which forced her to angle back. "Did you kiss him?"

"Hatfield?"

"Yes, Hatfield."

Roxie took her time licking her lips. Driving him wild was only fair. Tit for tat. He did it to her all the time. "Are you jealous?"

"Did you kiss him?" he asked again, deeper and slower.

She looped her arms around his neck. "You know that's not really your business."

"Roxanna—"

"What was it you said to me?" she asked without hiding her satisfaction. "Breathe through it. The pain will get easier in time, baby."

Mocking him was fun, especially when it was obvious that she was testing his patience. Damn, playing with him was exciting.

"One more time and then I throw him out an emergency hatch," Zairn said, maintaining his calm though the next question came out as something of a growl. "Did you kiss him?"

Tightening her embrace, she arched her shoulders back to ensure her breasts pressed against him. "Casanova," Roxie purred. "I'm hurt you don't know that I'm a one duck bunny."

"As you repeated several times earlier, we're not together."

"Doesn't mean I'd frolic with more than one playmate at a time." Her elbows were already at the curve of his neck, so she straightened her forearms upward around his head to let her fingers play in his hair. "Before I got sick, we were keeping our distance as much as possible. Wasn't that what we decided to do?"

"It isn't working."

"Sure it is," she said. It didn't feel that way in her gut, maybe saying it out loud would make it truer. "We haven't been in a position like this for weeks."

"Yet we find ourselves here again. We didn't fix anything, we delayed it."

Maybe. The strong one. Wasn't that her self-appointed title? Keeping their distance was supposed to be her responsibility. Except his "*fuck it*" comment often visited her dreams, both waking and asleep.

She took a deep breath. "All we have to do is delay another six weeks. After that, I'll go home and we'll never have to see each other again."

"That's not how this ends."

"I'm trouble," she said, reminding him. "It can't be like you picked the winner based on who was best suited to ride your cock."

His tractor beam gaze snared her. The stare went on forever, its hot certainty fueling the insanity between them. Both of them should be smarter than this.

Any conviction she hoped he might show was obliterated when he curled his fingers around her breast to squeeze and fondle her.

"You're temptation," he murmured.

"Of course I am, you've wanted me for weeks."

Just at that her bra clasp popped and the straps dropped from her shoulders. He'd just... her bra... While she caught up, he crouched to bury his face between her breasts. He breathed for a minute, then began to nip and suckle at her, kissing and using his hand to arouse her.

His ex had explained how he was with women. How careful he was about his hands and actions sending the wrong messages. He'd never been like that with her. Ever. Thank God. Their entitlement to each other, misplaced though it was, enlivened their attraction. Maybe he read something in her that told him it was okay, that he was safe. She hoped so but would never ask. The barriers to trust were still locked in place and always would be.

Except if he kept kissing her like that, teasing her body with his incredible mouth and those hands... Strong and bold, the way he touched her was more than arousing. He was devouring every secret part of her.

"Okay," Roxie said. Putting a stop to his exploration before it went too far, she pushed his shoulders to give herself room to hop down. "The breasts you can have; only because you were nice to me when I was sick." She tossed her bra to the vanity and threaded their fingers together. "Don't get excited, Casanova, my panties are staying on."

"Where are we going?"

She led him through to the other room. "You need to get some rest." Knowing she'd been taking up his bed since they left Australia, Roxie couldn't imagine he'd had time to sleep. "Which side do you prefer? Left or right?"

"Middle," he said, pushing her onto the bed. "I'll sleep so long as you stay in bed with me."

She crawled to the opposite side and tucked herself under the covers. "Deal."

They'd slept together before; it wasn't a big deal. Given how much she'd slept, there was little chance of them waking up at the same time anyway. He got into bed and without a word scooped her into the little spoon position.

This was cool, right? Nothing to worry about. No one could get into the suite and see them, that's what he'd said.

Opening her fingers over his, she closed her eyes when he slid his digits between hers. Okay, so, yeah, he was hard, which made her very aware of his nakedness. Even if he hadn't lost the towel before getting into bed, it wouldn't stay tucked in while they slept.

It didn't matter. That he was naked or that she wasn't wearing a top. It was intense and exciting, but natural too. Why was it so easy to relax around him? Why did he accept her sass? Her annoying habits? Her love of teasing and playing? For a serious guy, he put up with a lot of her BS. She tested his patience and got a kick out of it. And, apparently, so did he.

25

"I can sit here all night," Roxie said, pushing her breasts into her folded forearms on the table.

Retrieving Astrid from the lounge had been easy. Pavlovian actually. On command, the woman jumped to her feet and followed.

When led into the boardroom, Astrid's expression could only be described as one of mortification.

"Miss Kyst—"

Roxie blew a raspberry. "You've been spending too much time with the higher ups, honey."

Shoving her upper body off the table, Roxie spun her chair a quarter turn and reclined the back to raise her legs. With full entitlement, she propped her bare feet on the tabletop.

"Roxie…"

"Sit down with me," Roxie said, sinking deeper into the seat, extending her legs higher. "Kick off your shoes. Zairn wasn't sure on the wine, but he didn't say anything about tequila. I bet there's some on the plane somewhere. If I have to get you drunk to get the truth, I will. I'm ruthless. You better believe it."

Astrid crept a little closer to the table. "Anything you need me to do—"

"This isn't about what you can do for me." Roxie stood up to boost herself onto the table and scooched to the middle. "It's about what I can do for you. You're my friend."

"I've never seen anyone sit on that table."

"No one's here to tattletale," Roxie said. "The world didn't explode. You don't relax enough. You should have more time off…" Her head drooped to the side. "Do you get a day off? You should ask Zairn for more vacation days."

"Mr. Lomond, is a generous employer, who—"

"You're always so quick to defend him. Do you think he'll fire you if you have an opinion? I'd kick his ass if he tried that shit. You should too."

Astrid took another small step. "You're…" she stopped herself.

Widening her eyes, Roxie rolled them left to right a few times. "I'm… what?"

"You're just… you're so confident with him. Sean's seen him with everyone; he says you're different." Sean? Who the hell was Sean? He couldn't have seen that much if she'd never—oh, Ballard. Sean Ballard. She got it now. "Women are either clingy or aloof," Astrid said. "Most of them think they're better than us. They try to separate him for themselves… So many people want what he can give them, want his complete focus."

"Zairn is close to your cousin, isn't he?"

"Sean's the closest thing he has to family after Ogilvie. He did security for the very first Crimson."

"And you trust your cousin," Roxie said. "You should trust your cousin. I still don't understand why you're being weird with me."

"I didn't know you were…"

"I was what?" Roxie asked, planting her hands on the table behind her to throw her head back and growl at the ceiling. "Geez, finish a sentence, woman!"

"I didn't know you were with him," Astrid said in a rush. "I… I didn't know you were with him. I've never been around his girlfriends before… I'm new at this."

"Okay," Roxie said, shuffling to the edge of the table. "You were in the room when I said this before, but I had to say it a bunch of times to my girls too. Maybe it's just difficult for all of you to believe Z isn't nutso about me when he's clearly obsessed. But, yeah, we're not together. We're not in a relationship and not having sex… with each other anyway. What he does with his own fist…"

Showing her hands, Roxie waved them back and forth before slapping them together, gesturing washing her hands of the issue.

On an exhale, Astrid examined her. "Both of you glow," she said. "I noticed it, I think everyone did. I thought it was an attraction because you're both so confident and smart. He's gorgeous, I get why women fall over themselves…"

"Ah, ah, don't clam up, keep talking."

"I shouldn't be talking about this," Astrid whispered. "About his personal life."

The reddened cheeks and unfocused eyes were a clear signal, one Roxie had noticed before.

A mental lightbulb went on. "You're attracted to him."

"No!" Astrid exclaimed. "No, I…" Shrewd in her smile, Roxie let the assistant know it was a losing battle. Astrid surrendered. "Don't ever tell him. You can't ever tell him. I would never, ever tell him. He's my cousin's best friend and my boss."

"There's nothing wrong with feeling what you feel," Roxie said, grabbing Astrid's hands. "Hell, when I first met you, I thought for sure you and he were fucking…" Astrid's embarrassment burned her cheeks. "He is hot, you'd have to be blind or gay not to notice that. But I don't get it, why does that make you weird with me?"

"I wasn't weird."

Another untruth. "You were weird. Because you thought I was with him? You thought I'd be mad you were attracted to him? Girl, I have straight up sexual fantasies that star that man. Women all over the world have them. Celebrities and sports stars too. Hell, I'll bet presidents have imagined falling to their knees for him." She pulled Astrid closer. "Me and my girls talk about men all the time. When we start seeing someone, there's the deconstruct, we comment on how attractive our guys are. We talk about sex stuff. Offer pointers, take requests."

Astrid laughed. "Requests?"

"Sure! Toria has a thing for sucking fingers, don't ask why, I don't know why. But if me or Jane bring around a guy with strong fingers…"

"She sucks on them?"

"No!" Roxie said, laughing. "She asks us to, in private, whenever. Toria wants to know his response. I think she read it in a magazine, something to do with a partner's tolerance threshold or something. Speaking of magazines, if one of us is in a relationship and we read something about a new position or date spot, we're required to follow through and report back to the others."

"You must be close."

"We are," Roxie said, giving their joined hands an encouraging shake. "You can be part of our gang too. If it makes you feel any better Toria and Jane are crazy attracted to Zairn. We have a rule if we're all into a guy or making a play for him. As soon as one of us catches him, he belongs to that person. Catching him means an official date or his penis enters us anywhere. After that, for the rest of the group, he's hands-off forever."

"That's fair," Astrid said, nodding.

The door opened and Kael came striding in. He didn't acknowledge the women as he passed at the opposite side of the table to head for the master suite.

"Uh, where do you think you're going?" Roxie asked, spinning on her butt to look at him.

From the stunned confusion on Kael's face, she'd guess he hadn't expected to be thwarted. "There's a phone call for him," he said, revealing the phone he held against his shoulder. "About his next appearance on Talk at Sunset."

Roxie reached out, wiggling her fingers at him. "Give it."

"Miss Kyst—"

"Trust me," she said. "He knows to expect the unexpected with me."

"It's true," Astrid agreed, finally smiling.

Determined, Roxie kept wiggling her fingers until he relented and stepped up to the table to hand over the phone.

"Hello," Roxie chirped into the phone. "This is Mr. Lomond's gorgeous and glamorous assistant, one of them anyway. He has a whole squad of us. He's indisposed right now, how can I help?"

"Oh, we, just had a few questions," the uncertain guy on the phone said.

"I would think so, you are a talk show." Roxie laughed at her own joke. "What do you need?"

"We can call back at a more convenient time. I'm one of the producers here. I've spoken with Mr. Lomond a few times. He likes to field requests such as these himself."

"Hey! I've spoken to him a few times too. Something we have in common. I might have the answer to your question. If not, what's the harm in putting it to me?"

If they wanted to blindside Zairn with something, they wouldn't have called ahead to talk about it before getting him on the couch.

"It's about Roxie." Her area of expertise. "We held a spot for the winner on his return appearance and we just want to confirm she will be joining him."

"On Talk at Sunset? Yes!" she exclaimed. "Roxie will definitely be there." Her exuberance died. "Oh, wait, no…" Roxie shook her head. "No. No, she won't be."

"Why not?" the guy pleaded. "She's incredible online. The public love her."

"You wanted an answer. I gave you an answer."

"If I could just talk to Mr. Lomond—"

"You'd be able to persuade him? No. This is a hard no. No equivocation. Goodbye!" She hung up the phone and held it out toward Kael. "See, easy, fixed."

"You can't hang up on people who call for Mr. Lomond."

"Sure I can. I just did. The call wasn't about him. It was about me."

"You don't speak for Mr. Lomond."

On a groan, Roxie thrust the phone toward him again. "But it's okay for him to answer questions about me? I can't talk for him, but he can talk for me? What kind of chauvinistic crap is that?"

"We should discuss it with—"

"Ah, ah," Roxie said when Kael took another step toward the bedroom. She slammed the phone down on the table. "Do not go in there."

"He can't go in there," Astrid murmured from behind her. "He doesn't have clearance."

"Right," Roxie said, pushing her shoulders back in a triumphant show of confidence. "How about those of us who are allowed to walk into Mr. Lomond's private space while he's naked and vulnerable make decisions on who can speak for who? It's not like I'm suggesting we go look for Atlantis with his fortune. I didn't hatch some hare-brained scheme. The guy on the phone asked if *I* would be there. That's about me. I answered."

"Mr. Lomond may need you to be there."

Confident, Roxie shook her head. "He won't."

"You're popular right now, Miss Kyst. Your contract has provisions for promotional appearances."

"And if Mr. Lomond asked me to be there, I'd go."

"Which is why we should check—"

"But he won't." Kael's exasperation put a smile on her face. "Loosen up, Mr. Salad." Roxie spun around again to spring off the table next to Astrid. "Now we're going to talk about women things… at the bar."

"Okay."

After looping one arm through Astrid's, Roxie swept the other toward the door. "After you."

"You think I'm going to go in there after you leave?"

Going in without clearance might be impossible, but that didn't stop him knocking and waking Zairn up.

"I think if you try, I would be upset. You don't want me to be upset, Mr. Salad, believe me. I might seem like rainbows and unicorns, but as you pointed out, I'm popular right now and no one even knows who you are." If there was a stand-off, she wouldn't blink first. "Shoo, shoo, Mr. Salad. Get moving."

Though he grumbled out a sigh, he did relent and stomped back toward the door he'd come through. Zairn didn't rest nearly enough. While she'd been ill, he'd looked after her and made sure no one disturbed her. Doing the same in return was only right. He may not be sick, but he did need someone looking out for his wellbeing. It wasn't business. Wasn't the club. It was him and, to her, he was the most important thing.

26

"Heard you had some fun today."

Leaning in to the mirror in her new hotel bedroom closet, she couldn't see him. From the direction of his voice, she guessed Zairn was loitering in the doorway.

"I don't know what you're talking about," Roxie said, full of innocence as she swiped on some more mascara.

After spending the last few hours of the flight in the party room with Astrid, both conversing and assessing how ill the documentary guys were, the five of them disembarked and got into a car.

Once they were tucked in the vehicle, everyone else left the plane. Zairn lingered at the bottom of the stairs. A few seconds passed before he got into the second car with Ogilvie, Tibbs, and his two other Rouge guys. In that car, Ballard sat up front, on the passenger side it looked like.

"We went shopping. It wasn't a big deal," Roxie said to the man invading her closet. "I had nothing Italian to wear."

"That's right, I forgot you wanted to shop in Milan. We should've gone straight there."

"Rome was fine," she said without turning when he reached her side.

"You got your picture taken."

"I was safe," Roxie said, aware that pictures had appeared online because Astrid told her. "We only went to a few stores."

"I'll find out if that's true when the credit card bill comes in."

She tossed her mascara into her makeup bag and retrieved lip gloss. "No, you won't, 'cause I used mine."

"Why did you do that?" he asked, sounding oddly offended.

Slathering on the gloss, then checking the overall picture, she dropped the tube into the clutch next to the makeup bag. "Astrid bought lunch and dinner on your company card, if that makes you feel better?"

"That dress looks new."

Stepping back, she raised her arm to show him the crisscross cut outs up the side of the dress. "It is." Short and black, it had a straight neckline. "What do you think?"

The descent of his brow happened slowly. "I think you're not wearing underwear."

Roxie laughed. "We're in Rome! You know what they say about that." If there was anywhere to wear a daring dress, it was that city. "I'm looking forward to tonight."

"Shame I'll miss it, being a few hours behind," he said, pulling back his shirt cuff to show her his watch. "Seems while I was sleeping, someone changed the time on my watch."

Practically a whole day had passed since she'd adjusted his watch while he slept. She'd completely forgotten about her mischief. "Time changing fairies, ooh."

"Yeah," he said, his arm descending to his side. "Funny thing is, it's set on Chicago time."

"Best time in the world," she said, grinning when she flared her eyes at him. "Roxie time."

"Roxie time?"

"Yeah, I decided you can keep your time zones. I'm going to stick to my own time."

"In which case, you should be thinking about dinner plans, not going out to a club."

"I can party any time, Skippy," she said, fluffing up her hair to give it volume. "Morning, noon, or night. It's been almost two weeks. I am gonna dance 'til I drop tonight. Nothing will get in my way."

"Security will, actually." Roxie didn't follow or like the implication. "You can't go to any of the main floors," he said, sucking the wind from her sails. "It's too dangerous to have you in any kind of crush right now."

"Too dangerous? Why? What do you think will happen? Have Ballard watch me, you trust him."

"Ballard did the assessment," Zairn said, caressing her jaw with his thumb. "I knew you'd want to go down there. He checked it out. It's not safe. Even if we limit the numbers, we can't guarantee to keep everyone away from you."

"Hmm," she said, pushing her lips to the side. "I thought Ballard would've seized on any opportunity to get rid of me."

Zairn laughed. "Why would he want rid of you?"

Knowing he wasn't that stupid, she just gave him a look. "You may have noticed, we're not the best of friends."

"Doesn't mean he wants rid of you. You have to get to know each other better."

She scoffed. "No chance of that."

He rubbed her arm. "He's a good guy. He's seen it all when it comes to women in my life."

Folding her arms, she propped a hip on the vanity at her side. "You know, everyone seems to forget I'm not dating you. I'm a contest winner."

"Maybe people forget because you stand guard outside my bedroom scaring people away."

Hmm. "Heard about that, huh?" she asked, though wasn't ashamed of her actions or surprised he'd been looped in. "It was a stupid thing for Salad to get on his high horse about. I answered a question about me. I didn't speak *for* you; I was speaking for myself. Do you want me to go on Talk at Sunset with you?"

"No."

She presented a flat hand at him. "See. Thank you."

"Kinda hard to toe the 'no comment' line if you're sitting there next to me."

"Exactly what I thought."

"I know you now, Kyst. Putting you in front of a camera is a crapshoot. I choose not to be sitting next to you when you go off."

"You're just worried everyone will see."

The smirk on his face brightened. "See what, baby?"

She leaned in, failing to hide her immature smile. "Astrid said we glow."

"Did she?"

Nodding, Roxie rested her lower back against the vanity. "Apparently."

She sighed.

He came closer. "What was that for?"

"What?" Roxie asked, looking down at herself, righting the pendant over her breasts. "What's what for?"

"The sigh," he said, propping himself on the vanity, perpendicular to her. "If you're not up for this tonight—"

"No. No. I'm good," she said, quickly, laying both hands on his body. "I streamed earlier and everything."

"I saw you."

"You did?"

Her smile bred his and he nodded. "I set up an alert on my phone." Probably so they couldn't be caught in anymore accidental streaming situations. "I stop whatever I'm doing to watch you."

"To make sure I don't cause another crisis?"

"Yeah," he said on an exhaled laugh. "You did good. You brought up all the speculation and were clear you weren't going to talk about it, then pivoted to your day in Rome. Boundaries. You decided on your boundaries and stuck to them."

Something he'd been coaching her in since early in their friendship. Good word. Good ideology too. It allowed her to be honest without backing herself into a corner.

The strategy worked with her friends and family, including Astrid, and the documentary crew too. An especially large part of her remained separate from Hatfield and his colleagues. Their goal was to expose truth, so she was careful about which version they got.

She liked it when motives were clear. Even if they weren't altruistic, it was better to know where she stood. Knowledge gave her the chance to protect herself. That perspective added to her deep respect for Zairn protecting himself.

He'd never trust her. She'd known that since the beginning. Yet, that day, whenever she thought about him, something niggled at her. Whatever it was, it prodded at her again.

"I was thinking about that today," Roxie said.

"About what?"

"Boundaries. We talked about setting them for friends and family. About setting them with the public."

"Mm hmm."

Roxie raised her chin to meet his eye. "We've never talked about setting them for each other."

His arms closed around her. "And you think we should."

Maybe that was what bugged her. Either that they needed clear boundaries or that the idea of them unsettled her.

Whatever the reason, Roxie had brought it up. Which she shouldn't have. The air was beginning to fizz again. "Just something that was on my mind," she said.

"On your mind after your showdown with Fuller at my bedroom door?" She shrugged. "I wasn't mad."

"I knew that."

"Though you're not completely off the hook, Lola. I was mad that you snuck out and left me in bed."

"Us waking up together ends in trouble. You should be thanking me."

"I would've thanked you properly if we were in bed."

"Exactly the problem," she said, reaching around to take his arms away from her body to then step away.

He laughed. "You don't have to be afraid of me. Shit, Rox, you're not afraid of anything."

Except he was missing the point. Until Roxie knew that he understood, she couldn't play with him. "This is fun, right? I mean, we're just having fun, you know that."

Astrid didn't seem to believe it. No matter how many times Roxie said that she and Zairn weren't together, the assistant still spoke as if they were. Her girls hadn't believed it either. Not at first anyway.

"I'm the emperor of fun, baby."

"Okay," she said, hoping that was true. "Because it's your job to show me a good time… So technically…" Edging closer again, she touched one of his shirt buttons with a fingertip. "You work for me."

"Doesn't mean I'll let you loose on the Crimson dancefloors."

She huffed. "You're not supposed to be a fun sucker."

"You can have fun in our VIP room tonight, it has a view over the busiest dancefloor." Most of his clubs had a viewing area of some kind. "We have three Crimson Experience winners; they'll be there with their friends." Only one of the winners would spend the night in the VIP area, the other two would be trucked off back to the masses after their meet and greet. "And I have it on good authority that there are more than a few models in town tonight, looking for a way in."

"Easy pickings for you then," she said, still toying with his button.

"Female and male models."

She pushed out her lips. "Hmm, okay, that could be interesting." He had to know they were just having fun if he was joking about her hooking up with male models. "They're not baby models, are they? I like my men to be men."

"No one under twenty-five," he said. "I'll make sure they check ID."

"Under thirty," she said, switching to another button. "He should know what he's doing."

"Check," he said, enjoying her in the way that certain expression betrayed.

Whatever it said about her, she was getting used to his recurrent adoring amusement. "And I like tall men."

"Want me to organize a line up for you?" he asked, almost laughing at her. "They're models, not hookers."

"You saying you have to pay men to sleep with me?"

He bowed lower. "I would pay a fortune, if it would keep them away from you." He caught the section of her hair that fell over her temple to coil it around his finger.

"Except if any guy got a chance with you, he wouldn't give it up for all the money in the world."

She poked his chest. "Switch it off, Casanova. Business not pleasure."

He was still smiling even as he changed the subject. "Hatfield brought in a sub crew for filming tonight. So don't be surprised if a stranger sticks a camera in your face."

"Your face," she said. "They film and follow you when we're in Crimson." Which she liked because it left her free to go dancing, usually anyway. "You keep them entertained."

"If you hadn't noticed, there's increased interest in you, and in us, together."

Again, she shrugged. "We don't hang out when we're in Crimson. I shake some hands and throw out some air kisses, then grab a drink and go dancing."

"I can close the main floor if it means that much to you."

Roxie groaned. "That's missing the point entirely. For a party God, you really underestimate the power of losing yourself in a crowd."

"It's something I haven't been able to do in a long time."

Sad but true. She smoothed her hands up his shirt. "Aww, honey, you're rich and hot that's why people don't ignore you. If that makes you sad, I can ignore you, if you like."

It didn't take long for teasing to twist her lips.

Zairn crouched to grab her ass in both hands and hauled her close. "You've never been able to ignore me, Lola."

"Oh, I think I could," she said, looping her arms around his neck.

"Just to make me happy?"

"Your happy seems to have a lot to do with my ass and chest. You really don't respect me, do you?"

"I respect certain parts of you," he said, pulling her higher, bringing their mouths near to each other. "The fun parts."

"Yeah, keep it that way," she said, catching his jaw in her teeth for a fraction of a second. "The minute you start to show respect for my mind or wishes is the day I say sayonara."

"I would never do that to you, baby," he said, loosening his hold to set her back on her feet. Not because he wanted to put distance between them—no, absolutely not—but to free his fingertips to skim the cutouts that ran up each of her sides. "Who thought no underwear was a good idea at my club?"

She blinked. "Is there an employee at Crimson tasked with checking everyone is wearing underwear?" She sucked in an exaggerated breath. "If so, I would like to apply for that position."

"No," he said, laughing at her. "But that skirt is a hella short, Lola."

"And no underwear is the point of the illusion," she said, turning to the side and throwing her arm up over his shoulder to show him the effect again. "Gets your mind going, doesn't it?"

"In the direction of barring men from standing within ten feet of you, yes."

"Need to hire those hottie action heroes to secure my perimeter."

He stooped to get closer. "I don't want any guy getting inside your perimeter."

"No?" she asked, yielding when he threaded his fingers between hers.

"Stay close to me," he murmured, smudging his thumb against her chin to part her lips. "I'll protect you."

"You would be terrible at that job," she said, moving in close until her body touched his. "You can't concentrate when I'm around. You're too busy checking me out. Wanting me."

"If I wanted you, I'd have you."

"Convince me," she whispered, trailing the back of her fingers up his cheek before draping the arm around his neck.

The flash of a question in his gaze revealed the true implication of that request. Convincing her that he could have her if he wanted her? There was only one way to do that.

Someone in the doorway cleared their throat.

Ballard stood there, frowning at them. "Ready to go?"

"Heard you didn't take advantage of an opportunity to off me," she said. Letting go of Zairn to close her clutch and slip it under her arm, she started toward the bodyguard. "Thank you, Ballard."

"Gotta wait 'til you're out of the news to do that." Roxie paused perpendicular to Ballard, surprised at what she was hearing. "When nobody's watching."

Her smile concealed a swell of rising emotion. "Ballard," she breathed. "Did you just sass me? Oh my God."

"Told you he didn't want rid of you," Zairn said from right behind her, he linked their hands again. "Come on."

She fanned her face as Zairn tugged her out of the closet and through the suite. "I'm overcome," Roxie said. "I need a minute. I think I might cry."

Zairn swept her around in front of himself while opening the door to take her waist and push her out. "Cry in the car."

Ballard sassing her was a good sign. Either she was encouraging his smart mouth, or he was warming up to her.

In her opinion, the good life meant more than money and excess. She'd miss the lifestyle less than she would the people. In less than six weeks, Roxie would go back to her normal life. The people she'd got used to in the last month and a half would go on without her. Whatever happened, Roxie would cherish the people. They'd given her an unforgettable adventure.

27

Zairn kept touching her. It wasn't unpleasant but distracted everyone around them. Honestly, people had gone nuts. When they got out the car at the club, he'd been holding her hand. No big deal? Right? Except their physical connection stirred up their VIPs who insisted on showing them the online pictures just minutes after they got inside.

They were hot property apparently. People wanted them to be together. Strangers were invested in their non-existent relationship. People they'd never met and never would meet had an opinion on what should go on in their bedrooms. It mystified her.

"Babe?"

She and Zairn were sharing a couch in the Crimson VIP lounge. Sharing was a loose description. They were both seated in the middle, not a glimmer of light passed between them. For most of the night, his arm lay across her body, his hand resting on her opposite outer thigh. The three couches that made up the other edges of their square seating area were the same length, but all held more people. No one dared sit on the couch with them. Was that a rule she didn't know or because people just didn't dare touch the emperor without permission?

Come to think of it, he always sat alone on the head couch in every club. Sometimes people joined him, if he invited them to sit. With her routine being the dancefloor, she hadn't checked the relevant etiquette. In her defense, Zairn had pulled her hips down onto the couch when he sat.

"Lo?"

Yes, he was trying to get her attention. No one else had it, though the lights coming from beyond the glass did beckon. Being elevated from the busy party below didn't bother Roxie. Not as much as she thought it would. Still tiring easy, a night of just sitting, observing the fun, was probably a good idea. Not that she'd confess to Zairn he'd had superior insight.

His forefinger hooked her chin to draw her attention around to his. "You're ignoring me," he said, concern in his frown.

She grinned. "You're welcome."

When he caught on to her game, his concern evaporated to a smile. "Thank you," he said, not as gracious as he should've been. "You missing the party? Ready to kick everyone out and take over?"

"I'm okay here," she said, raising her glass to sip from the short straw. "I like Gin and It."

"Also known as Gin and Cin. I said you'd enjoy it," he said, squeezing her leg as he leaned in to kiss the top corner of her forehead. Angling away, she just blinked at him. "What?"

Oh, like that defiant smirk on his face didn't prove he knew exactly what he was doing. "We're kissing in public now?"

When he laughed, she just shook her head, amused by his audacity. If that was how he wanted to play it, she'd jump on board, but it could rock the boat for everyone.

He leaned in again, this time stooping a little lower to talk in her ear. "The guy near three o'clock has been staring at your legs all night." Extending her legs straight out, she caught her straw between her thumb and forefinger. "Yes, those legs."

Zairn didn't let her pins stay outstretched for long and slid his hand toward her knee to push them down. His new need to claim ownership was sort of hilarious.

He was kind enough to offer his ear when she turned. "Have you been glaring at him?" He shrugged, which was confirmation enough. She breathed out a short laugh. "The blonde next to him thinks you're checking her out. Would explain why she's been busting a gut flashing her tits at you all night. For a while there, I thought she had a tick. No one needs to toss their hair that much… Doesn't all the lash batting distract you?"

When she relaxed, he whispered in her ear again. "I didn't notice any blonde. You stare her out, I'll keep glaring at leg guy until he gets the message."

"He's a baby," Roxie said, stroking his thigh, then letting her hand settle on his inside seam. "You think he could handle me?"

"Lola, I'd be surprised if any man could handle you."

Holding her straw out of the way, she downed the rest of her drink and leaned over his arm to put the ice on the table. If kissing was allowed, so was dancing. It beat sitting there glaring at people who didn't have a chance of getting close to them.

Grabbing his hand, Roxie slid to the edge of the couch. "Come on," she said with a side-nod.

Dubious Zairn locked his fingers between hers and let himself be led. "Where are we going?"

The music wasn't as loud upstairs as it was in the main room below. Rome's VIP section was bigger than most of the others. The greater number of voices raised the usual volume level. On second thoughts, maybe the VIP area wasn't larger and Zairn had just allowed more people in so she could get her groove on.

Rather than dance as she usually would in a club, Roxie went to a quieter, darker corner and stopped to wrap his arms around her.

"Ah," his mouth moved in understanding before curling to a smile. "You want to dance."

Stroking his chest with flat hands, Roxie laid her head between them and closed her eyes. "You said we could."

His embrace was loose, yet it reassured her. The noise was irrelevant. The people. Even where they were. He'd said they could dance together in Crimson and was living up to his word. It didn't matter that their movement was contrary to the music coming from the speakers. It matched what she heard in her head. Obviously, Zairn heard the same tune because he was leading to perfection.

It was easy. Being with him. Existing with him was easy. So simple. Nothing about them was simple from the outside. Nothing about their lives or their personalities, but being held by him, that was effortless bliss. Zairn wasn't billionaire playboy; she wasn't a Chicago nobody. They were the same. Equal. Aligned. United.

Time ceased to mean anything, how long had they been slow dancing? She'd begun to forget where they were until Zairn stopped, breaking the spell.

Her senses were clouded by the intoxication of their intimacy. Tibbs was beside them, showing Zairn something on his phone. What was going on? Zairn bowed to say something to Tibbs. The assistant went one way and Zairn rushed her toward the exit.

"What happened?" she asked.

Like a man on a mission, he kept them moving without saying a word, through private passages and out a side door. Ballard was already outside in the alley, standing next to a car with the backdoor open.

Zairn urged her down into the car but stayed outside to talk to Ballard over the open door. Their car was only a few yards from the street. Through the windshield, Roxie could see lights coming from the sidewalk. There were people down there. Fun. Happiness. Festivities. Yet, they were in a shadowy corner, hoping no one would happen upon them.

She'd slid along the backseat expecting Zairn to get in with her. After giving him a few extra seconds, Roxie bent to the side to call out to him. "If you don't get in here and tell me what's going on, I'm getting out this side and going back to my drink."

She'd finished her drink, but that wasn't the point.

The screen between the front and back of the car ascended.

Less than five seconds went by, then Zairn got in beside her. Ballard closed the door and banged on the roof to get them underway.

"My purse is still in the club," she said.

Zairn retrieved his phone from his pocket. "Tibbs will get it."

"What's going on?" she asked, trying to peek at his screen, but that just caused him to turn it further out of view. "Fine, be a fun sucker. I was having a good time and you blew it. Couple more drinks and I might have—"

Zairn turned the phone toward her. She read the words once and again but still they didn't sink in. Without thinking, Roxie took the phone and cradled it in both hands to read the headline again.

"*Hot at the top.*" Underneath was a picture of an apartment block. One she recognized. Flames poured out the windows, smoke billowed toward the heavens. Inset in the bottom corner was a headshot of her ex, Porter Clement.

"Damnit," she murmured.

Yes, that was Porter's apartment building. The term '*narrow escape*' in the caption gave her chills.

"Did you know he was lead prosecuting attorney on the Gambatto case?"

"I knew he was on the team," she said, reading the story. Porter's apartment had been set alight. Only weeks after he'd been bumped up the ladder to First Chair. What happened to the original lead attorney? Yeah, according to the article, he'd been hospitalized after an unspecified attack. "He left a few messages when we were in Boston and Montreal. I didn't call back, I figured it was about the contest win."

Scrolling to the next part of the story, her whole body froze. There was a picture of them. Together. Her and Porter. Taken at a charity function they went to like a year ago.

Coincidence? Not likely. That picture would never have made the cut if it wasn't for Roxie's new notoriety.

"Oh God," she said, coming to realize what it all meant. "This will come back on you."

"Mm," he said, taking the phone from her.

Zairn had to think she'd set out to ruin his whole life. His reputation. His business. Goddamn, she was a calamity. Not even just one. Calamity after damn calamity.

When she buried her face in his shoulder, he put an arm around her to hold her there.

"Yeah, it's me," Zairn said. He didn't give Roxie much room; she only just managed to peek up to confirm he was on the phone. "What's Joe thinking, Trish...? What did Teddy say? Did he...? Yeah... Trish, honey, I can't... I can't see you right now... Yeah, there's always someone else... Yeah, that one... I don't care about that... I'm on the board, Trish, make sure he knows...Whatever it takes... Yeah." He hung up the call and offered her the phone. "You want to search for more stories?"

They'd all say the same thing, and she'd interpret them in the same way too: Porter was in trouble.

"Who was that?" Roxie asked. "On the phone? Who's Trish?"

"Trish Gambatto. Joseph's sister."

Sitting up, Roxie blinked at him, unable to believe her ears. "Joey Gambatto? The defendant Porter is prosecuting? The guy who killed Miss Illinois?"

"Ava Marilyn," Zairn said. "I met her."

"Met her or slept with her?"

From sitting quite loose with a distracted expression, he quickly zeroed in on her. The surprise in his frown caused her words to replay in her mind.

"Forget it," she said, sinking back in the seat, putting some space between them. "Sorry, just... forget it."

Taking out her issues on him wouldn't be fair. It didn't matter that she and Porter had broken up, she still cared about him. His boss had been forced out of his position, which had given Porter a leg up.

He could be in danger. The next story could be about his body being pulled from the river or him going missing, lost to some unknown fate. His career was important to him and without her, there was no one around to remind him of the big picture.

28

As soon as they got back to the hotel, Roxie raced up the stairs to hunt for her credit card. If she'd known international calls were on the agenda, she wouldn't have hammered it so hard at the boutiques.

Tugging her big purse from a shelf in the closet, she dumped it on the floor and began pulling things out.

"Babe, Tibbs's on his way."

"My phone won't be charged," she said, yanking out her makeup and sunglasses. "It's never charged."

Which never bothered her until she really needed it for something. Like right then.

"Use the hotel line."

"I will," she mumbled. "I need my credit card."

"Babe."

Her wallet was lost in the abyss. It had to be in there. Hadn't she just used it? Damnit. Weeks had gone by since she'd carried her big purse. Now a bottomless pit where she tossed things between various flights, it was a mess. Her focus was all over the place. Panic. Anger. Worry. Irritation. Every emotion wanted to agitate her.

Someone grabbed her arm and hauled her onto her feet. Zairn. Serious, holding a cordless phone out to her.

"Call him."

She exhaled some of her stress. "Thank you," she mouthed.

He touched her chin, then walked out, leaving her alone. The call would be expensive. She'd ask for the bill and pay it back. Getting through to Porter was more important than debt in that minute.

His phone rang half a dozen times. That was fine. Normal. Didn't it typically ring out for a while before he picked up? Porter put up with worse dating her. Despite always asserting that she'd charge her phone, the task always seemed to fall out of her head.

"Hello?"

A woman.

"Hey, is Porter around?" Roxie asked.

"Who is this?" the woman snapped.

Defensive much? Guess it made sense given what was happening in Porter's life.

"Check your phone, this is an international number. I'm calling from Rome. Tell him I'm returning a call."

Sort of the story of their relationship. More often than not she got his voicemail and called him back. It wasn't her fault cellphone batteries couldn't live up to the rigors of modern life.

"Are you from the media?"

"It's not like being a cop. I don't have to tell you the truth if you ask," Roxie said. "Though that's a myth, honey. That would be a pretty whacked-out loophole, don't you think?"

"Oh my God, you're Roxie. Famous Roxie!"

"Famous Roxie, is that who I am?"

"Lomond's Delight." Smiling, Roxie didn't mind being reminded of the name that flashed up every time she logged in to stream. "Porter, it's your girlfriend."

Ex-girlfriend, but whatever.

"Rox?"

Apparently, Porter wasn't seeing anyone because "girlfriend" was enough to identify her. "Are you crazy?" she demanded, jumping to the point. "You're First Chair?"

"Guess this isn't a congratulatory call."

"No, hello? This is your sanity speaking."

"You're my sanity?" he asked, incredulous and amused. "Boy, I must be in serious trouble."

"You know what didn't happen to my apartment last night? It wasn't torched. I suppose you're going to tell me your place being flambéed after you got a new job was a coincidence."

"No, it wasn't a coincidence," Porter said. "No way. But we want Gambatto coming for us, Rox. He's making our case for us."

"Great! I'll be sure to have that etched on your headstone."

"RoRo—"

"Your defendant isn't the only one you have to worry about. He's from one of the most influential families in the state and not in a good way. His family goes way back. They have connections—"

"I'm sorry, are you calling to interview?" he asked. "All positions on the team have been filled. Maybe if you returned calls, you'd have known what was going on at the time. Where are you calling from? Europe? Asia? You were never the type to be blinded by shiny things. How did he change you so fast?"

Her fingers curled around the shelf at her side. Her own sanity was slipping, and she really didn't want to explode at him. If they ended up in a full-blown row, his competitive hackles would ensure there was no chance of reason getting through.

"We're not talking about me," she said. "We're talking about you. About you nearly dying for a case. What about your sister? What about your mom? Did you think about them? What if we'd still been together? I slept over at your place all the time. What if I'd been in your bed when they torched it?" Silence. Good. That meant he was reflecting. "Is doing your job worth giving up your life? You're at risk. The people you care about, your staff, they're at risk."

"Someone has to do it, Ro," he said. "It's dangerous, but the city is protecting the people we care about. You're out of the country, I thought you would be okay."

"I'm in Italy, bright spark."

Where the Gambatto's network was probably as strong as it was in the Midwest.

"Hmm, so maybe you're not," he said. "I'll talk to Tim next time I see him."

Tim Unst being the State's Attorney. She sank down onto the floor to prop herself against the shelving unit while slipping off her shoes.

"You don't have to worry about me," Roxie said. "Zairn has his own security team looking out for me."

"You just met him. I don't know if we should trust him with your safety. I saw the video."

"Sure you did," she said, pointing her toes. "Half the planet has seen it."

"Did you get over your flu? Who gets flu in September?"

"Me, apparently," she said. "But don't change the subject. We're talking about your safety. You can't be casual about it."

"Why not? You are."

It was staggering. "No one's coming after me!"

"The press is," he said. "My alerts are flashing up your name every minute."

Aggravation stirred her blood. "Stop pivoting to me. You always do this, it drives me nuts. You're the one going after a murderer who has the reach to literally rip your limbs off. Who cares about the press taking my picture? You have to see that, in the grand scheme of things, this conviction means nothing if it costs you your life. If you die, where will your career be then? Huh?"

"You jetted off across the world with a stranger."

Bullheaded idiot. He infuriated her. Whenever he didn't have an answer, he'd ignore her and pick at something in her life instead. He picked and picked and picked.

"You never miss a chance to judge my actions," she said. "But this one is on you, Port. You can't just charge on; it could cause a lot of damage."

"Shoulda, coulda, woulda," he said. "You're talking about maybes. This is my job, Rox. I told you how it could be working in the SA's office."

"We never discussed arson. If you'd been staying with me, if they targeted you at my apartment, Toria and Jane—"

"That imagination, Rox," he said, laughing at her. "I always said you'd make an excellent criminal."

"I have an imagination, so that makes me a criminal? Is that judgment I hear again?"

"You called to judge me," he said. "It's a double standard. Isn't that what you always accuse me of?"

Roxie sighed. "This is going nowhere," she said, tucking her knees to one side. "It's my fault for thinking you could be civil."

"This is civil. Disagreeing is part of what I do."

"That doesn't mean you should take an opposing position for the sake of it. I'm calling to show concern and you dismiss me."

"Another thing you enjoy accusing me of."

"Porter," she growled. The pressure of frustration dammed in her chest; she exhaled to free it. "I shouldn't have called."

"If you want my help, I'll help you," he said. "I'll bring you home or organize security. I don't know how that works when you're on a different continent, but I don't want anything to happen to you."

"You just can't wrap your head around the fact I'm trying to tell you the same thing."

"Life isn't always smooth sailing," he said. "My job is dangerous. I was upfront about that."

He was a lawyer, not a trained assassin or even a Navy SEAL. At least those guys learned how to respect the threats they faced, Porter just brushed them aside.

"Okay, well if someone comes to murder you, I hope you remember in your last seconds that I told you so."

"Next time return my calls," he said. "You used to be good at it."

"I used to suck your dick too, times have changed."

"RoRo," he said on a sigh.

"See you around," she said and hung up.

Sinking forward, Roxie shoved the phone away across the floor as she stretched herself across it facedown. Porter was likely to get himself killed and she couldn't do a damn thing about it.

29

Still lying on her chest with her face buried in the carpet, Roxie wasn't sure she'd ever move again.

"I had sex with Dayah."

Zairn's voice drew her head around. Her damn hair was in the way, she tossed it back. He was propped against the corner of the shoe rack, just inside the door. He raised her purse to show her it was back and then slipped it onto the shelf.

"Several times," he said. "It wasn't a relationship, it was casual. I thought it was anyway. I was coming out of the intense, messy relationship with Kesley. I didn't want ties, I wanted something easy. So we messed around. I didn't want anything more and thought we were on the same page."

Roxie rolled onto her side and propped her head on the heel of her hand. "She wanted more?"

"Yeah," he said, crossing to sit on the floor in front of her. His shoes and socks were already gone and his shirt was looser than before. "We got into it. Argued. People saw us arguing at Crimson." Narrowing his eyes, he gestured shapes with his hands. "Crimson, LA has what we call 'private pods.' Individual soundproof spaces glazed front and back. Even the cameras don't have audio. It's to protect those inside. A lot of deals are done in those rooms."

"You argued in one of those pods?"

"Yeah," he said. "It wasn't an argument, we just... She asked for more and I was honest that I didn't want it. She got emotional. She was young, at the start of her career.

It didn't seem like a time she'd want to tie herself to anyone. She was supposed to be safe."

"Sometimes I think no one is safe," she said, laying her crooked arm on its side to use it as a pillow. "We can have the best of intentions and still wind up screwing someone's life."

Still serious, almost to the point of solemn, Zairn continued. "I drove her home. She wanted to have sex. I said it wasn't a good idea. That we should take some time. She got upset again, stormed into the house. After that, I don't know what happened. Police say it looked like there had been a struggle. My fingerprints were around the place, course they were, I'd been spending time with her for weeks."

From memory, the police hadn't specified cause of death. Or maybe they had, and she just didn't remember.

"How did she…"

"She cut her wrists in the tub. Ultimately, cause of death was exsanguination. The manner of death? Undetermined. Some say suicide, but the disarray of the house suggested foul play. And there were apparently inconsistencies."

"Isn't that what they always say?" Roxie asked. "And she was emotional. I've trashed my share of household property when I've been mad at a guy."

"Begs the question, doesn't it?" She showed an inquisitive frown. "Even if she was the one holding the blade, aren't I the one who drove her to use it?"

Guilt. That's what it was, but for all the wrong reasons.

Roxie pounced onto her knees facing him. "You are not responsible," she said, catching his jaw when it began to descend. "Zairn Lomond, you are a good man. Kind and generous. You couldn't possibly have known her state of mind would drive her to that. If you'd suspected for a second, you'd never have left her alone. You would've got help for her."

"How can you be so sure?"

"Because I know you," she said without a shadow of a doubt. "I know the real you. The man who covers up his kindness with the arrogant smooth operator facade."

His gaze became more probing. "You do know the real me, Roxanna," he said, taking her caressing fingers from his cheek. "I didn't think when we were bouncing around ideas for the contest that it would bring someone like you to me."

He'd been guarded about Dayah when she'd asked before. Why would he suddenly decide to offer details?

"Why the turnaround? Why tell me all this?" she asked. "Why now? Tonight?"

He stared into her for the longest time before answering with complete tender conviction. "I don't want any chance, even a slim one, that another guy might think he has a chance with you."

Confusion scrunched her face. "Because of legs guy?"

"Because you said you understood why I could never trust you. Since then, I've been obsessing about how to show you that I do. I do trust you, Roxanna. I don't have a damn clue why, but I do." His volume dropped. "You've been different since the beginning."

Their fingers played, coiling and caressing, but they never broke eye contact.

"You don't have to—"

"And because when I saw what your ex was involved in, I wanted to lock you up somewhere safe… I want the right to do that. To hash it out with you. Because, damn, baby, I know you'd fight any chains a man might try to put on you." He did know her; they shared a modest smile. Such a simple gesture, but it was all they needed to communicate. "I'm tempted to take out a hit on this Clement myself just to get you out of danger."

"Zairn," she murmured on a whisper of a laugh.

"I want you to be safe, Roxanna. I need you to be… because if anything happened to you…"

She wanted to assure him that suicidal tendencies weren't a part of her makeup, but that sounded glib even in her head.

"I'm safe," she said, shuffling closer. "Porter offered me security—"

"I'd buy you an army—"

"I know," she said, swaying closer. "I know, baby."

"Rox—"

"Enough," she whispered, sliding both hands onto his shoulders. "Enough."

Instinct took her mouth to his like there was no other place it should be. His didn't hesitate to respond. Their unity was its own language. Its own pursuit of what should be, what was right.

Pushing him to the floor, Roxie climbed on top of him, increasing the force of their kiss. Listening to his truth had changed something between them. What it was, she'd figure out later. They'd waited too long, *she'd* waited too long to taste the mouth that teased her. Judging by the determination of his urgent response, Roxie figured he felt the same. With one hand lost in her hair, cradling her head, Zairn curved the other around her and tried to roll them over.

She planted her hands on his chest to part their lips.

"You're not in charge here, Casanova," she whispered, tasting his kiss on her smile.

"Okay," he said, insinuating his thumbs under the hem of her tight dress.

As he pushed the fabric higher, he sat up, compelling her to rise to her knees, straddling him. Her body moved in a ripple allowing him to peel the dress away from her skin. He tossed it aside and captured her breasts in both hands to test and tease her flesh.

Relaxing her arms around him, Roxie sampled his mouth again. The novelty of the short, stolen kisses enraptured her. So much that when his arms closed around her and she was suddenly flipped onto her back, she shrieked in shock. Didn't take long for the sound to become a laugh.

"Found the reins," Zairn murmured above her mouth, brushing his nose back and forth on hers.

When her laugh gave way to an inhale, he kissed her again. Deepening their connection, his tongue pushed hers into her mouth, caressing and massaging her with a tender care his greedy hands weren't showing.

She understood the need of his touch. The pressure of her own desire was growing to a desperation. Pulling at his shirt, Roxie tried to loosen the frustrating buttons. The adrenaline firing her mind was screwing up her fingers. They wanted to work faster, but were fumbling, trembling, sensitive, like every other part of her being.

Hope of relief came when the weight of his body ebbed. She prayed he was going to vanish his annoying clothes from between them. His kiss stayed put on her mouth and sped up, taking, needing, hot and instant, mirroring the potent desire that scalded her from the inside. Giving up on being any kind of delicate, she yanked his shirt open, sending buttons flying. A moan of victory rumbled between them as they both fought to free him from the fabric.

Passion heated their furious kiss, but damn, he was wearing a belt. Damn stupid decision. Still, there was two of them and they were of the same mind. As his quick fingers worked on the buckle, she opened his fly.

Compelled to be filled by him, she arched up, longing for completion.

The moment his lips withdrew, hers grabbed for them again.

"I need a rubber?"

"No," she said, snatching for the back of his neck. "No. No. No…" A whine of impatient greed vibrated from her throat. "Z…"

Winding her legs around his, she pulled him to her, only breathing in when he pushed himself into her.

"Yes," was the first thing she said in a long slow exhale.

Her whole body ached, drowned in the wonderful, overwhelming ocean of pleasure. That was where she was supposed to be. Where he was supposed to be. He was more. It was the only word that matched her feeling.

Tingling, zapping shots of bliss flew through her in erratic, indulgent delight. He just kept on going, advancing his inches, proving his arrogance was rooted in his most carnal corner. Damn, she'd felt him hard against her before, but that was nothing to how his girth felt inside her.

Her body moved. Everywhere. Every muscle. She couldn't stay still. Roxie wanted to experience every second, feel every raw nerve stimulated to its peak.

Her eyes opened just a sliver when he retreated. It enlivened her to see the light of mischief in his gaze. There was the man who played off her. Who returned her banter with his own.

"Zairn," she said, draping her arms around his neck.

The swagger in his quick wink was too much. Her instinctive laugh was an odd juxtaposition to the ecstasy pouring through her. She was happy. In a way that was difficult to pinpoint. Relaxed in achievement, yet tense in the throes of possibilities.

If she had a choice, they'd stay there forever. Right there in that moment, locked together, feeding each other's cravings.

Minutes went by, maybe hours. Roxie didn't care. All she cared about was the man above her, inside her, satisfying her sizzling fantasies.

Humidity rose until she could barely breathe. It was coming, the apex he was racing her to. The crushing mass of climax took its time filtering through every atom of her being.

Fighting for oxygen, she panted and whimpered, begging for the pressure of release to capture her. It was there, right there, she hung on the cusp and then it burst within her, sending her whole body into the spasm of joy it sweated for.

The primal growl above enhanced her summit, deepening the release of zinging endorphins.

She groaned when he slid out. Though glistening and blissed out, she wasn't ready for the moment to be over. Yet, she couldn't move. It took some serious exertion to open her eyes and blink at the warm yellow light bleeding across the ceiling from the perimeter recesses.

"That was long overdue," he panted.

Yes. Definitely true. She blinked slowly, taking her time about returning to present reality.

"You know what I think?" she asked, her words lazy. "I think we have a thing for closets."

When he didn't say anything, she picked up her head to turn it his way and relax it again. He was smiling at her. His goofy expression called her a circus clown without using the words. She'd seen it before. A lot.

"You know you were only average," she said, returning her focus to the ceiling. "A six, seven at best."

"Really?" he asked. Rolling onto his side, he supported his head on a fist. "A seven, huh?"

"If I was feeling generous," she said, enunciating as she stacked her hands on her abdomen. "For a man who's had five thousand one-night stands in his life, I expected more."

He stooped to rest his lips on her forehead. "If I've had five thousand, you should've demanded a rubber."

She recognized his tease, but still sought his gaze when his lips left her skin. "I assume you had a medical exam when I was sick. To make sure you didn't catch anything." She inhaled and stretched her arms up over her head, testing her muscles. "Besides, if you give me a STD, I have a story to sell to the newspapers… and I can sue the hell outta you."

"Or I could pay for your silence."

"Pay me how?" she asked, rolling onto her front to prop her chin on his chest.

"Singles in your G-string while you shake your ass in one of my lounges. You'll need to support that kid I put in you somehow."

"Yeah, uh huh, I've heard of these gentlemen's lounges. Haven't been invited into one yet."

"I have access to security clearances through an app on my phone."

Rising to her knees, she slid one across him to straddle his torso. "Your point, caller?"

He pushed his hands up her thighs, squeezing and appreciating her. "If you're nice to me… maybe I hook you up."

"Now I understand how you convinced so many women to sleep with you. You bribe them with the promise of visiting your seedy titty bars."

"Hey, there's nothing seedy about my titty bars," he said, obliging by fondling her breasts when she leaned forward to present them. "I run sophisticated joints. Classy."

"I have no problem with anyone appreciating the female form," she said, arching into his caress. "It's just I'm all about equality. If you get a titty bar, we should have a… pecker bar." Both of them frowned as they tried to figure that out. Eventually she just shrugged it off and descended to kiss him. "You know what I mean."

"You have to work on your pitch, babe," he said, settling his grip on her waist when she rose again. "Most women score me higher than six or seven if they plan to restructure my organization."

"I don't want to restructure your organization. Just tweak it a little."

"Tweak it, huh? And that gets me a seven?"

"Don't worry," she teased, drawing random shapes on his body with her fingernails. "If you get me drunk enough, one day I might give you another shot at improving your score."

"Might?"

She shrugged and strutted a little, shaking her hair down her back "Yeah, well, I have to remain open for better offers."

"Better? Baby, there's no such thing."

No better because he could afford diamonds? Oh, wait… Her diamond. She grabbed for it over her cleavage, but it wasn't there. Panicked, her attention swung left and right as she scanned the floor, searching for it.

"Babe?"

"No. No," she said, clutching her neck.

Something glinted on the spilled fabric of her dress, which was strewn on the floor above his head. Scrambling up his body, Roxie was practically sitting on his face when she dropped forward to reach for the material.

"Not subtle, are you, Lo?" he muttered beneath her.

She swatted at his hands when he curled his arms around her thighs and tried to guide her higher.

"Stop it, I don't want you to eat me," she said, settling in her previous position, looping her pendant around her neck. "See..." Roxie nestled the gem in her cleavage. "Where it belongs."

"Looks good there," he said, pinching it between his thumb and forefinger.

"I'm surprised."

"That it looks good?"

"That it granted me access to the emperor himself."

"Baby," he said, coiling the chain around his finger to draw her lower. "The emperor entered you."

His smile seemed different. Maybe it was just the angle. Taking his face in both hands, she tilted her head and kissed him again. On more than one occasion, they'd been close to sharing the simple act. She could never have imagined it wouldn't be like kissing any other man.

Zairn Lomond had probably kissed more women than she'd had meals in her life. Roxie was just like any other. A set of lips, a tongue, tits and ass. He could catalog her features, slot them into the directory of others he'd experienced.

Roxie could view him as just another guy. She couldn't quite figure it out yet. Maybe it was because they'd been strangers thrust together without much of a transition. It could be that his lifestyle, so different from any she'd ever lived, was a novelty that she was still getting used to. Whatever it was, Roxie was grateful that they'd met.

He brushed her hair from her face, pushing it back from her cheeks to hold it against her head. "Want to take this to your bed?"

"There's something sexy about doing it on the floor."

"We've done on the floor," he said. "Now I want to do you everywhere else."

"Have you got a list?"

"In my head."

"We can take it to *your* bed."

"My bed?" he asked. "What's wrong with yours? It's closer."

"You think I invite just anyone into my bed? What will the maids say when they find my soiled sheets?"

Her mock outrage seemed to tickle him.

"Maybe they'll think you're irresistible."

"Oh, and that would excuse a man wheedling his way into my bed?"

"Is that what I'm doing? Wheedling?"

She pushed away to climb to her feet and looked down at the man still lying on the floor between her legs. "If you don't want me in your bed…" Roxie took her time about running a toe down his sternum before twisting to sashay away.

"Hey, now, baby," Zairn said, scrambling up from the floor. She kept on going, but he caught her in his arms and buried his face in her hair. "I definitely didn't say that."

Being held by him from behind, they went from her closet into his bedroom. The master was bigger than her room. Much bigger.

"I don't think we should share a suite anymore," she said, screaming when he scooped her legs out from under her to toss her onto the bed.

"You're right," he said, kneeling on the bed to move toward her in the middle. "We should be sharing a bed."

"Ah-ha," she laughed, resting her forearms on his body when he reached her. "You're a comedian."

Coiling his arms around her, he lowered her onto her back, slower than the flip stunt he pulled in the closet. Though there was nothing subtle about it.

"I've got no hang ups about the size of my cock, baby, but I have to admit to limitations. It can't stretch from one room to another."

"Just because you get some action doesn't mean you can shout about it from the rooftops. Didn't think you'd be the type to kiss and tell."

While she wound her legs around his, Zairn's frown bloomed. "You don't want people to know?"

"You shouldn't want people to know," she said, running her fingers through his hair. "This is a PR exercise. I am a PR exercise. And if people found out you screwed your PR exercise, you'd wind up facing a firing squad." Widening her smile, she tilted her chin higher. "Be a good Casanova and fuck your PR exercise… discreetly."

Did he get the hint? Roxie had no plans to subdue her pleasure. If she wanted to scream, she'd scream… while they were alone in the suite.

They offered each other overdue comfort. She didn't read too much into it. Zairn was the emperor of fun and that's what they were: fun. And nothing more.

30

She'd never dreamt of white dresses and fancy houses. As a kid her dreams were only of happiness and leisure. The idea of travelling the world inspired her. Though backpacking and bunking in hostels had been more common in her mind's eye than five star and caviar.

Lying in bed, next to Zairn, her fingers feathered across his cheek. He was perfection. The perfect specimen of man. Tall, chiseled, strong, alpha, in charge. He had his flaws. No one was perfect. But the world thought different. They adored him from afar. Coveted his life and attention.

The world didn't know him. People thought he was chasing the proverbial high. Sleeping around. Partying all night. Extravagant. Gregarious. Wild.

He wasn't.

She'd dated the party boy in college. More than one of them actually. The party boy didn't care about details, not the ones that counted. He was irresponsible. Unreliable. Tiresome.

Zairn Lomond would never abandon someone for a better offer or a good time. He didn't care about the party. He cared about people. About their good time. About their needs and fulfilling them. He lived a glamorous life of luxury. No one could deny that. A literal highflier with the world at his disposal.

Yet, she hadn't seen him once do anything that suggested he treated his life with anything less than the respect it deserved.

Yeah, okay, so he'd shipped her friend's homemade soup across the globe. He'd summoned a doctor at God knows what expense when she was sick... Crimson had deep pockets, or Rouge did, whoever was picking up the tab.

But it wasn't about the money. It was about the man.

Those across the world who swooned after him saw the flash, the charisma, the square jaw and designer clothes, the swagger.

They didn't get it.

The fun. The tease. The wit. How he could pull her close and arouse her with just a look. To say he had depths would be a cliché. He was real. That was it. He wasn't the flat, one dimensional playboy fangirls believed him to be. She didn't judge them. It was cool, fun, to know something the masses didn't. Something her girls didn't.

Zairn Lomond.

Being honest with herself, getting horizontal with him was inevitable. They'd been dancing around it long enough. It was a bad idea. She was his PR exercise, a contest winner. The Crimson crew must have seen the way light scampered around them... or maybe they hadn't. In company, they were usually occupied by other things. Their verbal sparring sessions, the moments when they got closer than they should, happened in private, behind closed doors.

Hmm, except, didn't Salad believe she had access to naked Zairn? Yeah, maybe not so smart.

But it wasn't a lie.

Drawing a fingertip down the center of his chest, she flattened her hand to let it slip under the sheet onto his abs. She had access alright. To the stores. Before her hand got there, she withdrew it.

While he wasn't a frivolous playboy, he also wasn't Mr. Forever. A life on the move every day, every minute, was taxing. He'd done it for so long, lived under the constant burden of corporate decisions, affecting hundreds, no, thousands of lives, that it was second nature. He was used to being in demand, being everywhere all at once, and carrying on from day to night without any hint of a break. Any inkling about remaining switched on, even in tough times or those of exhaustion, was nothing to his reality.

He was invulnerable. Powerful. Relentless. Giving and giving to everyone around him without pausing to think about himself. Like Kesley said, he didn't know what he wanted.

Maybe it was going through the motions. He did make life seem effortless, but he couldn't have gone from six mil to billionaire without smarts and hard work.

In his bed, happy and warm, she appreciated the moment. Absorbed it all. They were just blips on each other's radar. Spending a night with the Emperor of Fun, given the circumstances, seemed like a rite of passage. One day, in the distant future, she'd confess to her girls what really happened between them. How they played together, how gravity weakened when they were caught up in each other. Life, and many of its experiences, were temporary, often fleeting. This was one of those experiences. If they hadn't given in to it, they'd always have wondered, or she would've, about what it might have been like.

Now she knew and wasn't disappointed. Grabbing opportunities, living the chances despite the risk, it was what life was all about.

Porter was the only guy she'd been with for almost two years. Zairn was a palate cleanser. A gorgeous and delicious palate cleanser. He'd freed her from what was and given her to what could be.

Carefully boosting higher, she kissed his cheek, lingering for a second before slipping out from beneath the covers.

If they weren't on the road, they'd have somewhere to go alone, back to their homes or hotels. Loitering in his bed would lead to another calamity. No one could know what they'd done, sure, but she also didn't want it to get awkward or weird between them. They could still flirt and play. Would it be the same or would the buzz be gone?

Tiptoeing into her room, it took a few minutes to find her phone in the closet and another few to locate and connect her charger. While it did its thing, she washed up and got into her pajamas. The phone remained in the basket of her hands after she sat on the floor, her back to the vanity in the closet where she and Zairn had…

The phone vibrated and powered on.

She dialed home and waited. The cellphone bill would be epic when it came in. Used to seeing her girls every day, it wasn't easy having limited, and expensive, access.

"Hello!" Jane chirped.

Cyndi Lauper was playing in the background—the girls planned to hit the town.

"How long have you been waiting for Toria?" she asked, smiling.

Picturing the scene was easy. Music, drinks. Jane tidying. Toria flitting in and out of the bathroom doing this and that with her makeup and hair. She'd have at least three wardrobe changes too.

"Oh my God," Jane said. "Toria! Toria! Get out here! How are you doing, honey?"

"Good," she said, an odd heat gathering at the corners of her eyes. "I miss you. Both of you."

"It's Rox," Jane whispered, obviously to Toria. The music volume dropped. "Where are you?"

"Rome."

"Hey, did you hear Porter got smoked out?" Toria asked. "Put her on speaker." There was a beep and the audio changed. "Porter's apartment is toast."

"Yes, I heard," Roxie said. "We get the news here."

"We tried to call," Jane said. "A whole bunch."

Her cellphone charges weren't the only ones that would come due at the end of the month. "Don't rack up the bill," Roxie said. "I told you. We can't afford it." Though their apartment was lying vacant because of her Sydney stream. No one was using the phone there. "Not at home or on your cellphones. I'll call when I can. You don't need that hanging over you."

Toria snorted. "Who cares about the phone bill? You're coming back with fifty grand."

In theory.

"What did Zairn say when you told him about the fire?" Jane asked.

Porter. Right. So much to catch up on. "I didn't tell him, he told me. He rushed me out of the club and—"

"Yeah, we saw online," Toria said. "The pictures of you going in."

"He was holding your hand," Jane squeed.

"And then you were dancing… there's cellphone footage." Great. Hatfield would be thrilled to hear that. "You know, for a couple who aren't together, you do a lot of together things."

"You have no idea," she mumbled and sighed. "I want to talk about you guys. Keep me in the loop, what's going on at home?"

The last time she'd called, it was to tell them that she wasn't sleeping with Zairn. This call couldn't be more of the same. They were developing some nasty habits.

Her friends weren't as interested in updating her, they wanted updates themselves. "What did Porter say when you called about the fire?" Toria asked.

"How do you know I—"

"Because we all know you did."

Her friends knew her so well. This was why she needed them, to keep her grounded. Her sanity was beginning to fray. "Yes, I talked to him and he was a pigheaded idiot… as usual."

"He's not dropping it?"

"No, which doesn't surprise me," she said. "For a guy who's so damn smart, he's also damn stupid a lot too."

"What did Zairn say?" Jane asked. "When you talked to Porter?"

"He was… supportive." About the conversation anyway. "Are you two safe to go out? I thought the press were harassing you."

"They've lost some interest now you're in the picture again," Toria said. "Your parents and Sonia went home earlier."

Jane gasped. "Zairn paid for a new fence around their yard and state of the art security," she said in a rush.

"Rouge pays," Roxie said. "It's on the company dime."

"Wherever it's from, he had to authorize it, right?"

Maybe. She didn't know the specifics.

"Stop helping her change the subject," Toria said. "Zairn and Porter."

"There's nothing to tell. Zairn's people got the news, he told me, and we came back to the hotel. That's when I called Porter."

"And he pissed you off," Toria said. " 'Cause the guy's an ass."

There had never been much affection between Toria and Porter, even at the height of the relationship.

"I just wanted to check in. To let you know I'm safe… and I miss you."

"We miss you too," Jane said, making kissy sounds.

"Home is always here if you need it."

Sometimes Toria was too astute.

"Thanks. I love you ladies!"

They hung up. She put the phone on the floor by the outlet.

Home felt far away. Very far away. And that was nothing to do with geography.

Like she'd said on the plane. Delay. They were more than halfway through the tour. Another few weeks and they would never see each other again. They had to go back to distance. Anyone finding out about their physical encounter could spell disaster. It had worked for them before she got sick. Distance. Delay. Words to live by.

31

Adjusting the thin neck scarf so the knot was at the side, there was bounce in her step as she left her bedroom the next morning. Zairn stood at the other side of the living room, next to a stack of papers on the short bar.

Why was he—oh, there was a phone at his ear.

"I have to go," Zairn said. The tickle on her skin came from him watching her cross the room. She didn't have to look to know it. "Yeah, maybe... Not tonight."

She stopped at the bar next to him, peeking at the cups on a tray by a half-full French press.

"You snuck out on me," Zairn said. To her? It didn't sound like something he'd say on the phone. His hand slid onto her shoulder. "Lo..."

"Is this coffee still hot?" she asked, touching the side of the French press with the back of her fingers to find it was warm.

Zairn gathered her hair away from the side of her neck. When the heat of his lips met the spot he'd uncovered, Roxie smiled and picked up the pot to pour the coffee into one of the empty, but used, cups.

"Feeling frisky today, Mr. Lomond?" she asked, putting the coffee pot down.

"If you play your cards right," he whispered in her ear, then returned to kissing her neck, tucking a finger under the scarf to ease it out the way.

His lips trailed to her shoulder. "I'm French today," she said. His hands crept around to massage her abdomen beneath her striped Bardot crop top. "I should get a beret. Do they sell berets in Italy?"

"I'll take you to Paris," he murmured. "There's something French we can do all the way there."

"You flirt," she said, easing out of his embrace to spin and hop up on one of the bar stools. She leaned against the low back, holding the coffee cup's rim with just her fingertips. "You better not be suggesting what I think you're suggesting."

Pointing the toe of her maroon heel toward him, he thought nothing of catching her ankle to coil her leg around his.

He closed in on her. "I'm suggesting anarchy," he said, his fingertips gliding beneath her skirt to her inner thigh. "Let's take off. Go lie on a beach somewhere."

"We have responsibilities," she said, capturing his hand to push it out of her skirt. "Besides that, tongues are already wagging about us."

"With reason."

True. Roxie straightened up to tuck her legs in and turned the stool to face the bar. She drank some more coffee.

"Astrid texted to say Greg and his guys want to meet today," she said, putting the cup back on the tray. "It's great that they're feeling better."

His gaze grew more discerning as his eyes narrowed on her. "How are you feeling?"

She didn't have to ask what he meant; he wasn't talking about the flu. "Last night was amazing," she said at the same time someone knocked on the door. Twirling the stool away from him, she hopped off the seat in a flourish, and called back to him over her shoulder. "Just because it happened once doesn't mean it will happen again." At the door, Roxie paused to glance back. "Emperor of fun, right?"

Wearing a broad smile, she opened the door to welcome the usual suspects. Ogilvie and Ballard were first, closely followed by Fuller, also known as Salad, and Terry Elson, who she'd met only once. Astrid and Tibbs were at the rear.

Roxie closed the door and took Astrid's hand to swing it back and forth. "Thought the docu guys were coming."

Astrid glanced toward the bar. "Mr. Lomond requested we delay them."

"Oh," Roxie said and turned his way. "We don't need to delay."

"We do," Zairn said, setting his focus on Ballard. "Tell me."

"My guys will land in a couple of hours."

"If this guy's so good, why the delay?"

"He had prior commitments and has a family... His wife likes to check the protectee out."

"Why does his wife care?" Elson asked.

"That her husband is jetting across the world to join the entourage of the world's foremost playboy?" Fuller asked. "If she's seen Roxie, the woman would be smart to be concerned."

Roxie's brow dropped to an instant frown. "What does that mean?"

Concern flared in Fuller's expression. His focus jumped between the others. If he was hoping an ally would save him, he was disappointed.

"Nothing offensive," he said.

"Roxie's attractive," Ogilvie said, his attention on Zairn.

Actually, make that everyone's attention. Every person in the room was focused on him, even when talking about her. Were people afraid of her... or were they assessing his reaction? His feelings were more important than hers. These people would have to live with each other after she went back to the real world.

"She's bold too," Fuller said. "If she wanted the guy, nothing would get in her way."

"So I'm hot and pushy," Roxie said. "You guys are sweet to flatter me so much."

"Are you saying they're wrong?" Ballard asked.

When he put it that way...

Leaving Astrid, Roxie sashayed across the room between all the people to take a spot in the middle of the only free couch, the one nearest the terrace doors. Though, unfortunately, the doors were closed. She could really do with the air; the room felt smaller than it had yesterday.

"I guess with the way you're talking that I'm the protectee," she said. "If this is about the Gambatto case, I don't think it's that big a deal. We're thousands of miles from that."

"They have connections here," Ogilvie said. "The Gambattos can get to you."

Her instinct was to say if that was true, they should leave Italy. Except they'd already missed half of Australia and hopped right over Tokyo. Her track record wasn't so great. She was supposed to improve the image of Crimson and instead, her involvement made Zairn and his people less reliable.

"Okay, so they watch me. They're like security guards or something?" she asked, to which Ballard nodded once. "But from far away, right? They won't be on top of me."

"Stone's recommendation will be the one we follow," Ballard said. "He'll make his assessment."

"I thought you already did that," she said. Stupid new setup wouldn't get her back on the busy dancefloors any time soon. "I sorta think maybe it's time to consider cutting your losses."

"Meaning?" Ogilvie asked, not the only one confused.

The oppression of Zairn's reaction was so heavy she didn't have to see it to register it. "First the screw up with the stream, then I got sick, forcing you to cut a whole country from the tour. I'm more trouble than I'm worth." She smiled at Ogilvie. "You were right. I was wrong to argue with you. That's not something I often admit."

Ogilvie laughed, which was so unexpected, she froze, stunned. "Roxie, you are trouble. Yes, I was right. But I was wrong too, you're the right kind of trouble."

"The public love you," Astrid said. "Almost unanimously."

That wasn't entirely accurate. A whole folder of emails said otherwise.

"Your connection to the Gambatto case makes you more sympathetic," Elson said. "That your ex is taking him on shows you've got spunk."

Jerking forward a couple of inches, she pointed at herself. "I've got spunk? Me? I called him last night and told him he'd be an idiot not to drop it. He's going to get himself killed. I have no doubt about it. He doesn't see the whole picture. He gets blinkered and…" Blowing out her frustration, she held up a hand. "Don't get me started."

"Your profile has raised his," Elson said. "There's already talk of him running for office."

"Will be hard for him to do that after he's dead," Roxie said, unimpressed by the optimism in the room. "It's people like all of you who get other people killed. People like you fill heads like Porter's until they start to think they're invincible."

"You're really worried about him?" Astrid asked. "Do you still have feelings for him?"

"Of course I have feelings for him. He was a big part of my life. Just because we're not together doesn't mean he suddenly evaporates from existence."

"Enough about this," Zairn said, startling everyone with the abrupt interjection. "Roxanna is our concern. If you say Stone will keep her safe, I'll trust you, Ballard. I've heard about his work. He is impressive."

"He knows what he's doing," Ballard said.

"And he knows cost is no barrier?" Zairn asked. "You have a blank check on this."

"He knows."

Ogilvie was next to join in. "We could limit Roxie's exposure. If we take her out of public view, their appetite for her will increase."

"That could produce a powder keg," Ballard said. "If Gambatto or his people are focused on her—"

"I talked to Trish," Zairn said. "They know we're in the mix."

Ogilvie voiced his opinion. "Joey Gambatto was never a fan of yours. He felt threatened by you. Everyone else showed deference, not you."

Zairn's tension seemed to be rising. "I don't give a damn about Joseph Gambatto," he snapped. "As long as he keeps his sights away from Roxie, he can rot or go free, I couldn't care less."

"Maybe there's a deal there," Elson said. The look exchanged between Ballard and Ogilvie was intriguing. They weren't obvious allies, yet there was something between them. "Throw your weight behind him, maybe he leaves Roxie alone."

"Og can call the lawyers and—"

"No," Roxie called, bouncing to the edge of her seat. "No way. You can't do that."

"Undermine your ex-boyfriend's case?" Zairn sneered. "I don't give a shit about his political career."

"Do you give a shit about Ava Marilyn?" she asked, resenting his glare. "I know you, you don't like to lose. If you take this on, he will go free. Where's the justice in that?"

"To be fair, we don't know whether he's guilty or not," Elson said.

Roxie heard him but maintained her focus on Zairn. Slowly, her head began to shake. "Don't do it. You have to let justice run its course."

"There is no justice," Zairn said, cold in his delivery. "Money breeds power, it wins every time."

"No," she said. "Some things money can't buy."

"You've made that perfectly clear, Miss Kyst."

What was going on? Where did his disdain come from? The guy standing there in Zairn's skin wasn't the one she'd been getting to know for more than a month and a half.

Rising to his feet, Ballard side-nodded at Zairn. "Can I talk to you?"

"We don't have—"

"Now, Z," Ballard said and turned to stride in the direction of Zairn's bedroom.

That wasn't his security agent and underling, an employee would never command a boss like that. But Zairn deserved it. Asshole. Huffing and puffing and snapping. Someone needed to put him in his place.

Despite exhaling like he had enough annoyance to refuse, Zairn stalked off after his friend. A few seconds later, the bedroom door slammed.

It didn't make sense. Where was the guy who'd been kissing her neck, talking about Paris just a minute before everyone arrived? Why was he in such a foul mood? Who was this new guy? He could go back to wherever he'd come from as far as she was concerned.

"Did something happen?" Astrid asked.

With Zairn out of the room, everyone's focus switched to her.

"He was fine when I was here earlier," Ogilvie said. "Did you fight?"

Did they fight? No. His only comment was that she'd snuck out on him. On the plane, when she'd done the same thing, he'd claimed to be mad but wasn't really. Why would it be different now? It wasn't like she'd left his bed before he finished. They had sex twice more before he'd fallen asleep. She'd only gone to her own bed after. She hadn't gone to Mars or immediately online to share every detail.

A crash in the bedroom put her on her feet. Whispers followed as she hurried toward it. Without even thinking, she opened the bedroom door, swerved around it, and kept the inner handle in her grip when she dropped her weight against it, shutting them in.

"What is going on in here?" she hissed, observing the scene.

Ballard was closest, Zairn was at the other side of the bed, near the broken lamp pieces scattered on the floor.

"None of your damn business," Zairn snapped.

"Oh no?" she asked, shoving away from the door. "You're making it everyone's business with these theatrics."

When she was about to pass Ballard, he took hold of her arm to keep her next to him. What the hell? Why was he touching her? Grabbing her? If he wanted her mad too, he was going the right—the heat of Zairn's ire grew. Ha, she got it. Idiot. Ballard thought he was protecting her.

Relaxing, Roxie breathed out. "You think he's a threat to me?" she asked, a laugh in her voice. "Please." She landed her own glare on Zairn. "You know, I thought I didn't recognize you. For a second, I couldn't figure out how the guy I've been spending so much time with, the gracious gentleman who's always willing to play with me, became this unrecognizable person. But I do know you. We have met before. I met you before I met my Zairn."

"Your Zairn is a myth," he retorted. "He doesn't exist."

"Apparently," she said, folding her arms.

"I don't know what the hell went on between the two of you," Ballard said. "Whatever it was, I don't care. You need to cut this shit out. Both of you. The whole damn planet might be in love with you now, but that can change in a hurry."

"Nothing to worry about," Roxie said. "I have zero interest in spending any time near this Zairn."

"Good," Zairn said, marching toward them. "That's all I needed to hear. Keep her alive, Bal."

Both she and Ballard moved fast to let him pass. His momentum didn't give them a choice. Throwing the door open, he departed, leaving her and Ballard looking at each other.

"You don't have a damn clue what you've done, do you?" Ballard asked, with resignation not anger.

"I didn't do anything," she said. "He's the one in a crazy snit. I didn't do it."

"Yeah," Ballard said on an inhale. "You did."

All the blame landed on her? That was unfair. She didn't go smashing lamps and storming off.

"Can we just get this over with?" she asked, leaving the bedroom to return to the living room. When she got there, one notable absence stalled her. "Where's Zairn?"

"Gone," Astrid said.

The solemn expressions around the room didn't bode well.

Ballard appeared at her side. "Shit."

"Yeah," Ogilvie agreed. "My sentiments exactly."

Roxie wasn't exactly sure what they were referring to, but it wasn't good. Wherever Zairn was, it couldn't be anywhere his friends and colleagues wanted him to be. She hadn't meant to upset him. Her attitude was automatic, and he'd never hesitated to rise to it before. She didn't get it. What had changed?

32

"You're not yourself."

Her wandering mind took a second to catch on that Greg was speaking. "Sorry," she said, tossing her hair away from her shoulder. "I'm focused. Ask me again."

He laughed, in a polite way. "We're off our game. It's been a while since we did this."

Being interviewed by Greg was a more pleasant experience in Rome. Regal furniture just lay about all over the place. Each of them had their own embroidered settee. A carved coffee table with an engraved glass top took up the space between them. Everything was just... fancy.

"It's gorgeous around here," Roxie said, admiring the cornice on the ceiling. "The whole place is like straight out of history."

"You like Europe?"

"I do," she said, widening her smile. "I want to explore every corner."

"And, unfortunately, Zairn is keeping you on a short leash."

That was a joke. Wasn't it? Taking it that way was better for him. And for her. Her capacity for any extra negative emotion was limited.

Anxiety wouldn't leave her alone. His phone was on the bar. Why was she obsessed with that? She wanted to talk to him. His phone was on the bar. Wanted to ask why the hell his mood soured so fast. His phone was on the bar. His goddamn phone was on the fucking bar.

"There are security concerns," Roxie said. "He takes his responsibility to his people seriously."

"You're not just one of his people though, are you?" Greg asked without disguising his implication. "You're special to him."

"Ah, now…" she said, trying to maintain the jovial mood. "I can't tell you what is in Zairn Lomond's head." Never had that been truer. "I can only tell you that I've always received the greatest of considerations. He's generous and very, very good at his job."

"What about you?" Greg asked. "Can you tell us what's in your head?"

"My head's full of joy and happiness," she said, exuding nothing but positivity. "I've had an amazing time. I have to say sorry again. I can't say it enough to those who missed out on their Experience because I was sick. It was all on me. Completely my fault."

"You have my sympathies. We were all floored by it."

All except Zairn, it seemed.

"It was nasty. I just slept. We should talk about something else. I've talked about the flu on my stream plenty. I'm sure everyone is sick of hearing about it."

"Never," he said. "Since you've been back with us, you haven't said much about your relationship with Zairn."

"And I won't," she said. Boundaries. "I'll talk about Rome all day long though. There's still so much to see!"

The door opened, drawing everyone's attention. Ballard slipped in just enough to gesture to her.

She leaped to her feet. "Can we take a break?"

Although phrased as a question, she didn't wait for agreement. She hurried over to Ballard who stepped back to hold the door open for her.

Alone in the hallway, Roxie stepped in closer, laying her hands on his waist. "Did you hear from him?" she asked without caring that it sounded desperate.

"Don't expect to," Ballard said. "Stone and his guys are here."

He started to turn away; no way was the conversation over.

Roxie dug her nails in and stayed put. "Wait, no," she said and swallowed while searching for her words. "When will he be back?"

"Rox, I wouldn't expect to see him again. Period."

Her heart stopped. Maybe it didn't. How to breathe... She couldn't... He couldn't mean... "What?"

"You think you know him, Roxie. You don't. Not like the rest of us do."

And she didn't get it. He said the words, yet... "You don't sound mad, but those aren't happy words."

"I don't know what happened and I don't wanna know," he said. "My loyalty is to him and I'll do whatever is necessary to protect him. But I follow his orders too, and he wants your safety to be the priority."

"Ballard," she said, pulling him back when he tried to turn away again. "I would never do anything to hurt him."

"I guess you weren't paying attention earlier," he said. "The guy who walked out of the suite, that guy was hurt."

Ballard walked away. Her arms dropped to her sides. Hurt. He'd been angry. Resentful. Venomous. They'd had an amazing night together and somehow, without meaning to, she'd hurt him. Damnit. Screwing him up without any ill intentions. Her special skill. She really was her own worst enemy.

33

The remaining time in Rome was torturous. After two nights of not sleeping in her own bed, Roxie switched to sleep in the master. On the night they'd had sex, Roxie hadn't slept with Zairn. Maybe her subconscious regretted that decision. Sleeping in his bed was the best way to ensure she wouldn't miss his return.

The days passed and eventually the time came for their group to pack up and fly to Barcelona.

A new city.

For the first time since starting the tour, moving to a new city wasn't exciting. In fact, she flat didn't want to go. Making a scene wouldn't get her anywhere, except embarrassed. Resisting would be crazy anyway, it wasn't like Zairn didn't know where to find them.

The wheels had to keep on turning, even if the leader wasn't at the helm. His team were practiced. The machine never stopped moving. Like clockwork, night after night, the Experience winners met her at Crimson. The Casanova-4-Lola merchandise many flashed at her was fun, or it would be if it didn't sour the back of her throat. They should never have been so stupid. Sex wasn't just about them, the whole world wanted front row seats.

Zairn was all the Experience winners wanted to talk about. She was no substitute. Yeah. Yeah. She got it. In one respect, it was a reprieve. In their exuberance, the winners ended up chattering with each other, saving her from dodging too many questions. Each night, she arranged for the secondary winners to stay in the VIP area. The more people around, the less pressure to maintain the façade of joy.

Surrounded by security guards, she couldn't go to the dancefloors to lose herself in the music or go sightseeing either. Keeping her safe meant restricting her so much that the delight was sacrificed. Depressed wasn't a word she'd ever use to describe herself. Yes, in the right context, cynical maybe, but overall, she tagged herself as optimistic. Maintaining any kind of positive attitude was difficult when she couldn't be herself anymore.

Having been returned to a modest suite with a single bedroom, the message was clear. The Crimson crew didn't expect to see Zairn again during the tour, just like Ballard said. It ripped her apart. Forgetting was impossible. It wasn't right that their final interaction should be so angry. That didn't reflect what they'd been. That shouldn't be their legacy.

Shaking off her melancholy, Roxie clicked the stream button and waited for the numbers to tick up. In the time between click and transmit, she didn't say much and used the camera to check her hair and makeup. It was a sort of joke, just her way of being silly.

A few minutes went by, people were watching and ready.

She straightened up and smiled. "Hello, Crimson Delights," she said, bubbling with faux glee. "Still in Barcelona and loving it! I'm moving here, I've decided."

If only that were true. Her security detail kept her inside all day, the city was a mystery. Roxie got why. If anyone shot at her, they'd likely hit one of the agents tasked with protecting her. Their diligence made sense.

At the start of the week, for a brief moment, she'd hoped a new city would mean less restrictions. Nope. Nice try. No dice. Italy, Spain, it didn't matter. Security ruled and that meant confining her.

Now out of the loop, she wasn't privy to discussions at the top. Astrid's answers were vague, but it basically boiled down to one fact. With Zairn out of contact, no one was willing to loosen her chains.

"I wish you could be here," Roxie said, beaming at the camera. "It's amazing."

During the day, Greg and his crew would go out and shoot the sites, then they'd come back and show her the footage. In his way, Greg was being sweet, indulging her. Her Delights probably recognized that there was no streaming out and about. As it went, there was nothing anyone could do about that.

"I said I would answer questions today," Roxie said. The questions were stacking up in the comments tracking up the side of the screen. "I see most of them refer to the Emperor…" what she'd taken to calling Zairn. "Is he alive?" She laughed. "Do you think I'd sit here smiling at you every day if he wasn't?"

If nothing else, the tour had taught her how great an actress she could be.

"What else do we have?" she asked, reading the questions. "The hotties watching my ass? Yes, they're security brought in to keep an eye on me. You, Delights, should know by now that left to my own devices, I'm a danger to myself." Another laugh. "I know you are desperate to see Zairn in the pictures appearing on the web every day. Unfortunately, he has a business to run. If he doesn't make all those spondoolies, how will he keep lavishing us with a good time?" A few of the questions were beyond personal. Those ones got a wide berth. "Do I miss him?" Roxie scoffed. "Only every single second." That truth was painful. The next question to catch her eye took her mood to a more somber place. "Do I have a message for him if he's watching?" If only she believed he might be. Wherever he was, it was far from anything that might remind him of her. "I'd tell him it wasn't a myth. It really wasn't."

A knock on her bedroom door snapped her out of a daze.

"Oh, one second," Roxie said to her stream watchers. "Let's see who's come to visit."

Crossing to the door, she peeked out to find Astrid on the threshold.

"Ah!" Roxie said, throwing the door open to pull her friend inside. "Miss Astrid!" Putting an arm around

Astrid to draw her toward the computer, it was great to have a break from questions. "Say hello to our wonderful audience! Astrid is my best buddy here on the trail."

Astrid blinked about ten times and settled her wide eyes on the camera. "I... I..."

"Relax," Roxie said, giving her a sideways shake. "We're all friends here. It's not like I haven't let people in on my private moments before." She winked in the direction of the camera. "Do we have secret business to discuss?"

Astrid squirmed. Her obvious discomfort set Roxie on edge. Oh, God. Had something happened...? To Zairn?

Concealing her worry wasn't easy. Sickness churned in her belly as she returned to her seat in front of the computer. "Sorry, Delights, I will have to cut this one short. I'll be back tomorrow and will answer all of your questions, promise!"

She blew a kiss to the camera and clicked the button to end the stream. The stream was off. Yes. Check once and again, always. Closing down the computer was the best way to make certain there wouldn't be any accidental streaming.

The moment the screen blanked, she closed the laptop and twisted around to look at Astrid. "Tell me," she said, hooking her linked fingers over the back of the chair. "Is he hurt?"

"No!" Astrid said, rushing closer. "No! It's not... I have no idea where Mr. Lomond is, I... I promise."

Breathing out, relief rose first. Anger wasn't far behind, but she damped it down. Astrid didn't mean to scare her, edginess was just the young woman's way.

"Then why the scary expression?" Roxie said, her heart rate not yet ready to climb down. "Geez, woman."

Leaping from her seat, she ran her fingers into her hair. Shake it off. Shake it off. No need to panic. Ignore the spine-dancing spiders and the tightening heartstrings.

"Sorry," Astrid said. "You wanted to speak to Ogilvie."

Hope overshadowed anxiety. "Yes?"

"He's on a conference call but said he'd come down after. You can talk before the club."

"Good," Roxie said, nodding. "That's good. So I should get changed?"

Astrid scanned her figure. "I think you're ready."

Hmm, yeah, the open back red dress was her apparel for the club. The plan was to leave right after her stream. Though the stream was supposed to last more than six minutes. Now she was at a loose end.

"Right," Roxie said, the sensation of being off-kilter was unsettling.

Another knock on the door brought the women's eyes together. Astrid quickly turned to hurry over and open it. Rather than Ogilvie, it was Ballard and Stone, the new head of her security detail.

"Are you hungry, Roxie?" Astrid asked as the two men came in. "You haven't eaten anything today."

"No," Roxie said. "I'm not hungry." She frowned at Ballard. "What do you want?"

"That's nice," he said.

"You don't usually come just to hang out," Roxie said. "The only time you come near me is if you have to."

"Luckily for you, I was looking for Astrid," Ballard said and side-nodded at the assistant.

Astrid was quick to hurry out with her cousin.

"Subtle," Roxie murmured, returning to sit in front of the computer again.

"Subtle?" Stone asked. "Cutting you out?"

"Just the way it is."

Before Zairn disappeared, she was in the master suite, a part of decisions, in the club.

"This will be their world long after you go back to your life," he said. "I wouldn't take it personally."

Hooking her linked fingers over the backrest of the chair again, she rested her chin on them. Stone wasn't wrong. Whether it was personal or not, soon everything would go back to normal for everyone.

Listening to her breathing, she was sick of dwelling on things out of her control.

Her focus switched to the hottie guarding her. "Did I hear someone say you were married?" Roxie asked, having not spent any time getting to know the men tasked with protecting her.

"I am." Her gaze dropped and she craned to seek his hand. He raised it up to show her his bare fingers. "My wife has the ring."

"You don't wear it in public?" she asked. "What's the point of that?"

"Neither of us wear them on our hands."

Odd. "Why not? Because both of you like to play away?" She gasped. "Do you have an open marriage? I have never, ever met anyone who's cracked that. What's the secret?"

The semi-smirk he wore suggested she was off track. "My wife works with her hands and what I do is too dangerous to wear a beacon that might endanger her," he said. "Dusty wears both of them on a chain around her neck."

"Oh," Roxie said, resting her cheek on her fingers again. "Secure woman. I wouldn't send my husband across the globe without tattooing his marital status somewhere for the world to see."

"She has nothing to worry about and knows it… The guys on my team keep her updated with any details I might forget to share."

Subdued amusement seasoned his words. If the idea of him straying was so hilarious, his wife had good reason to be confident in their relationship.

"Why didn't you bring her with you? If you're so loved up and secure? She wasn't pissed you got to come to Europe and chose to leave her behind? Might be the only chance she gets to see any of this continent."

"She is European," he said. "And who said I didn't bring her?"

Roxie perked up. "Can I meet her?"

"No."

Simple, clear answer.

"Why not?" Roxie asked. "Afraid I might corrupt her?"

"Miss Kyst, you are not renowned for your ability to stay out of trouble," he said. No, the opposite was true.

"And I am not renowned for my ability to keep my eye on target when my wife is in the field."

Good reason.

The door opened without any knock preceding it. Astrid came back in with Ballard, Ogilvie accompanied them.

"Roxie," Ogilvie said. "What do you need?"

Wasn't that the sixty-four-million-dollar question? She got up to head for the bedroom. "Can we talk in private?"

He followed, both of them went inside and she closed the door. She could've chosen the hallway but had learned a few things about discretion and suspicion. Anyone could be listening any minute.

If Zairn Lomond and Crimson had taught her anything, it was to be aware. Boundaries. He'd made her a more guarded person. Hardened her. Damaged her.

"What do you need?" Ogilvie asked when she turned to face him.

"Nothing," she said, folding her arms. "I just wanted to tell you something."

"Okay," he said, probably thinking of ten other places he'd rather be.

"I'm getting off the train after Barcelona."

Startled, his wandering concentration became keen. "I don't know what that means. I don't speak Roxie." It wasn't a surprise to find out the others had their own terms to explain her. "What is getting off the train?"

"I'm going home," she said. "I've had enough." Concern deepened the lines between his brows. "No one needs to do anything. I am waiting for the airline to get back to me with available flights. I'm happy to pay my own way home." Thankfully, on her instruction, Astrid returned almost everything that she'd purchased on her card in Rome. Almost everything. Anything she'd been photographed in was hers for keeps. The credit that had been refunded to her card would be just enough for a flight home. "You don't have to keep paying for security either, I'll talk to Porter about that when I'm home. I wanted to tell you in person because I figure you're the most senior person still around. I didn't want to do it in front of the group." Not that she got to see everyone as a group anymore. "It's no big deal." She smiled. "That's it."

When she started for the door, Ogilvie stepped into her path. "Wait a minute, you can't just... You can't just go home."

"I can," Roxie said. "I took my time reading the small print when it was first given to me. There is a distinct clause that allows me to leave any time I want. It states I will forfeit all or a portion of the prize money and additional prizes. I'm happy to tell you to keep it. All of it. I don't want money or tickets for the New York club or the resort. Please don't concern yourself with confidentiality either. I have no intention of sharing any details or answering questions about my time with Crimson." She exhaled a laugh. "Let's face it, the sooner we can all forget this ever happened, the better."

His lips began to move, but his words didn't take form. The phone in his hand chimed. Saved by the bell. She waited while he read the screen.

A flash of something other than concern crossed his face. "Excuse me," he said and hurried out of the room.

34

Ogilvie never moved that fast. Rather than be offended, her curiosity ignited, luring her into his wake.

"Turn it on," Ogilvie yapped at Astrid in the living room, waving his phone at the television.

The assistant did as told. Ogilvie grabbed the nearby remote to punch in a channel number. The screen switched to the news.

"...Kesley Walsh. Reports are unconfirmed at this time," the news anchor was saying. The screen showed images of Zairn and Kesley leaving a building and getting into a waiting car. "The pictures were taken by a member of the public twelve hours ago. We have confirmed that both Zairn Lomond and Kesley Walsh are sharing his usual suite in Las Vegas. Attempts to contact either of them for comment have been thus far unsuccessful."

Ogilvie's arm shot out to point at Astrid. "Where's Tibbs?"

"U... up... upstairs," the stunned Astrid stuttered.

"Bring him here," Ogilvie said and looked to the TV again.

Astrid scarpered, running out of the room to follow instructions.

"...Mr. Lomond has been MIA for just over a week," the anchor said. "We're going to go to our reporter who is in Las Vegas right now. Fiona?"

"Yes," the voice rose just a second before the picture switched to that of a woman standing by a barrier outside a hotel. The hotel she'd stayed in while in Vegas.

"Hello, Christina. Yes, I am here outside the hotel where it has been confirmed that Zairn and Kesley are sharing a suite. From what we can gather, they arrived together the night before last. Staff are tightlipped about what may or may not be going on in the suite and the couple's reasons for coming to Vegas."

The screen split in half, so the woman in the studio and the one in Vegas were both visible. "The pictures of them taken last night seem to explain that."

"At the moment, we are trying to confirm through official records, but, yes, their attendance at the wedding chapel last night does speak for itself."

Her mouth opened. Some sound must have left her lips because the men present turned to her. She couldn't rip her eyes from the screen. Married? He got married? What the...? What in the actual...? Rage burst within her. Not because he owed her anything. No. Because it was insane. Married? To the woman he'd dumped because the relationship couldn't go the distance? Asshole.

"Do we have any corroborating evidence from his camp?" the anchor asked. "They're usually quick to react to these kinds of developments. They're no strangers to scandal and intrigue."

"No," the reporter said. "Though in an interesting turn, Roxie Kyst was streaming from Barcelona not long ago. She cut the stream unusually short when an assistant came to her with news. Roxie and Zairn Lomond have, of course, been romantically linked. Until this news, it was believed that the two were involved in an intimate relationship. Who can forget that video accidently streamed just a few short weeks ago? Lomond's representatives wouldn't comment on that relationship either."

"Which is odd, right?" the anchor asked. "He's always been open about who he's seeing."

"So we thought," the reporter said. "We do have to wonder if his relationship with Roxie was genuine. If it was, what caused the sudden turnaround? Why is he now back with his ex-girlfriend? Possibly married to her? And how is Roxanna Kyst reacting to the news? Did she know this was his plan or was she as in the dark as the rest of the world? Lomond definitely has a lot of explaining to do."

Astrid came rushing back into the room with Tibbs not far behind. Ogilvie's hand jerked in the direction of the television. It took a second to realize he'd muted the screen.

"Get him on the phone," Ogilvie barked at the young man.

Tibbs's eyes flared while at the same time his form shrank in submission. "I haven't spoken to him for twenty-four hours."

"I don't give a damn!" Ogilvie roared.

Did she hear that right? Twenty-four hours? All the time everyone was telling her Zairn was lost, Tibbs had a connection with him?

"He's blocked all calls to the suite."

"You knew he was in Vegas," Ogilvie demanded, bearing down on Tibbs.

"Yes," Tibbs answered, nodding. "I… I did."

"And you didn't think that was a red flag?"

"I didn't know he was with Miss Walsh."

"Now Mrs. Lomond apparently," Ballard said, calmer than she'd have called given the situation.

Ogilvie began to bluster. "Balla—"

"It's done or it's not," Ballard said. "We get on a plane with Elson and Fuller."

"We won't get there until tomorrow."

"And?" Ballard said. "They're holed up. Only places they'll go are her place in LA or his in New York. Easy diversions."

"Honeymoon," Roxie heard the word in her own voice almost like she was out of body. "He'll take her on honeymoon." She closed her eyes in a blink and opened them again on Stone. "Your guys ready to saddle up?"

"On standby."

"Good," she said. "Let me grab my purse."

Roxie went into the bedroom to retrieve her purse. When she turned around, intending to return to the living area, she stopped at the sight of Ballard closing the bedroom door, trapping both of them inside.

"I've made it a habit to never get involved in his relationships with women," Ballard said.

"That is an excellent habit," Roxie said. "And one you should stick with."

Except when she tried to go to the door, he stayed in her way. "What happened?"

The deep, grumbled words were loathed. It was obvious he didn't want to be in his current position. But, hell, neither did she.

"Rome is in the past," she said. "For all of us. There are three more Crimson nights in Barcelona, including tonight. When they're through, I'm on a plane back to Chicago."

He frowned. "You worked that out with him?"

"With Ogilvie, just before this," she said, grateful her intentions got voice before the marriage announcement. "It's all planned. I'll get a flight myself and keep my mouth shut from now until forever."

"Does he know? Zairn. Does he know that you're leaving the tour?"

She laughed and opened her arms. "Look around you, Ballard, the tour is over. It's finished. It's done."

"He goes off the reservation sometimes. It's happened before. Usually when there's some kind of stressor in his life. Not pressure. He can deal with business and expectations. It's always something unexpected. Something personal... Something happened that last night you were together in Rome."

Stay put. Stay strong. Ignore the mental images of Zairn from that night. Don't give up any ground.

"I just want to go home," she said. "I can see out these last three nights or I can go now, your call."

"Without his protection, you're toast," Ballard said. "Gambatto was one thing, but this... If he married her while the world thought he was with you, you're the wronged woman. Sympathy for you will skyrocket; both of them will be demonized. You'll have dozens, maybe hundreds of paparazzi on your tail, camped outside your building, chasing down everyone you know. Your family and friends will need his protection too, you do know that, right?"

The truth was frustrating. "What do you expect me to do? Cower and hide? I have to live my life."

"We'll come up with a strategy. Something that—"

"That what? Extricates me from this mess? How likely do you think that is? Really? How does this get better for me? You made it clear your loyalty is to him. All of your loyalties are. Where does that leave me?" Roxie hoped she was better than Ballard at hiding her thoughts because she saw the truth behind his eyes. "If I am in a prison, it is of his making. Before this I was nobody. I want to be nobody again. I want my life back."

"What happened in Rome, Rox?"

"Nothing to what happened last night in Vegas. I didn't ask to come on this trip. It was sold to me as a once-in-a-lifetime opportunity. Something I'd be a fool to pass up." Her eyes narrowed. "Do you know how close I was to walking away in Boston? Before that even." She showed him an inch of space between her thumb and forefinger. "This close. I was this close to just going with Toria and Jane when we took them home. This close to not getting back on the plane at all."

"Because of Vegas," he said. "It started fast between you. It's been years since he did the casual one-night stand thing, but with you… No one thought they had to say you were off-limits because he was always smart when it came to women. Always. He has a sixth sense about it. At least he did before he met you… You were—"

"A PR exercise, I know."

"Yeah, but that put you in a category, for all of us. You were glass with a wide perimeter. You weren't allowed to get close—you weren't *supposed* to get close." He took a breath and ran a hand over his hair, which was the most frazzled she'd ever seen him. No, it was the only frazzled she'd ever seen him. Ballard was always composed. "I saw it in LA. You got your hooks in. He asked for the room and I… None of us should've walked away. The forbidden thing has never been his deal. I don't know what made you different."

"You expect me to respond to that?" she asked. "This whole trip has been a head fuck. I should've known the minute I lied to my friends about him that going any further was a bad idea. I shouldn't be here. I want to go home."

"I can't let you go home," Ballard said. "It's not safe."

"So? What do you care?"

"The last order he gave was to keep you alive," he said.

"Going home to be hounded by press won't be fun, but I doubt it will be lethal."

"Do you want to take that risk? Going back puts you on Gambatto home turf."

"We don't know that he wants to hurt me. Porter and I aren't together anymore. There are more relevant targets. Besides…" Roxie sucked in an exasperated breath. "He married Kesley Walsh! I don't think he gives a shit where I'm at or what I'm going through."

"You think he doesn't care?" Ballard asked. "He left because of you. Because of whatever went on between the two of you."

Sex made him leave? That was good to know. She'd said since the beginning that he was the wham, bam type. Though even she hadn't believed he'd leave his own tour to save himself from dealing with the one-night stand.

"Whatever," she said, waving the statement away. "It doesn't matter. Like you said out there, it's done or it's not, right? All we can do is react to it. My reaction, even before the marriage news, was to leave. I want to leave."

"Who else knows?" he asked, suddenly more discerning. "About the two of you."

"Jesus," she groaned. "First Zairn and now you, there is no two of us! There never was a two of us! There's him. There's me. We had fun! That was it. Fun!"

A little out of breath, her chest rose and fell as she waited for him to get it. A kind of understanding she didn't expect relaxed his expression. Slowly, his eyes closed and he pressed the end of his middle finger above the bridge of his nose.

"Fun," he murmured. "And you said that to him?"

"What? Yes! What the hell, Ballard, can we just get over the past and move forward?"

"Yeah," he said on an exhale and backed off to return to the living room.

Roxie went after him, expecting to go to the club as planned. But when she tried to pass, Ballard caught her arm and kept her next to him.

"What's going on?" Ogilvie asked.

The television was still on mute. To her chagrin, the news was now playing her stream.

"She's going to London," Ballard said to the room. "Stone, get your guys ready to protect your primary in a private residence. We own two apartments; you should be able to keep a tight hold on our space. I'll give you full security clearance. Whatever you need."

"London," Ogilvie said. "You're sending Roxie to London?"

"Yeah," Ballard said. "The rest of us are hitting Vegas."

"You want Roxie leading the Experience while we're over there?"

"No," Ballard said, shaking his head, then looking to Tibbs. "We'll take her to London and fly to Vegas from there. Call Dennis."

Tibbs nodded and already had his phone in hand before he left the room.

"Would you like me to make the arrangements in London?" Astrid asked.

"Yeah," Ballard said. "Don't call ahead to Vegas. Get everything here packed up ASAP."

Astrid accepted that and followed Tibbs route out.

"I need to bring Elson and Fuller in," Ogilvie said, leaving the room too.

Roxie wasn't sure what was going on and no one seemed interested in looping her in.

"Lacie and Junior still at her folks?" Ballard asked Stone.

"Yeah."

"You'll have almost nineteen thousand square feet to do whatever you want with. I don't know how long this will take. They're welcome to stay with you if you'd prefer it."

"Are they in danger?" Stone asked.

"Nothing you can't handle. I'd expect paparazzi hounds more than snipers, but I know you'll prepare for anything."

"Appreciate the offer, but they're better where they are." Stone shrugged. "They didn't travel alone."

"Ah, Sorcha?" Ballard asked and got a look from Stone in return like that word was explanation enough. "And the earache of Sorch and Shep is enough to put you off?"

"I try to limit my son's direct exposure to Lulu," Stone said.

Ballard laughed. Wow. She didn't know he was capable. "I hear you," he said. "You'll be in charge... of your primary."

"Treat her as my very own."

"If she was yours, we'd never have got into this mess," Ballard said.

His tone piqued her curiosity, why did he sound so circumspect?

"I'll round up the guys and get her to the airport."

"I'll stay here. Come get her when you're ready to roll."

"Twenty minutes," Stone said, striding to the door.

"Uh, I don't need to be babysat," Roxie said to Ballard as Stone departed, paying her no heed.

"You're a danger to yourself," Ballard said, all of a sudden angry. "Go pack your shit."

"I'm going home. Not London. You can't take me prisoner."

He closed in on her. "You wanna bet on that?" he asked. "You've seen Stone's guys, right? You're under contract." His phone made a noise, taking him away from her. Probably for privacy, he wandered across the room, but she heard him mutter, "He just hasn't told you yet."

The world was going mad. Sometimes she'd think it was just her. Not today. No, it was definitely the world. It was going to hell and taking her right along with it.

35

London.

A beautiful city. History. Drama. Architecture. Fashion. Fascinating… though less tangible when viewed on a cellphone screen. Browsing was her only entertainment on the drive from the airport to the covered side portico of a tall, odd-shaped building.

As she left the car, Stone's men surrounded her to escort her inside. They blocked her view of everything until one of the guys leaned over to press the top button in the elevator. The top floor. The best. Just like she expected from Crimson.

It was crazy.

Travelling the world was supposed to be freedom and it felt like she was on her way to the gallows.

Stone led the apartment entry. She was put in a grand bedroom and ignored while the guys went in and out of every space, learning it or checking for the boogeyman, could go either way.

Eventually, Stone came to her in the window overlooking the park.

"There's some staff guy, butler person in the foyer. He wants to speak to you. One of us will be outside the front door at all times. There is service access from the kitchen. We'll be on that door too." So much for trust. "You need anything, just open the door, we'll be there. There won't be a breach, but I'll say this because I'm thorough. If there's a breach, go into the hers master bathroom." He pointed to a door on the other wall. "Lock the door and stay there."

Despite recognizing the master suite, she'd chosen not to explore. It wasn't just the master suite, it was Zairn's master suite. Whether it belonged to him or Rouge, he'd slept in the room, spent time there… maybe with a parade of different women. If walls could talk…

That was a thought for another day, a day when she was alone.

"Roger," she said, saluting with two fingers. "Go settle in, I'll talk to my butler."

With lots of big arm gestures, she shooed Stone to the foyer and out of the front door. The male employee was there, waiting.

"Miss Kyst—"

"I don't need staff." His mouth closed. "I need the Wi-Fi password. That's it."

"It's on the welcome pack in the kitchen."

Who had a welcome pack in their apartment? Zairn, apparently. It wasn't the start of a joke, though it should've been.

"Great!" she said, plastic smile in place. "Then we're all good."

"Miss Kyst, we pride ourselves on—"

"I'm sure you're really good at your job, but I don't need a staff."

With a hand on his shoulder, she directed him to the door.

"We can cook, clean… whatever you need."

Roxie opened the door. "Thanks for the offer, but no."

The real world was her permanent address. Fending for herself was nothing new. London wasn't Chicago, but it gave her the opportunity to grab for some normality. The last hope for her sanity.

Turning the lock on the door, the snick was reassuring. Free, she kicked off her shoes and ran through the apartment seeking the kitchen. Of course, it was at the other side of the apartment. She got lost more than once trying to find it but whatever.

The password, check. Next thing? Her phone. For once, she knew where it was and got through putting in the password when… the battery died.

"Damnit."

The adapters wouldn't fit the outlet. Stupid things. They had them for the EU and for Australia. Why did the UK have to be different again?

Throwing the phone and charger to the floor, she shot to her feet. Freedom meant nothing if she couldn't share it with her girls.

What was she supposed to do? Just sit there. In the apartment. Zairn's apartment? Until what? When…?

"Fuck it," she said, using Zairn's words.

Sitting around, unable to talk to her friends or family, would drive her nutty. Hell, she was already there. A hornet's nest of buzzing exasperation stimulated every infuriated inch of her. Zairn had ditched her. Fine. He wanted to close the book. It was closed.

She needed to let loose. The glorious darkness of the new city held one opportunity for her: Crimson. Time zones rocked. The flight from Barcelona was two hours, but they jumped back an hour in London. Plenty of time left to party!

After changing into the open back red dress with its single spaghetti halter meant for Barcelona, Roxie found a mirror. She fished the diamond from her cleavage and checked her appearance.

"Good enough," she said to her reflection and headed to the front door.

As soon as she opened it, one of Stone's guys got in her way.

"What do you need?"

"Nothing from you," she said, sidestepping, but he mirrored her. "Listen…" She laid a hand on his arm. "We can either work together or I can own your ass." His brows rose as amusement twisted his lips. "All I want to do is go to Crimson. Not any scary place where your guys don't have clearance. Crimson. I want to dance and drink." She showed him her purse. "I carry Visa. I'll take a cab. Easy. I doubt the press even know I'm here." He didn't appear convinced.

"Think about it logically. I let loose tonight, I'll sleep all day tomorrow… When I wake up, I'll cook all of you a nice steak dinner. I'll even be a sport and do it naked if you guys want the visual." When his head tilted, she smiled. "Call your boss."

Crimson, London was the perfect medicine. The minute Stone and his guys shuttled her into the highest tier VIP area, she was home. It was small, intimate, had a private bar and a sound system. What else did she need? She'd thrust her purse at the closest guy and raised her arms over her head to declare that the party had arrived. After that, one drink followed another and things began to blur.

Peeling her eyes open and her tongue from the roof of her mouth, Roxie couldn't quite manage to focus. Where was she? Where had she been? What day was it? What continent was she on? Her head was pounding, but she had to move.

Rolling onto her back, her arms fell open at her sides, or they tried to. The bedcovers were in her way. Bed… she blinked and raised just her head to look around. It was familiar, that was something. Familiar…

Her head dropped back into the deep pillow. "Zairn's," she said on an exhale.

While loitering in the apartment at the time they arrived, she'd vowed not to sleep in the master, no matter what. But that was definitely where she was…

What had happened? Drinking. Drinking and dancing. Her lips curled. For the first time in too long, she'd let loose. The demure, too-cool-for-it celebrities in the VIP area either threw in with her or went on their way. Fine by her.

Her smile dropped when she remembered screaming about champagne for everyone… on her. Sitting bolt upright, she looked around, where the hell was her purse?

Someone came into the room. What in the…? Jerking back, she monitored the woman's progress.

The stranger was calm, modest, young. Why was it so cold? Ah, that might be because the ladies were on display. She grabbed the covers to hold them against her breasts.

Who the hell was this person? Didn't Jeeves get the message about staff? She didn't need them.

"Uh… hello?" she said to the stranger ignoring her.

The woman looked up. Had she even known the bed was occupied? "Miss Kyst."

"And you would be…"

"Marita," the young woman said. "I am on the building's staff. Here to provide anything that you need."

"I need clothes," Roxie said, sniffing the air. "Is that coffee?"

"Yes," Marita said, going to a tray on the nightstand that Roxie hadn't noticed.

Marita picked up the tray, unfolded legs from beneath, and reached over to set it next to Roxie on the bed.

Coffee. Croissant. Some kind of eggs. Whatever. Coffee. Coffee was definitely first.

"How did you get in here?" Roxie asked after enjoying some java.

"Mr. Stone requested someone stay with you. To check on you while you slept."

So she didn't choke on her own vomit or something. Stone could keep her safe from external threats. From herself? Yeah, that wasn't so easy.

"How did I get naked?"

"You did that yourself… After Mr. Stone carried you to bed."

Embarrassing much? "After he left the room or…" Marita cast a glance her way. The twist of her lips was enough to answer the question. "It's okay, he's in an open marriage."

"Yes, ma'am."

The young woman went to the seating area at the other side of the master suite. While drinking her coffee, Roxie observed Marita's movements. Tidying up… Hmm, she and Jane would get along well. Marita bent down and stood back up with… Was that her cellphone?

Just another disappointment she didn't need reminded about. "I need a damn adapter for that thing," she grumbled.

On her approach, Marita turned the device to show Roxie the lit screen. "We provided an adapter and charged your phone for you."

Hot hope flooded her. "Oh my God, thank you!"

What the hell kind of country was this? The best damn country in the world, that's what.

Marita handed over the cellphone and charger. "I'll give you privacy," she said, fading from the room.

The woman hadn't cared about privacy when Roxie was flashing her tits. But, whatever, she had nice tits.

Gulping the coffee, Roxie used one hand to navigate to her contacts. She needed to talk to people. Needed to loop people in. To find out what the hell was going on.

Autopilot, for some stupid reason, took her to *Casanova* first. The time on her phone said it was just after five p.m. Had it auto-adjusted or was that Marita too? If it was five in the evening, the breakfast food was a little odd. *Casanova.* If the others had arrived in Vegas, which they should've, he'd have his phone back. Wouldn't he?

For over a week, she'd wanted to call him, and he hadn't been reachable. Now there was a chance he would pick up and she was hesitating. Why? Because of his new wife? Because if she called and Tibbs or Astrid picked up, she'd be embarrassed? Unlikely. Roxie didn't get embarrassed by things like that. Or she never had before.

Because if he had his phone and still chose not to call...

Damn, no more dwelling.

Shaking off the confusion, she went into an app and used the Wi-Fi to call both women in the group chat. If she'd bought champagne for everyone in Crimson, there wouldn't be anything available on her credit card. No more overseas calling without Wi-Fi for her.

"Rox?" Jane answered the call. "Oh my God, is that you?"

"Yeah, is—"

"Roxie?"

Toria.

Smiling, she sank back against the pillows and put the phone on the tray, so she could enjoy her coffee with both hands.

"Oh, I'm so glad to hear your voices," Roxie said, already feeling more centered.

"What the hell is going on?" Toria asked. "It's mayhem."

"Tell me about it," Roxie muttered, closing her eyes.

"Are you okay?" Jane asked. "Where are you? Are you still in London?"

One of her eyes opened before the other. "How do you know I'm in London?"

"Are you kidding?" Toria spat, sort of laughing in her incredulity. "Uh, maybe the footage all over the internet of you dirty dancing with Logan Lowe? What the hell?"

Oh, shit… Gulping the coffee could come back to haunt her. "Footage?"

"Yes, filmed in Crimson, London last night," Toria said. "You two were flaming hot. The paps got you leaving the club with him too."

"Did you sleep with him?" Jane asked in a whisper.

"No!" Roxie exclaimed, checking around the bed just to be sure. "I didn't sleep with him." Putting a hand over her eyes, she cradled her head when it sank down. What the hell had she been thinking? "It's online?"

"It's everywhere! Both of you are," Toria exclaimed. "Did Zairn really get married? Is he in Vegas?"

"I have no idea," Roxie said, her head falling back against the headboard. "I haven't spoken to him in… a long time."

"I don't understand, if he's in Vegas, why are you in London?" Jane said. "Aren't you supposed to be together?"

"That was the plan," Roxie said. "The whole thing's gone to shit. I wanted to come home yesterday and then the Vegas thing happened."

"If you wanted to come home, why are you in London?"

Good question. Why had she been left behind? Not taking her to Vegas, yeah, that made sense, but leaving her in

Europe? Some bizarre force connecting her mind to reality conjured an answer. A text message, hmm…

> ### Need to meet ASAP. Greg x

"I have to call you back, guys," she said, hanging up and dialing Greg fast.

"Roxie?"

"Yeah," she said. "Where are you?"

"In London," he said. "We were brought to a hotel from the plane and didn't have a clue what was going on. All this stuff is all over the television and—"

"I know, I'm just catching up. Let me shower and we'll meet. Send your location to my phone. I'll come to you."

They hung up and she leaped out of bed. For a quick second, she thought about turning on the TV but decided against it. This was not a see it to believe it situation. She was already hyperaware of the particulars.

Left, right, up, down, backwards, forwards, dodging the world's notice wasn't easy. Zairn had been attempting it for years and hadn't managed it. His life was lived under a microscope and thanks to him, Roxie was on the same slide now too.

In the back of the car on the way to the docu crew's hotel, Roxie's phone rang. Astrid. Shit. It was Astrid's number.

"Astrid?" Roxie answered.

"Roxie, hi," the assistant said quickly. "How are you? Are you doing okay?"

"That's a loaded question," Roxie said, relaxing her shoulders. "I'll live. How are things there?"

"Uh… everything here is good. I tried to get hold of you earlier."

"I didn't have my phone until after I woke up. I'm on my way to meet with Greg. Do you guys have a line for me?"

"Uh… Hold on a second…"

A scuffling noise was followed by the clack of heels on what sounded like tile. That was soon replaced by air crossing the microphone.

"Astrid?" Roxie asked, craning to hear.

A few seconds went by before she got a response.

"Roxie? Sorry, I was with everyone. Oh my God, Roxie, it's crazy."

"Tell me about it. What is going on?"

"He went berserk. Crazy. Like I've never seen him... Well, heard him. We got here and he was like ready to receive us. I don't know how he knew what... He talks to Tibbs, so... I don't know when he knew that we were—"

"Astrid," Roxie said, bringing her friend back to the point. "He went berserk?"

"Yes! Him and Ballard and Ogilvie went into the other room. There was shouting. They were arguing. Ogilvie came out. Mr. Lomond and Ballard were in there forever. It felt like a zillion years."

"And?" Roxie asked, her heart pumping hard in her chest. "Then what happened?"

"You were all over the TV! Everywhere! You and that music guy."

Logan Lowe. Yeah, she'd been briefed.

"So?" Roxie asked. "Who cares about that?"

"Everyone!" Astrid said. "It's crazy. There's a really weird atmosphere. It just feels... wrong."

A lot of that was going around. "What do you want me to say to Greg? No comment? You've left him here, I'll have to tell him something."

"Hold on," Astrid said.

Waiting. Sitting there. Roxie got antsier with every second that passed.

"Rox?"

Ah, now the male Ballard.

"Yeah?" she asked.

"You don't get laying low, do you?"

She took a breath. "Maybe I just wasn't sure which low you meant. Logan Lowe wasn't who you were getting at?"

"Please do not tell me you had sex with him at Zairn's place," Ballard said.

"What do you take me for?" Roxie asked, adjusting her shoulders against the seat.

That wasn't enough for Ballard. "Rox?"

"No," she said. "Geez, Ballard. What am I doing here? Where's Astrid?"

"I'm here," Astrid said, suggesting they were on speakerphone. "What should she say to Greg?"

"It's easy to toss me aside," Roxie said. "But even if I go home tomorrow, the docu crew still expect to get footage. They get it here or they get it there, which do you prefer?"

"Are you offering to stay?" Ballard asked. "To help us out."

"I wouldn't go so far as to say that last part, but yeah, Crimson has taken too much of a hit already. Someone has to steer this in a straight line. I don't know what's going on over there, but we lost most of Sydney, all of Tokyo, and just walked away from Barcelona too. There's a chance of showing some stability in London."

"She's not wrong."

Ogilvie. Damn, how many people was she talking to?

"It's not like you to be accommodating," Ballard said. "This just so you can hang out with your new boyfriend?"

"It might have something to do with my potential credit card bill and my need for the prize money." That was only partially true. The bill was still a mystery, she hadn't mustered the courage to check it yet. "I'll stream from London. Do the Experience with the winners, maybe do some sights with the docu guys. It's business as usual as far as they're concerned. Stone and his people are still here watching my ass, you don't have to worry about me being offed."

"London's all cameras," Ballard said. "There's CCTV everywhere."

While he went to security concerns, Ogilvie went another way. "Nothing worse than the British press though. They'll be all over her."

Apparently, Ballard wasn't worried. "Stone can handle it. And they do give cover against anyone Gambatto might send."

"He shouldn't try anything in London," Ogilvie said. "Okay. Finish out London then it's an overnight in New York."

"After that she'll be in Vegas anyway," Astrid chimed in.

Everyone considered the situation for a few seconds.

"Damn, we must be in one helluva sorry state if Roxie is our stability," Ballard said.

Roxie couldn't say he was wrong. "Funny," she replied, smiling at the parallel. "My ex-boyfriend said something similar not so long ago."

"No more dirty dancing with high-profile people," Ogilvie ordered. "I don't know if I like leaving you in charge over there... You're changing the tenor of what it means to be a Crimson VIP."

"Nothing wrong with mixing it up," she said. "Don't you worry, baby. I got this."

The final words came from Ballard. "You need anything, call Astrid. We'll keep in touch."

That would be nice, to hear from the other cogs in the machine.

After ending the call, while moving in the gentle rock of the car, she admitted her cowardice. Asking about Zairn wouldn't make any difference to what had or hadn't happened. Something he said on the last night they were together came back to her. He wanted to have the right to lock her up and keep her safe, wanted the right to hash out the situation with her.

Whatever Zairn was going through, Roxie didn't have the right to involve herself in it. It wasn't her place to offer two cents. Putting him out of her mind was the best way to maintain the status quo.

36

Roxie was given the same suite in Vegas as she'd had last time Crimson hosted her there. Sleeping in that room would be a novelty. The last time, she'd slept in the Platinum Suite... Probably where Zairn and his people were that minute.

The last few days had been manic. After flying from London to New York, she'd been delivered to the Rouge headquarters. There, a long-legged blonde took Roxie and the docu guys on a tour of the unopened Crimson, New York.

The flagship venue was situated in the same skyscraper as Rouge HQ. The club itself was massive. They didn't get close to seeing the whole thing. Over several floors, it offered everything any Crimson establishment did. A bunch of floors contained hotel rooms to boot. Party and sleep in the same building. Heaven. Rouge was run from the rest of the tower. Everywhere except the top two floors, which were Zairn's private residence, apparently. They didn't go there, thank goodness.

Exhausted, they crashed in Rouge hotel rooms. After, they met around dinnertime to eat and then boarded the flight to Vegas. The Triple Seven had been returned to London for their comfort. Somehow, it just wasn't the same without the usual people around, so Roxie stuck to the party area.

It felt good to be back in the States. Keep on track. Positivity. Home soil. She could do this. Sticking to the mantras, she readied herself for another night in Crimson.

Las Vegas. The same Crimson she'd snuck away from to meet Zairn in his suite. Man, that felt like a lifetime ago. How long had it been?

Three months.

Six nights in Vegas. Five in LA. Then it would be over, and she'd be on a plane back to her life. Everything would go back to normal.

In theory.

A knock on the door spurred her to action. Knowing the drill, she grabbed her purse, pasted on a smile and went to answer it. As expected, Greg was there with his crew, camera trained on her. A couple of Stone's men loitered in the background. Another two would be elsewhere in the corridor. All of them knew their starting positions in the grand and ridiculous production titled, *"Her Life."*

"Time to party," Roxie said, slipping out of the room and starting down the hallway.

"Are you looking forward to Crimson, Vegas?" Greg asked.

"Yes," she said, pressing the call button for the elevator. "I've been here before, it's familiar."

"That's right, after you were arrested in LA, you came to Vegas. Was it a memorable night?"

She smiled, to herself more than them. "Yes. It definitely was."

A night spent with Zairn. The first time they slept together… in the literal sense, of course.

If she was an ordinary human being, walking to the club would be a given. Unfortunately, photographers and fans would keep up if she tried to walk down the street. At least that was what Stone said while ushering her into a car.

They arrived at a side entrance, as always, and were granted access. Last time, she'd only been to the Regular Joe part of the club. Thank God Stone and his people studied the floor plans of every Crimson and knew how to get to the VIP zone. Following their lead always got her where she had to be. They'd take the safest route. Although not Roxie's usual MO, she'd learned how to be a little more accommodating. Just a little.

When they got there, the VIP section was already teeming. It caught her short. Not the people. The place. They were in the glass cylinder suspended over the writhing, gyrating bodies below on the public dancefloors. The room. The one she'd spotted the brooding Zairn in all those weeks ago. From down below, she'd texted him. Told him to meet her in the suite.

"Rox?"

Greg's voice pulled her back to the moment.

"Yes," Roxie said. "Yes, sorry. Are our people here?" Six people bouncing and brimming with unrestrained joy were bunched tightly together near the center of the space. "Never mind." Widening her smile, she went over to them, arms open, ready to deliver her speech by rote. "Welcome to Crimson!"

"Eek!" the woman nearest her actually said the word. "It's Roxie!"

"Oh my God!"

"I love you!"

"You're amazing!"

So many compliments in such a short time.

"Thank you," Roxie said, dizzy with the positive outbursts. "I appreciate your support."

"You really are amazing," a brunette with thick bangs said. "You've gone like all around the world." An audible gasp rippled through the group. The brunette's friend began tugging on her sleeve. "To like every single Crimson there is."

"Except Tokyo." Zairn. Right behind her. Damnit. How was she supposed to pretend it was no big deal when her pulse kicked up like that? "Take a seat. We'll get you drinks. My associate will show you."

Tibbs rushed past her, herding the contest winners to a collection of curved couches arranged in a broken circle.

"I didn't know you'd be here tonight," Zairn said.

Damn. Her eyes closed slowly. The intimacy of his deep voice vibrated through her.

"We flew in tonight," she said without turning around.

"We assumed you'd take the night to settle in."

No one had suggested that. Or if they had, she'd missed it. "Do you want me to leave?"

"I didn't say that."

Inhaling her courage, Roxie turned around to look up at him. He was there. Right there. Almost in her personal space. Almost, but not quite. "Z…" His attention was fixed over her head, most probably on the contest winners. "Zairn, will you look at me?"

"You know everyone will be watching this," he murmured, his mouth barely moving. "The whole world is waiting with bated breath."

"I don't care," she said, snagging his hand. His surprised gaze jumped to hers, giving her reason to smile. "I don't care, Casanova." In response, his fingers twined between hers. "What happened?" The open acceptance of his expression altered to something wary. Still, it didn't seem to know what to portray. "I was so mad at you and then I was just confused… Talk to me."

"Not here," he said, taking his hand from hers. "I have guests to entertain."

He walked away to do his job. She couldn't be mad about that. Talking in Crimson would be difficult. It just wasn't the place. If she'd wanted to talk to him, she could've called. Should've maybe. But he didn't call her either. Maybe what they were was just done. They didn't need to worry about months stretching in front of them, they had only days left. He'd said "*not here*" not "*no*." Still, maybe there was no point. It would probably be best to leave the past in the past. Roxie was no one to him; he owed her nothing.

Dancing felt different with Zairn in the room.

Just like in London, the music was turned up and Roxie threw herself into the groove.

The glass cylinder room was connected via floating stairs to a bar area. It just so happened that her purse was stowed at the bar. Another habit picked up in London. As she scrolled through texts, the bartender brought her drink. These days, there were always so many messages. People she hadn't spoken to for years were suddenly compelled to contact her for some odd reason.

As she scrolled, a message came through, appearing at the top of the screen.

> Platinum Suite. Alone. X

Zairn.

The corners of her lips rose. Taking her time, she swung around to lean back on the bar. Across the room, he sat on the head couch, his attention trained on her. Scores of other people drifted around the dark space. Lights flashed and music played. Bodies moved. Female bodies, much closer to him than hers, yet he fixated on her like she was the only one in the room.

Breaking their stare was difficult, but she had to text back.

> Stone's men guard my door. But I am on my way to the restroom. X

She pressed send and took her time about drinking to make sure it got through. By the time his attention dropped to his phone, she'd already put down the glass and slunk away from the bar. Above the elevated door in the back corner was a restroom sign with an arrow next to it. The perfect reason to wander out of the VIP area and into the long hallway beyond. The corridor turned ninety degrees; the ladies' room was at the head of that turn.

Taking her time, she peed, checked her makeup, applied more gloss… No Zairn. What did she expect?

Crimson belonged to him. If anyone was allowed to swan into the ladies' room, it was him. Still, no show. He wasn't squeamish, being in female personal space wouldn't put her off. Something could've happened. Some drama or maybe someone noticed her sneaking off and him trying to follow. Ballard had figured it out before.

The opportunity was missed. She'd given it a shot. On strolling out of the restroom, all thoughts of dancing disappeared when she spotted a shadow at the far end of the descending hallway.

Zairn.

He paused, then disappeared into a room. That was deliberate. No way it wasn't. He wanted her to see him.

Walking down the slope of the hallway, taking her time, she wouldn't appear too eager or risk being intercepted. A fast pulse of anticipation tried to hurry her. It was insane. Desperation fired her need to be alone with him. They'd taken that privilege for granted when living together.

By and large, anxiety wasn't a part of her life. Not until Zairn. A jitter filled her belly. The agitated butterflies were scared he'd be a stranger, yet adrenaline-fueled excitement battled to dominate. Just a few feet and then…

The moment she pushed the handle down, the door was yanked out of her grip from the other side. Someone snatched hold of her wrist and hauled her inside. Oh— what—the perpetrator rushed her up against the door, using her body to shut it fast.

Zairn.

Yes, it was Zairn.

His cologne. His breath on her temple. It was him. Yes. Her body recognized him. His touch was unmistakable.

He kissed her temple, her cheek, his mouth descending toward an obvious target.

Giving in to their physical need would be easy. But she couldn't, they couldn't. Not if…

"Wait," Roxie gasped in a whisper, his mouth hovered above hers. "Did you marry her? We can't do this if you're hers."

His fingers slid onto her jaw, tipping her face up. "Lola."

That was enough; it was all she needed. His word. That word. It was enough.

Her mouth snatched his, devouring him with the intensity of a first union. But it wasn't like their first kiss. No, it was faster, hotter, much more urgent. She didn't fumble with his belt, her mission was to liberate him from his pants as he picked her up and dumped her onto the closest surface.

Yes, it was all she needed. He was all she needed. Everything would be okay if only he could be inside her again. Desperation meant nothing until that minute. Need. Desire. Yearning.

Her legs wound their way around his hips, begging him for more. He delivered. Rough, dominating fingers plunged beneath her skirt to force her underwear aside. He surged forward, filling her up in one sure thrust. That was it. Oh, God. Like that. Need overflowed. Nothing else existed in the ecstasy of this completeness. All that mattered was this. Him. Zairn fucking himself inside her.

Made to comply, to fulfil his desires with her own satisfactions, she didn't care that anyone could walk in and catch them. Didn't care about the sounds of their bodies meeting or the pulse of the furniture hitting the wall over and over.

Truth. Heat. Passion.

"Z," she called for him, balling her hands in the fabric of his shirt, pulling him closer, arching nearer, opening more of her body to his.

The smack of sudden, perfect orgasm raised his name to her lips again, much louder and certain than before. A long whine of reckless desire ended more like a groan, vibrating her whole being. The primal sounds in both their throats were the same rung by lovers since the dawn of human existence. Yet, it felt new. Like they were the only two people in the universe who knew how to connect this way.

"Baby," he huffed into her hair, his hand somehow cupping her neck and sliding up into her locks. "Lola Bunny."

His fingers closed in a fist to yank her head back as his tongue delved deep into her mouth. He thrust into her, filling her with the truth of his desire.

His tongue ebbed, but his mouth stayed. They breathed, lip to lip, absorbing each other. Coming to terms with their actions, they gave their bodies time to dial back on the surging hormones and hammering heart rates.

His hand slipped free of her hair at the same time he took his mouth away.

Roxie was sitting on a low shelving unit, it looked like anyway. Pushing down her skirt, she closed her legs, watching as he fastened his pants, his back to her.

"How was London?" he asked, clearing his throat after speaking, which was a shame, she liked it when his voice went husky.

"Good," she said, swinging her legs a little. "Would've been better if I had my playmate around to share it with."

"Logan Lowe wasn't playful enough for you?"

He turned to the side to look her way.

"That was nothing. It was one night in the club and nothing happened between us," Roxie said, surprising even herself with the candor.

Why was she explaining herself… or was she making excuses? Why would she do either?

"I know," he said. "Stone kept Ballard in the loop."

"I figured," she said, curling her fingers around the edge of the shelf beneath her thighs.

"You're okay with that?"

She shrugged without letting go of the wood. "He's on your payroll. I know how it works. I know how some of it works. The way you left Rome—"

"Was ridiculous, I know," he said. "I'm sorry. After that departure, I felt the only right thing was to give you your space."

"Z," Roxie said, dipping her head lower in an attempt to catch his eye. "Look at me." He did, though reluctantly. "It's me."

"I'm embarrassed by my response to your honesty."

"You should've called," she said. "You sleep with me then split only to shack up with an old girlfriend? I didn't know what the hell was going on."

"It was petulance," he said, sauntering closer. "Immature and absurd. The truth is, I…" He put a hand on the wall behind her. "I'm used to getting my own way. Used to getting whatever I want."

"The price of success," she said, opening her hands on his chest. "I knew that about you. And sex with me wasn't your own way?"

"Paris didn't tempt you. The offer of a tropical island... You blew me off." He raised a brow to her confusion. "Just because it happened once..."

Ouch. Okay. Yeah, now she was getting it. Damn her. She was the asshole. "Sometimes what I say comes off as glib. I'm sorry. I don't mean to be insensitive."

"Don't apologize," he said, brushing her hair away from her temple. "You are who you are. You have always been clear about what this is."

"I bruised your ego. I didn't think..." Even though it wasn't her intention to hurt him, she had. Turned out Ballard was right. "I missed you." Her hands leaped up to link her fingers at the back of his neck. "If that counts for anything."

"It does, Lo... Will you come back to the hotel with me?"

So polite. "I would. But I have several shadows everywhere I go," she said. "Stone's men are always on me. And I don't think it would be a good idea to give the press more to speculate on... Is Kesley in your suite?"

"She went to LA," he said. "She's having issues."

"And you are the issues fixer," she said, her leg moving higher as it coiled around him.

"For everyone except myself," he said, ducking lower to rest his forehead on hers. Her eyes closed; they breathed together for a minute. "I want to spend the night with you."

"We're in separate suites now and the docu guys—"

"Want us in the same suite. The plan is to meet tonight when we all go back to the hotel... Hatfield already put in a request for things to go back to the way they were."

"He's doing his job for you... I said you were bribing him, didn't I?" Teasing him felt so good. "I guess you'll have to call off Stone's guys," she said. He rose to meet her eye. "I don't need them. I'm safe under Ballard's umbrella. And what's going to happen anyway? I'm too much in the public eye to be a valid target." Had she convinced him? Maybe he was swaying her way; maybe he wasn't all the way there yet. Roxie tipped her head back. "You want sex more than you want to keep me alive."

"Hard to have sex with you if you're dead," he said and exhaled. "Stone is crisis and event security, temporary, not permanent." Meaning they'd have to give them up soon anyway. "But you will have a permanent team when you're home." Her mouth opened to object. "Until the Gambatto trial is over."

"That could be months!"

The trial hadn't even started yet.

"Then months it'll be. Lo…"

Just the severity of his finality prompted her to surrender. "Fine," she said, looking around for her purse. "You send them home and I'll spend the night with you."

She eased him back to hop off the shelving. Ah! Purse—on the floor by the door.

"The whole night, Rox," he said. "You sleep in my bed. We have eleven days. After that you're due to go back to your life." Yes, she was. In eleven days, it would all be over. "Give me eleven days and I promise you'll have fun."

Because he was the emperor of it.

With him or without him. Eleven days was it. All they had left. The options were leap in or back away. Their limited time was a gift, she couldn't throw it back at him.

"We have to be discreet," she said. "I don't want anyone cornered or lying for us… and I don't want you cast as the villain when this is over. What we are is not their business."

"Never," he said. Walking to her, he ran a hand over her hair. "Eleven days?"

"Eleven days."

Then they would fade from each other's lives and it would be over.

37

"I'll be back in LA tomorrow," Zairn said into the phone. "Yeah, tomorrow, Kes."

His phone hit the nightstand. She didn't open her eyes or lift her head from the pillow to check. Over the last eleven days, the sound had become familiar. Guy was like always on the phone. Even at stupid o'clock.

He smoothed a hand over her hair and down beneath the covers to stroke her bare back.

"You know, this might be kinda obvious," Roxie mumbled, her mouth half buried in the pillow. "But I think it's time someone let you in on the secret."

"Okay," he said, his mouth just above her ear. "Let me in on it, Know-It-All."

"You're in LA now." She adjusted the angle of her head to peek up at him. "I'm sorry to be the one to tell you."

He swept her hair from her face and sank lower to kiss the corner of her mouth. "Thank you for your honesty."

His smirk was a familiar sight in their bed. Somehow, still, he was amused by her. Wriggling onto her side, they adjusted until they were sharing a pillow, their faces just inches apart.

"Kes still having issues?"

"Denise is adamant that she doesn't need help," Zairn said. "Nothing Kes can do to change that."

One of Kesley's best friends was a top industry makeup artist. Or she had been until meeting the man of her dreams and running off to Vegas with him.

"It's love," Roxie said. "We can't live our friends' lives for them."

"She's giving up her career in a highly competitive field."

"Maybe," Roxie said, tipping her chin up as she swayed closer to steal a kiss. "But it's Denise's choice to throw her lot in with a guy who's happy running the Love Chapel."

"You think if Toria left a promising career in Hollywood to marry a backstreet Vegas hustler, you'd have the same attitude?"

She laughed and wriggled closer, enjoying how his arm tightened to pull her body against his. "Have you been paying attention, Casanova?" she asked, opening her mouth around his jaw. "If anyone is going to run off with the backstreet hustler, it's gonna be me."

"I wouldn't let that happen."

"No?" she asked, raising her brows. "You think you could stop me?"

"If I showed up and turned it on, you'd forget all about the hustler, baby."

"Hmm? You think so," she teased, accepting his kiss. "Guess it would depend if his score was better than yours."

"You'd leave me for eight or higher?"

"In a heartbeat," she said.

Using his body, he rolled her onto her back and took his familiar place above her. They'd had their eleven days. Just eleven days. Over in a snap. It had gone by in a flash. Yet, looking at him there, on top of her... The view was as familiar as her own reflection... Saying goodbye wouldn't be easy. She appreciated him. Valued him. Had connected with him in a way she'd never connected with anyone.

Not that she'd ever say that to him.

What did it mean? Nothing. So what if they'd gotten used to being around each other? So what if her body craved his with a potent need she'd never experienced in her whole life?

"We only have a couple of hours."

"I know," she said, running her fingers through his hair, imprinting the memory as deep as she could.

"Are you ready?"

"I did most of my packing yesterday. Figured we would want to maximize our time today."

"Excellent plan," he said, kissing her. "What would maximize this time? What do you want to do, baby?"

"Tic-tac-toe?" she asked.

His lips twitched before a laugh seized all of him. Such a wonder. His joy reached every crevice of their intimacy. Marveling at him was one of her favorite pastimes. His lips found hers again. Any kiss could be their last. Why did that thought keep coming back? So many times since Vegas.

The way he'd left in Rome… shaking that off wasn't easy. Delete. Delete. Delete. Ha, how many times had she tried that? Memories sucked.

They were at the end. "*Rox, I wouldn't expect to see him again. Period.*" Ballard was right. Maybe not when he'd first said the words, but they were true now. No longer just a possibility, the prophecy was fulfilled. In a couple of hours, she'd be on a plane back to Chicago and it would be over. Her Crimson adventure would be done. Her friendship with Zairn would be finished. She'd never relied on a man. Never given up any of herself to another person.

Lying there under him, enjoying his kiss, his hands, his whole being… he'd always have a part of her. And, for the first time, that was okay. Keep it. She wanted him to keep it and maybe, sometimes, he'd appreciate the gift. Would he ever think of her again after she was gone?

They shouldn't have stayed in bed as long as they had.

In the closet, the last minute packing was coming to a head. Ready. Packed… Was she packed? The stupid zipper just wouldn't…

Zairn walked in. What was he doing? He better not plan on doing anything.

Sitting on her suitcase, zipper in hand, panic put her on ready alert. "What are you doing?" she asked, rife with suspicion.

He stopped. "What am I doing?"

She pointed at him. "Show me your hands."

He opened both, snickering at her. "Won't be the same around here without you, Lo."

"Okay, you're fine," she said, blowing out a relieved breath. His hands were empty. Good. She flicked her hair back over her shoulder. "What do you need?"

"What did you think I was holding?"

"I don't want to go to the dinner," she said, opening an honest hand. "That's all. No big deal."

"Okay," he said, clearly not following her meaning.

"It's not that I don't like dinner food. I do. Obviously. Everyone does. There are a lot of dinner foods."

"Mm hmm," he said, approaching to offer her a hand.

Taking it, she let him help her up. "It would just be weird is all." Being in a room full of women who may or may not have slept with Zairn. "What do you need?"

"Hatfield's finished setting up."

For her final interview. "Okay," she said. "This stuff has to go to the car. The suitcase won't shut."

"Ballard will take care of it," he said, caressing her face. "I don't like how this feels."

"It's the end. We knew it was coming. We've known it the whole time."

"We have," he said, slipping his fingers between hers. "You are a force to be reckoned with, Roxanna Kyst."

"That's right," she said, prodding his arm. "Don't you forget it."

"Forgetting anything about you is impossible."

"Good," she said, freeing her hand to sneak around him. "Because I know where the bodies are buried."

He laughed. "You do."

Not all of them. By the time they got back to the suite late every night, sex was a higher priority than talking. Zairn's days were business and hers were occupied by the documentary crew.

In the living room, the couch had been moved closer to the window. The view provided the backdrop. Nice.

"Rox," Greg said when he noticed her. "I can't believe we're all the way at the end."

"All good things and so on," she said, going to stand in front of the couch. "You want me here?"

"Wherever you want, though we did wonder…"

"About?" Roxie asked, pausing with her hands smoothing her skirt to her thighs.

Greg twisted to look at Zairn who'd just joined them. "About interviewing you together. You've never done it together."

Sealing her lips, her cheeks puffed out. Oh, that was a hard one to let slide. The double entendre… If Zairn looked at her, she'd break.

"Yeah," Roxie said, smoothing her skirt as she sat. "That's not happening."

"It would be great to—"

"We've spent the last God knows how many weeks ignoring the news media's ridiculous"—not-so-ridiculous—"ideas about us," she said. "I'm not sharing my final spotlight with him."

Because their electricity would be impossible to hide from the camera. They were a whole room apart and somehow it still reached her. That buzz in her gut, the awakening of her core, the desire that bubbled around her heart. Damn, she couldn't concentrate. Don't look at him. If they made eye contact… she'd see the reflection of her own soul.

"I just think—"

"She said no," Zairn said in that final word tone that tempted her to tease him.

Anyone else heard it and did exactly what he said. Not Roxie. She needled him. Mocked. Teased. Jeered… or seduced him. In the last eleven days, she'd learned what it was to have influence with the monolith. She didn't push, not for anything outside the bedroom. He was her plaything and she was his. Or they had been. No more.

"Okay, we have to film the presentation."

"Presentation?" Roxie asked. "What am I being presented with?" Her focus leaped to Zairn. "You are not putting anything in my hair."

Tibbs suddenly appeared with Astrid. Both assistants went to Zairn to hand over a leather binder.

"This isn't going to be a big deal," Zairn said, taking the binder then walking her way. "Rox'll need to make a speech."

"Why do I have to make a speech?" she asked, eyeing what he held as she stood up again.

"Because you're supposed to be grateful for the tour you just embarked on," he said, opening the binder when he stopped next to her.

"I'm grateful," she said, rising on her tiptoes to try peeking over the top of the binder.

"You ever hear what curiosity did to the cat?"

He'd said that to her before, but it didn't dissuade her. "The cat wouldn't have to be curious if she was satisfied."

Frowning, Zairn plucked something from the binder: a red plastic card. "She doesn't need this," he said, tossing it away.

"It's for the—"

"I know what it is," Zairn said. "But she has her diamond…" He looked to her. "Show me your diamond." Roxie plucked it from beneath her neckline. "She's good."

"You want this back?"

"No," Zairn said, glancing around. "I need a pen."

"I don't have a pen," Roxie said, even though he'd been appealing to the others in the room.

He cast his eyes to her for a brief amused second. "I wasn't talking to you. I know better than to ask for anything from the woman who can't charge a cellphone. Just stand there and practice being silent."

She scoffed. "Yeah, like that'll happen."

Tibbs came rushing over, pen in hand.

Zairn took it and signed something in the binder. "Okay, ready."

"What are you signing?"

After Tibbs scuttled out of view, Greg stepped back and Tevin raised the camera to his shoulder.

"Miss Roxanna Kyst," Zairn said, startling her with the professional tone. "On behalf of everyone at Crimson and Rouge, our parent company, I would like to thank you for your contribution and companionship on our Crimson World Tour. You have been a magnificent comrade. You've touched the lives of every person you met. We couldn't be more grateful to you for your involvement." He held the binder out to her. "A token of our gratitude."

"What is it?" she asked, taking the folder. "Your home phone number? Can I sell it on the internet?"

Teasing him in front of the camera probably wasn't fair. Wasn't so easy to maintain that professionalism when she made jokes, huh, Skippy?

"This is the rest of your prize," he said, clearing his throat to hide his smile. "Your prize money and your tickets for New York and the resort."

"Oh," Roxie said, inhaling the word. "I forgot about that."

"Do you have anything you'd like to say?" Greg asked. "About the past few months?"

Did she have anything to say? Had he met her? Except, hmm, it was becoming quite a solemn affair.

"I have to be honest…" she started.

"Unlike you," Zairn muttered, earning him a glimpse of her smile.

"Before this journey, I hadn't thought much about Crimson. I certainly didn't spend any time thinking about the people who kept the cogs turning. I've learned so much…" She hugged the binder to her chest, raising her focus to Greg. "They're good people. All of them. To them, Crimson isn't just a good time. It's not a never ending party. They work hard to provide the best experience for their customers, all of their customers. Even if it means sacrificing their own experience. Crimson gave me a gift. One of understanding and delight. I'll miss Crimson… and those it introduced me to. Thank you doesn't seem to quite cover it, but that's all I have."

She ended on a shrug.

Greg smiled. "I love it. Now… you're sure you don't want to do the interview together?"

"No!" Roxie and Zairn said in unison.

"Okay." Greg laughed it off. "Roxie, if you'd like to take a seat."

Greg went off to seek a chair for himself while Tevin attached the camera to a stand.

Zairn's hand brushed hers; she got his message. He was grateful for her words. They were true, all of them. What she'd gone through had changed her. How much? That wouldn't become clear until after she got back to her life. Her life. She'd wanted it bad, so many times. Normality was a long way away. How long would it take her to settle back into it?

38

"We've done it in the car before," Roxie said, struggling to liberate her hand from his grip. He wasn't giving in, stubborn jerk. Pushing up higher, she flicked his earlobe with her tongue. "Your cock has been mine to play with anytime we've been alone for days. Aren't we alone, baby?"

"When we got in the car, you said you wanted to make out."

"Making out leads to other things," she said, sliding her legs over his lap. "I've been trying my best to educate you about the ways of women. You're not too sharp."

"Sharp enough to have you soaking your panties," he said, gifting her a kiss. "You're getting pretty desperate."

"Desperate?" They kissed again. "Please. Bedding you is my contribution to society. Someone has to lower themselves to do the dirty jobs."

"It's always dirty with you," he growled and stole another kiss.

Curling her fingers around his lapels, she pulled him closer. "Only when you're playing hard to get."

His arms wound around her, scooping her against him, slanting her back. "I like to drive you wild, Lola."

"One more time," she whispered, opening her mouth under his. "Please let me feel you once more, Casanova."

"Wish granted."

Instead of taking things up a notch, he sat up, righting her with him.

Uh… how did he plan to do her? "Baby—" The car stopped. That was quick… Wow, they were at the airport already. "Where's your plane?"

Ballard appeared on the other side of the tinted glass to open her door at the same time the driver opened Zairn's. Ballard offered a hand to help her out. The plane at the other side of the red carpet wasn't their usual Triple Seven. It wasn't a Triple Seven at all.

"This isn't his plane."

"I'm taking you home in style," Zairn said, reaching her side. "Say goodbye to Ballard."

"*Sending* me home in style," she said. "You're not coming with me."

Dismissing Ballard was unheard of. Zairn bailed alone, sure, but he didn't leave his trusted friend and colleague behind when the plane was right there.

"I'm trusting you to send him back," Ballard said, laying a hand on her shoulder. "If you don't put him on the jet, he'll just camp out under your bedroom window."

"You can't come back with me," Roxie said, touching Zairn's torso when he put an arm around her.

"Nothing for the next four hours," he was saying to Ballard without paying her any attention. "I don't care if the damn sky is falling in."

"Yeah, I know," Ballard muttered. "Take care of yourself, Little Rox. What am I talking about? You're invincible. It's the rest of the world who needs to watch out."

She grinned before letting go of Zairn to throw her arms around Ballard. "I knew you'd come around to me eventually."

Squeezing him tight, tears pricked her eyes. Saying goodbye to Astrid had been difficult, really difficult. She'd made the assistant promise to visit when she next got vacation time, which, knowing the Crimson schedule, may be never. But saying goodbye to Ballard, she hadn't expected that to be so hard. Maybe it was because he was the only one who knew about her and Zairn. The most aware one anyway. The others maybe had their suspicions. Roxie hadn't confirmed or denied anything because no one had brought their curiosity to her. Zairn hadn't mentioned anyone approaching him either.

"Okay, enough hugging," Zairn said, extricating her from Ballard's embrace.

She sucked in a fortifying breath and raised her chin to look Ballard in the eye. "Look after him," she said. He bobbed his head in response. "I mean it." She socked his arm. "He'll be a mess without me. Inconsolable. Moping around. Not getting anything done. You have to support him. To cover his ass. I'm sure everyone knows he's nutty about me. It's not like he hides it well."

"Okay," Zairn said, taking her shoulders to pull her back against his chest. "We're leaving now." He kissed the top of her head. "Say goodbye, Lola."

"Goodbye, Lola."

Ballard shook his head at her, though she didn't miss the smile tugging at the corners of his lips.

"I'll be back tonight."

"I'll hold both of you to that," Ballard said. "You have Sunset tomorrow night, Z. If you don't come back, I'll send the world's media to your doorstep."

"Better make sure I hide us well then," Zairn said, directing her toward the aircraft.

It was smaller than the Triple Seven. Much smaller. She went up the stairs and smiled at the pilot standing to the left of the door. Dennis. Zairn's most trusted pilot. Sometimes she'd seen him every day. For months, he'd been conveying them from one location to the next. She'd entrusted her life to him and… After that flight, she'd disappear from his life for good.

The cabin to the right was like a living room, with couches, a coffee table, even a chessboard. Before the contest, she hadn't known it was possible for jets to look like anything other than… jets. A smoked glass wall behind the entertainment unit divided the space. Opaque, hmm, tilting to the side, she wanted to see through the gap at the end.

Zairn closed the door behind them. "Come on," he said, taking her hand to lead her to the opening.

What was beyond? A curved couch, like a chill-out area. Next was an office, a sort of workspace with chairs in each corner, one behind a desk. Another smoked glass wall blocked their route. Zairn pressed a touch panel and a section of glass slid away. Inside…? A readymade bed jutted into the width of the space. Whoa, boy!

"Oh my God."

"That comes in a minute," Zairn said, pressing something on another touch panel.

The glass slid shut, isolating them from the rest of the plane.

Opposite the end of the bed was a closet. As for the door at the other side of the room? She'd guess it led to a bathroom. While she was busy checking things out, Zairn went over to flip back the bedcovers.

"Hey…" she said, dragging out the word. "Is this the infamous Zee-Jet?"

He came back to take her hand. "One more time?"

"We have four hours," she said, kicking off her shoes and unzipping her dress. "I think you can do better than that."

Dragging him away from LA only to send him back did seem insensitive, but that was it. Their last chance to be together. Roxie wasn't selfless enough to take a pass.

"Imagine we'd died," Roxie said, lying on her back in the sumptuous bed. On his side, Zairn loomed over her, stroking her hair away from her forehead over and over. "You're a bad influence. Imagine not putting on a seatbelt for descent."

"You're beautiful, you know," he murmured, examining her hair. "There's something about you. An impervious quality that makes me forget to compliment you like I should."

"Like you should?" she asked. "I'm hot and I know it."

He smiled, still stroking and scrutinizing her. "I know about bravado, baby. You say it, but it sounds like a joke. It's not a joke. You are hot."

"Flattery won't work," she said. The plane was on Chicago tarmac. They both knew it. Nothing could turn back time. These seconds were their last. "I already made a deal to sell my story, so it's too late."

"Oh, yeah?" he asked. "Shame about that pesky NDA then, isn't it?"

Roxie cupped a hand around her mouth to stage whisper. "I signed it Lola Bunny. I'm in the clear." He laughed. "You should fire whoever was responsible for checking that, by the way. Unless it's Astrid. I like Astrid."

"How will we get by without you around, Roxanna?"

She shrugged. "Everything will go back to the way it was before."

"I don't think anyone can ever be the same post-Lola," he said. "You crawled inside me, babe."

"Yeah, that's just my way of increasing the final settlement amount. I've definitely been traumatized by the Crimson Experience. You'll be hearing from my lawyers… or you would be if I had lawyers."

On another laugh, he descended to kiss her. The gentle sensation of his lips deepened. But it was time for retreat. For both of them. She pushed his shoulder to break the kiss.

"I'm not done," he murmured. "I want more."

"The meter ran out, baby," she said, caressing his face. "It's pumpkin time."

Wriggling out from beneath him, Roxie shuffled to the end of the bed. The plane wasn't moving anymore. They'd arrived… and she was still naked.

Oops.

Quickly leaping up, she started to dress. Zairn opened one of the nightstand drawers to retrieve a pair of sweats. He lay down to put them on, then sprang to his feet.

"I lost my panties somewhere," Roxie said, zipping her dress. She swiped her bra from the floor and tossed it over his shoulder. "That one you can keep for fun." She twisted to poke at the touch panel on the wall. "Which one of these lets me out?"

"Babe," he said, catching her hand to pull her around to face him.

"We don't have to do sappy," she said. "And you shouldn't come with me. There's a car out there for me, right? Doesn't matter, I'll grab a cab. The real world awaits!"

"I planned to take you to your front door."

Roxie shook her head. "We don't know if there's press around. And the flight crew will—"

"It's only the pilots," he said, hooking the long chain of her diamond pendant around her neck. Where did he find that? The floor? The bed? It was anyone's guess. "And they used their real names on their NDAs."

"You think."

He smiled and swept a hand across her cheek. "Damn, this is hard."

She crooked a brow as her gaze descended. "That's a quick turnaround," she purred.

Given he'd still been inside her when the wheels hit the runway, being ready for another round would be quite incredible.

"Baby," he said, gathering her into his arms. "This is the big goodbye scene, no more jokes."

"I like jokes."

"I shouldn't have to say it, but I will anyway," he said, ignoring her comment. "You know if there's ever anything... anything at all, you have my number. I want you to call."

"Thank you. I won't. But thank you."

He frowned. "You won't?"

"No!" she said, disgusted by the idea. "I won't be one of those people who use you whenever it's convenient for them."

"Is that what people do?"

"Yes!" Roxie said, pushing on his chest, but that only served to tighten his embrace. "I've been living in your pocket for more than three months, I have seen it all when it comes to the way people treat you. People adore you for only as long as it suits them." She relaxed. "Which I guess I did too..." Horrified, her attention flew to his. "I used you for sex!"

He snickered. "That's something you can do anytime," he said, crouching for a short kiss. "I was a willing participant." Keeping his words low and soft, he brushed his nose across hers, tempting her mouth higher. "I adore you, Roxanna Kyst. You're an incredible human being."

She looped her arms around his neck and stage whispered, "You're supposed to use the pick-up lines before you get into a woman's panties."

"Who needs pick-up lines with a woman as easy as you?"

She smiled, appreciating him lightening the intense tone. "You have my permission to use memories of me when you jerk off."

"Thank you," he said, kissing her again. "At least once a day."

"Don't injure yourself," she said. "You have to find someone to help you practice all I taught you. Be ready for her."

"I don't think there's a woman alive who can follow my Lola Bunny."

"It'll be tough," she said, nodding. "But thankfully you travel a lot, search far and wide."

He cupped her face in both hands and crouched to her eye-level. "Anything you want, Roxanna. Any time. This isn't the end."

Except it was. They had no reason to be around each other. Not for anything. If she had an excuse to see him again, it might be too easy to take it.

"Thank you for everything, Mr. Lomond."

One corner of his mouth rose. "You got it, Miss Kyst."

He kissed her again, lingering much longer than normal. Although it was wrong, Roxie relished those seconds. If she had the ability to pause the moment, she'd probably have stayed there forever.

Keeping her eyes closed, she turned to the exit. Zairn reached past her to press the button to open the door. Counting her steps, one, two, three… something felt off. On step six, she paused. Something was holding her back. What was it? Some part of her wasn't ready to walk away. But why?

With all their joking and teasing, it was easy to pretend none of it meant anything. But it had. It was easier to be playful than to open herself up and show anyone her secrets.

Her heart was pounding hard. She couldn't do it. She couldn't leave without telling him that whatever they were wasn't just some big joke.

Spinning on the spot, she moistened her lips. How did she tell him? What should she say?

He was there, in the open doorway, sensing her ambivalence. "Anything you want, Lo."

"You were a twelve," she admitted, shivering in the breeze of vulnerability. "A hundred and twelve. There isn't a better man. He doesn't exist."

His lips curled just a little. "I know."

His wink relaxed her. He didn't judge or exploit her. As always, he was just what she needed.

"Bye," Roxie mouthed.

She turned around to leave. Her Crimson Experience was over. She was his no more. Not that she ever had been.

Leaving the plane and slipping into the waiting car didn't feel right. The heavy pit of her stomach churned. It was over. All over. Forever.

Thank you for sharing this adventure!

Sign up for Scarlett's newsletter and read excerpts from all her novels on her website: